FOLLOW YOU

ALSO BY RICHARD PARKER

Stalk Me
Stop Me
Scare Me

RICHARD PARKER

FOLLOW YOU

bookouture

Published by Bookouture
An imprint of StoryFire Ltd.
23 Sussex Road, Ickenham, UB10 8PN
United Kingdom
www.bookouture.com

ISBN: 978-1-78681-998-7
ISBN: 978-1-78681-171-4
eBook ISBN: 978-1-78681-170-7

To The Plump Duck

CHAPTER 1

The only parts of her body Meredith Hickman could move were her eyelids. She could just blink them against the matted ends of her blood-soaked peroxide hair.

The barbed wire that tightly coiled her naked form to the cold stone pillar lacerated the bridge of her nose and held her head rigidly in place. It restrained every muscle and painfully secured her arms, which were crossed and pinned firmly to her chest.

Her teeth ground the taut metal that cut deeply across the corners of her mouth, and Meredith gagged as she tried to position her tongue against the sharp spikes. Dirty tears diluted and leaked dark mascara down her cheeks. She attempted to swallow but one of the barbs was already stabbing her throat.

The area beyond Fun Central's derelict concrete walkway was in darkness. Perhaps she was going to be left here until one of the crackheads found her and let her go. Or did what they wanted to her. She prayed that's what would happen.

She felt goosebumps prickle her pinioned shoulders but not from the freezing air. Meredith knew she was going to die. And in her twenty-six years she'd never left Broomfield.

The person who had taken her had been a shape at the periphery of her vision outside the bathroom of the fried chicken place before a sack that stank of paraffin had been put over her face. Then something heavy had slammed into her scalp. Meredith could feel the bruise pound under the raw and broken skin, still taste the vinegary Buffalo wings she'd been eating. She breathed out and flinched as the spiked metal pierced her stomach.

Movement behind her – whoever had stripped and bound Meredith was the other side of the pillar. She gasped as the wire cut deeper. They were pulling and tightening it. The tops of her arms throbbed as the blood was trapped and the steel points dragged and tore at her flesh.

Meredith struggled to shape her guttural pleas but agony squeezed them flat. Was it going to get any worse than this? She closed her eyes and kept them shut even after the wire had stopped contracting. Her wounds trickled warmth down the inside of her thigh.

'Meredith,' a calm voice whispered in front of her.

She cracked her eyes at the hooded person standing in the shadows. They took a step forward into the dim light, head bowed as they focussed on something in their gloved hands.

Meredith looked down and saw it was a tiny tube of glue. They unscrewed the cap and then moved the nib across the area under each of her eyebrows. She could only grunt incoherently and stare at their throat.

She could smell the cool solvent on her skin before the leather pads of their thumbs curled her false eyelashes against it and pressed them hard in place.

She couldn't shake her forehead as they pushed it harshly against the pillar. A few moments later she was released. Meredith could feel the air on her exposed eyeballs and them quickly drying out as her lids fought to blink. Now she had no choice but to look at whatever they were going to do to her.

The hood spoke to Meredith through her tears and agonised begging, so she only heard some of what they said. But it was enough. They retreated back into the gloom when she understood. She couldn't accept what they'd told her. How could she have brought this on herself?

Meredith waited for them to return but their footfalls faded before she heard a car door slam.

She was still going to die; nobody would find her and cut her down in time.

An engine started. They were leaving.

Her circulation coursed irregularly through her constricted limbs. Meredith sucked in air through her nose. Unconsciousness began to release her.

But the black haze was quickly bleached out.

Meredith Hickman was illuminated and couldn't seal her eyes against a blinding set of headlights turning square in her direction. The car accelerated, hurtled through the main entrance and rocketed straight at her.

CHAPTER 2

Hazel Salter yanked on the frosted entrance door and breezed through the downstairs reception as quickly as she could. 'Hey, Rena.'

The pink-haired, twenty-three-year-old intern looked up from her granola and magazine with barely concealed hostility. 'Hey.' Rena had the kind of indolent arrogance that stemmed from the belief she had so many years ahead of her she was bound to be spectacular at some point.

'You've beaten me in again.'

Rena grinned inhospitably. 'When don't I?'

Hazel couldn't blame her for being spiky. She was a UCLA graduate who had been employed by her for seven months and had been tucked downstairs since she'd started. She hit the button for the elevator and willed the doors to open.

'Hazel?'

She turned and rapidly blinked at Rena as if startled from her thoughts.

'Just wondered if you've interviewed for another receptionist yet.' Rena knew Hazel hadn't. She signed everyone in.

'I'm still looking at applicants.'

Rena nodded but knew she was being fobbed off. 'I have a friend who's interested. Maybe then you could put me to better use.'

'Great. Get her to email me her résumé.'

Rena knew it was another stalling tactic. 'She's in town today. I could get her to swing by, if you're not too busy... ' she said significantly.

Hazel had one solitary meeting that day, and Rena knew it. She'd orchestrated this perfectly.

'Sorry, I'm locking myself in the office to work on some new proposals. But if she can leave her details with you, I'll get back to her as soon as I can.'

Rena's eyes instantly glazed. 'Sure.'

'Any messages?'

Rena shook her head once as if it was becoming a tiresome ritual. 'Mail's on your desk.'

The elevator doors parted, and Hazel stepped inside. She wouldn't have to run the same gauntlet for much longer and had been half-expecting to find reception empty for the last couple of weeks.

The other floors of the office block were unoccupied so she'd had to put Rena there as sentry. Seven months ago she'd genuinely believed in the chemistry she'd felt when the girl with the bowl cut of pink hair had walked into her office fresh from campus. When Hazel had interviewed her, she'd said she needed a general factotum but that there'd be plenty of opportunities to gain valuable production and post-production experience. Now Rena was her only employee – today, at least.

The doors separated, and she echoed through the oversized second empty reception, past the six unoccupied desks on the production floor to her expansive office beyond. Hazel had no choice but to give up her Sunset Boulevard business address at the end of the month and go back to working from home. However long she owned that.

Hazel regarded the pile of envelopes on her desk and knew exactly what they were. She flicked through them, holding her breath as she did. A final rent reminder and demands for business utility bills with red stamps all over them. After spending her teenage years with her British mother in the UK, Hazel had lived in LA for just over a decade, but, wherever she lived, she'd always had a tendency to ignore everyday responsibilities.

She didn't even look at the Emmy on the cherrywood wall unit any more. It had been her talisman when she'd moved Veracity Media to the next level, and now the golden angel with the atom within its grasp was a gilded joke.

Even though it was only the September before last, picking up the award for *Isil Brides* seemed like it had happened in somebody else's lifetime. It coincided with her thirtieth birthday, and her agent at the time had told Hazel everyone was talking about her forthright interview technique and that she had to step up to the plate and capitalise on the exposure. Now her office was about to shut down, and the bank was going to foreclose on her house. She'd used it as collateral to start up Veracity Media.

She hadn't got complacent. The number of meetings she'd had after *Isil Brides* picked up its award for best documentary had been dizzying – big studios, big talk. Seven months ago she had so many projects pending she wondered if her office space was going to be big enough to cope. Now even the secretaries of the execs had stopped returning her emails, and the only people still in touch with Hazel were her crew.

Isil Brides had been made with caffeine and goodwill. Most had worked for nothing and had stuck with the project above and beyond the point most professionals should have. She loved her crew but now she couldn't make good on the promises she'd used to entice them on board in the first place.

Hazel knew she could do it again. Some of them would come back, if not all. But how could she replicate the optimism and belief that there was no limit to what they could achieve next that she'd engendered on the Syrian shoot?

She'd been here plenty of times before, but on her earlier projects she hadn't been an award winner with overheads. Ironically, the industry now thought she was too big a producer/director for indie money, but not big enough to helm upscale projects for the majors.

Picking up the remote, she switched on the news channel, turned her back on it and took a jar of instant coffee out of her handbag. Moving into the galley kitchen she filled and switched on the kettle and waited while it strained and wheezed. Hazel wondered if she could get any money back on the cappuccino machine that had been installed. Jesus, had it really come down to this?

For a while her mind searched for a gear. The kettle boiled, and she made her drink on automatic pilot. As she stirred her coffee, the words of the male newsreader gradually filtered into her thoughts. He was talking about the 'Be My Killer' story.

Several people were dead after they'd responded to a dare to put their names into a Twitter stream supposedly for serial killers to select their victims. She sipped her coffee but it was piping hot, and she was just struggling to open a new milk carton when Hazel recognised a name he mentioned and walked quickly back into the office, her attention on the screen.

A twenty-six-year-old woman, Meredith Hickman, had been brutally murdered in Broomfield, Vermont.

Hazel examined the photograph on-screen and saw, behind the make-up and wear of twenty years, a girl whose shrieks and laughter and cherry lip-balm scent had mingled with her own as they'd chased and weaved through the broken benches of Blue Grove Park.

CHAPTER 3

'Yes?' Detective Jared Bennett's flat tone said he'd run out of excuses not to speak to Hazel.

She hadn't been expecting him to pick up and tucked her short ash-blonde hair behind her ear as she sat down on her desk. 'I've left a ton of messages for you.'

'You always do. What can I help you with this time, Miss Salter?'

'My crew are travelling to Broomfield tomorrow. Just wondered if you'd reconsidered.' She already knew what his response would be.

'I've got nothing to add since the January press release.'

'It's March now. No progress since then?'

'I've got a bunch of other things on my plate.'

'It's been five months since Meredith's death. Don't you think participating in my documentary would be an opportunity to rekindle interest in the investigation?'

'Why don't you speak to the FBI? Since they assumed control I've probably had as much luck getting them to pick up the phone as you.' Detective Bennett had been uncooperative since Meredith's murder had been tied in with the 'Be My Killer' hysteria. That's when it had become much bigger than just a small-town homicide and, after his department had been ridiculed for their handling of the case by the media, it had been swiftly wrestled from his hands.

'I'm just asking you for an hour or so of your time.'

'Yes, you and all the other TV people. Just let me get on with my job, Miss Salter. What I don't need is you and your crew picking over a cold crime scene.'

'We've got permission.'

'I don't doubt it. But we've only just seen the back of all the cameras and TV crews. Everyone here went crazy with that. Wait, I've got another call.'

Hazel's eyes came to rest on the photo of Meredith Hickman stuck to her pinboard. 'I promise I wouldn't be pursuing this if I wasn't wholly committed to this story.'

'If you want to help the investigation, just keep your crew away from Broomfield.' He hung up on her.

Hazel set her iPhone on the desk, stood and walked to the pinboard. Over the past months she'd immersed herself in the chain of events that had followed the 'Be My Killer' Twitter craze.

The Twitter account @BeMyKiller was supposedly set up as a prank. Millions of people had responded to the dare and put their names forward using the hashtag #BeMyKiller and included a message goading their potential murderer.

Four people had died after using the hashtag. She examined their faces. Denise Needham was a pretty twenty-three-year-old nanny working for a wealthy family in Belle Meade, Tennessee, who, on Halloween, had baited her killer with the words

Take your best shot #BeMyKiller

Two days later, three armour-piercing bullets fired by a sniper through a kitchen window fatally wounded her.

One day later, in Clearwater, Florida, thirty-one-year-old Caleb Huber's

Want a piece of me? #BeMyKiller

message was taken very literally. His younger sister, Eve, found his mutilated remains in their backyard. His pockmarked features sneered crookedly at Hazel from the wall.

She took in the gaunt expression of twenty-five-year-old Kristian O'Connell. A couple of hours after Caleb had died, he'd been stabbed thirty-six times in an alleyway in Cheyenne, Wyoming.

He'd tweeted the @BeMyKiller account but was the only victim who didn't include a message for his killer. Kristian was a heroin addict.

Three days later, Meredith Hickman had been murdered only two hours after her

Hit me up #BeMyKiller

invitation in Broomfield, Vermont.

Hazel's eyes returned to her toothy smile. It was the photo they'd used on the news, and there was a doleful vulnerability in her regard that hadn't changed since she'd first met her.

It was why Hazel had taken her under her wing. The other kids that played in Blue Grove Park had teased Meredith. She was weak and they'd all sensed it. Meredith had been four years younger than her but Hazel had given her one of her woven rainbow friendship bracelets and shielded her from the bullying of the others.

Her parents never picked Meredith up from the park so Hazel often walked her to the gates because she knew she was reluctant to go home. Meredith had two brothers but they were much older and had already been getting into trouble with the police.

Having researched her background Hazel hadn't found any surprises in the trajectory of her life. Both her brothers were now serving time on drug dealing charges, and her parents had substance abuse histories. Meredith had grown up in a criminal family. Maybe the simple truth was that she'd been doomed because of her upbringing.

She'd spoken with Meredith's father, Wade Hickman, via FaceTime, after he'd agreed to take part. Her mother, Tamara, had been vehemently against the documentary being made and had only conceded after it was clear the shoot would go ahead. Hazel had decided against mentioning to them she'd been a childhood friend of Meredith's.

That was something Hazel hadn't declared to her crew either. She didn't want them to think her connection to Meredith would cloud her impartiality.

Statistically, out of the eight million people who had used the #BeMyKiller hashtag, a small percentage of them would have been murdered in any case. But the similarity between the nature of three of the deaths in the US and what the victims had specifically said in their tweets was irrefutable, and the FBI investigation was still focussed on catching multiple perpetrators.

It had ground to a halt, however, and Hazel was exploring an alternative: that, despite the fact that each murder had occurred in a different state, one individual committed all the crimes. This 'lone tourist theory' was popular online but had been dismissed by the official investigation because the time-frame of the murders didn't allow for one killer to travel to all the locations.

But in light of a recent revelation, Hazel believed it would have been possible. And to her it seemed plausible that the murders were the work of one person rather than #BeMyKiller inspiring several people to kill in the space of one week.

The killing stopped at Meredith Hickman. By then, Twitter had shut the account down for breaking Twitter Rules. Meredith Hickman's horrific execution had put Hazel's anonymous home town on the map in the worst way possible. They'd both grown up in the same place. Both played in Blue Grove Park. Hazel had been lucky enough to move away to the UK with her mother. If she'd stayed she doubted she would have had the same fate as Meredith. But if she'd remained in Broomfield, could she have saved her?

CHAPTER 4

FUN CENTRAL

The words of the stilted sign were plastered over balloons that Hazel remembered used to be different hues but had now been faded a uniform blue by the sun. She swung her car onto and climbed the ramp before levelling off in front of the condemned domain of mirth. It was part of a shopping mall, and bleached stars were also dotted over its teal aluminium roof. A familiar orange Toyota and a vintage motorbike were parked near the main entrance. Looked like some of the crew had beaten her.

Positioning herself in a space nearby, she switched off the engine, got out of her grey Mazda and took in the building while the chill March wind blasted through her black puffer jacket. She recalled her parents driving her out here on weekends to shop, and her father buying her a malt shake while they waited what seemed to be an eternity for her mother.

After the bigger mall was built on the east side of Broomfield, however, Fun Central struggled to survive. Many of the chain stores relocated and, although it attempted to entice families back with its go-kart arena, it never recovered. Hazel couldn't believe it had hung on so long. But after Meredith Hickman was murdered the place had been closed down for good leaving it to skulk emptily on the edge of town, an unwanted reminder of what could happen right on your doorstep. From what her location manager told her, Fun Central had been moribund before the homicide; the waste dump behind it and the stagnant pond nearby a hang-out for junkies and the criminal dregs of Broomfield.

The sliding main entrance doors parted and Cox trotted out into the parking zone. 'Haze.' He quickly covered the distance between them with strides of his spindly legs and hugged her. The location manager's long auburn hair smothered her.

'I thought I'd be the first here.' She'd wanted a little time on her own to explore the exterior before Cox arrived with the keys.

'We were lucky with the traffic.'

The soundman, Weiss, ambled out of the building to join them. The blonde German was leaner than Cox but squeezed her as tight. Behind him was the cameraman, Lucas. He waited his turn. She wasn't sure she liked him with his head so severely shaved. It seemed even less likely a smile would break out on his stern, meditative features. He'd always been her cameraman. And even when they'd become closer, their relationship had remained professional.

'I must be a glutton for punishment,' Lucas quipped in her ear.

She embraced him but for a shorter time than the other two, and they diplomatically parted.

'The others should be arriving over the next few hours but I really want to thank you guys for this.' She made eye contact with each one.

'How could we possibly pass up on such an exotic location?' Lucas gestured around.

'Ready for the tour?' Cox held up a bunch of keys.

Hazel followed her core crew to the entrance. It was so good to see them again. And she already felt guilty she had no immediate budget to pay them with. She was working on that but, for the moment, they were back where they'd started. The tacit notion of their hard work on *Isil Brides* being a springboard to bigger things was now a little frayed around the edges. After the Emmy, everyone believed the days of shoestring gigs might be behind them and Hazel felt she'd let them all down. Now she was determined to reward her crew in the way they should have been last time around.

'Come see the shrine.' Cox strode ahead. 'It's sadly beautiful.'

Her head spun towards a sound to her left. Crows suddenly took off from the branches of the trees on the edge of Holtwood Forest. She'd been a little girl the last time she'd ventured in there but it still seemed as foreboding.

The doors parted and Hazel was walking over the dirty peanut butter tiles of a wide concourse that smelt strongly of bleach. A row of glass-fronted and numbered fun zones stretched away from her on the far side, and the leaves that had blown in were piled in their doorways. It was difficult to square the scene with the one she'd visited in her childhood. She tried to spot the shake place.

It looked like it had been replaced by a ball pit and, as she squinted through the dirty window, Hazel could see the grubby red rope climbing frame and the slide leading down to its full pool of gaudy plastic fun. To the right of it was an entrance to the mini go-kart arena, 'Speed Zone'.

Looking left she saw a large, empty space bordered by low, plastic green hedges emblazoned 'Bounce Zone', where, she assumed, various inflatables used to be positioned. Shops and a shuttered fast-food outlet, 'District Burger', were to the left of it. Next to them were the bathrooms and a row of three grabber machines. There were only a few faded cuddly toys left inside each one, and their reinforced glass cases were distressed where vandals had failed to break them open. One was blackened from fire damage.

MEREDITH SUCKED DICK FOR CHANGE proclaimed the graffiti words over a crude phallic drawing sprayed on one of the support pillars to her right. It seemed such a vile desecration: scrawling that where Meredith had lost her life in such an abhorrent way. Hazel hadn't found any evidence of prostitution in Meredith's background. Only a record for petty theft and under-age drinking. She identified the pillar shrine straight-ahead – votive candles in jars, shrivelled dead flowers, soft toys and pictures taped around its base.

As she followed Cox, Lucas and Weiss, the photos of Meredith's beaming face emerged from the cluster of tributes and handwritten messages. They depicted her at various stages of her life. Same smile in all of them that couldn't conceive of her horrible end there.

Hazel had seen the pictures plenty of times but it was only contemplating her callow image in such a squalid place that accentuated how alone and helpless she must have been. And even though it was twenty years ago, Hazel could still vividly recollect handing her the rainbow friendship bracelet and Meredith's expression of undiluted relief when she'd accepted it.

CHAPTER 5

As the crew continued their survey of Fun Central, Hazel excused herself and stepped back outside for a breath of fresh air.

This had taken her by surprise. She hadn't envisaged how returning to Broomfield would have affected her in such a way. Even standing in the parking zone she felt claustrophobic. So much had happened in her life since she'd last walked through the doors of Fun Central but suddenly it seemed as if none of it had.

If her father hadn't died when she was ten years old, would they have stayed? And, if so, who would she be now? Perhaps she'd be living in town, working in Stooky's bar or one of the other dives.

She wondered if Meredith had ever yearned to escape. But her parents had owned the turkey farm here. Work and family – for most people – that was usually reason enough to stay. But she'd seen Meredith picked up from Blue Grove Park by police and driven home enough times to know that her domestic life had been pretty unstable. Hazel could see how easy it was to get trapped.

The media attitude towards Broomfield had been pretty bromidic. Patronising reporters insinuating the 'Be My Killer' craze would be seized upon by disaffected kids in small towns. Hazel knew it would be a mistake for her own investigation to make the same facile assumptions.

She turned on her heel and looked through the glass panels of the doors to the shrine. Meredith hadn't been her responsibility for two decades. They'd both made a lot of choices in the meantime. Even if Hazel hadn't left and remained as her friend, she suspected they might have grown apart. Or could those photos around the shrine just as easily have depicted her own face?

CHAPTER 6

Henrik Fossen had a dusk view of the fallow fields of Broomfield from both sides of the cab.

The driver was in his forties and blinked at Henrik in the mirror through thick lenses. 'They making a movie about the girl who died?'

'Something like that.' Henrik glanced right as they turned at the huge Fun Central sign and climbed the ramp.

'How long they gonna be here?' The driver parked up.

'Not my department, sorry.' Henrik got out of the car and dragged his single bag with him. He peeled off enough bills from his wallet and thrust them through the window.

'Only asking,' the driver grumbled.

'I really am the wrong guy to talk to.'

The driver pocketed the money and didn't offer him change. 'Who then?'

'Her?' Henrik indicated the pink-haired girl who had emerged from the entrance to the complex and was doing one of those elbow walks that looks like running but actually isn't any faster. As she approached, he tried to maintain eye contact with her and not look at her breasts' jiggling, independent rhythm.

'Henrik, hi.' She was carrying a clipboard that held a thick yellow itinerary. 'I'm Rena, AP,' she said breathlessly.

He frowned.

'Associate producer,' Rena explained, as if it wasn't the first time she'd had to. Most of her freckles had hibernated for the winter but were still visible across the bridge of her nose.

'What are you folks shooting here?'

'Documentary,' Rena answered the driver.

When she didn't elaborate, he gave them a sour look and swiftly reversed his cherry Chrysler away.

They both watched him go.

Henrik turned to Rena. 'Hazel said I could claim any travel expenses.'

'Absolutely. Just give me any receipts and I'll get straight on it.'

Henrik looked back at the receding car.

'Right this way.'

Henrik tried not to focus on the cellulite of Rena's denim-clad butt as she led him across the parking zone. His brother could always find something he found attractive, some physical characteristic he appreciated in every girl he met. Henrik had a talent for the opposite. He caught up with her.

'You're the first interviewee to arrive. Hazel wanted some one-on-one with you before the others get here,' she informed him over her shoulder.

Henrik nodded uncertainly as the entrance doors to Fun Central shakily slid open.

'I know this must be a… significant moment for you, Henrik,' she said as they approached the shrine.

He hung back and didn't reply.

'But I think Hazel wants the camera present for the tour. If you wouldn't mind bypassing this… '

Bypassing it was what he'd been unsuccessfully trying to do for the past five months – why he'd taken the overdose of flunitrazepam pills, and why his last seizure had made him nearly bite his tongue in half. Meredith Hickman, a complete stranger to Henrik, had been kidnapped and mutilated twenty feet from where he was standing, and the finger of blame had been pointed firmly in his direction. All because, out of sheer boredom, he'd created the @BeMyKiller Twitter account.

Henrik moved tentatively forward again.

'The crew will be done soon. Hazel's in a production meeting with them now… '

Henrik was mesmerised by the images of Meredith Hickman.

'Hazel, sorry, Henrik's here. You might want to head down.'

Rena's phone conversation receded as he reached the pillar. In between the tiny champagne tiles Henrik could see a dark residue and deep dents in the plaster. He knew exactly what had made them.

'Henrik.' Rena was behind him. 'Hazel said take as long as you need.'

CHAPTER 7

When he walked into the production office, Henrik Fossen was much taller than Hazel expected from her FaceTime conversations with him. But despite that, the twenty-four-year-old's hooked posture made him look like he'd been punched in the stomach and was nursing the blow. A brand new pair of white Reeboks flashed under the flares of his jeans. It was difficult to believe the awkward individual in front of her was responsible for all of them gathering at Fun Central.

The crew took his entrance as their cue to swiftly wrap up the meeting. There was no furniture in the damp-smelling upstairs room so they stood from their leaning positions around the graffiti-daubed walls and moved towards the door.

Hazel firmed her lips at Henrik. 'Everyone, just quickly say hi to Henrik Fossen. He's just flown in from Saratoga.'

They all nodded at him as if they didn't know exactly who he was. He smirked a greeting, his goatee tightening up his haggard face.

'Henrik, this is Lucas, Weiss, Sweeting, Cox and Keeler, and they'll be so in your face for the next couple of days you'll have nightmares about them. Their hygiene standards are evolving though,' she joked, perfunctorily.

Henrik pursed his lips as they filed past him.

'I'll let you guys eat and then we'll block out tomorrow. Sorry again about the catering situation. Rena's sourced some delivery menus and will take your orders. Beers in the cool box.'

The crew grunted. They were used to living on pizzas and cold dough balls but it was late March and freezing so the alcohol wasn't going to be the recompense it usually was.

Hazel moved across the office and held up her finger to Henrik. 'Sorry – one minute. Lucas? I can sweeten the pot with a bottle of Glenlivet if you can give Rena a ride into town.'

He ran his palm over his shaved head. 'No problem.'

Hazel handed her credit card to Rena. What the hell, she had expenses debts from *Isil Brides* she was still making minimum payments on. 'Henrik.' She took his hand and it felt like a cold rock. 'Thanks again for agreeing to take part. Rena tells me you've just seen the shrine.'

He met the gravity in her gaze and nodded. His matt green eyes were emotionless, however: no indication of how the encounter had affected him.

Hazel was still disturbed every time she walked by it and saw Meredith's familiar smile in such a godforsaken place. She filled the awkward gap. 'It's an arresting sight.'

'I'm sorry. Rena said you wanted to record it.' His Norwegian accent was barely discernible.

'It's me that should be sorry. I should have been there to chaperone you.'

'I got an earlier plane. I hope my turning up early hasn't spoilt everything.' He released her hand.

She couldn't yet tell if the apology was genuine or if he still had the vague disdain for the project Hazel had sensed in their FaceTime conversations. 'Of course not. I really don't want you to be uncomfortable with anything we're doing here, but my job is to capture as much of the reality of this place as I can.'

Henrik nodded impatiently. 'You mentioned I could claim for my expenses.'

It wasn't the response she expected but confirmed to her what the main motive for his presence was. 'Just give any receipts to Rena.'

'I'm afraid I wasn't aware of that when the cab dropped me here.'

She reached for her handbag. 'Sure. Let me reimburse you for that.'

Henrik made no attempt to stop Hazel retrieving her purse.

'How much?'

'Thirty… and tip,' he said, with an air of entitlement.

She knew all about his wealthy background and how his behaviour had impacted his father's business empire. Hazel handed him forty, and he pocketed it.

'I was told there was accommodation on-site?'

'Yes. You have the rare pleasure of bunking with us. It's actually ideal and means you won't have to get up early in the morning to travel to location.' She could see from his expression she hadn't sold it. 'We've converted the admin offices and storerooms up here into sleeping quarters. The crew are sharing but you get your own room. I'm hoping you're going to be too busy to spend much time in it though.'

Henrik grimaced. 'There's nowhere in town?'

'Yes but, logistically, it's better that you're here. Look, I want to be honest about the resources we have at our disposal, and by that, I mean we're running on a very tight budget. The crew won't be paid until we sell the project. Nor will I, or any of the other participants. I'm just paying their expenses like you.'

Henrik said nothing but inhaled slowly.

'I need you to make this work, Henrik. We're going to ensure you're as comfortable as possible, and I'm hoping being part of this project will compensate you way beyond any financial rewards.'

Henrik closed his eyes and nodded reluctantly.

Hazel felt a small surge of relief but immediately sensed this was to be the first of many similar conversations. 'Good. I'm really grateful for you flying here to be with us, and I genuinely believe you're going to benefit from this experience.'

'I'm not entirely convinced of that… Hazel.' His use of her name sounded strange. Like he was bolting it on to mimic natural conversation.

'Let Rena show you to your room so you can settle in. You can join us for dinner or we can give you your privacy. I can't promise this won't be difficult. Tomorrow will be particularly hard. But you can trust me because I'm looking for the same answers as you.'

'So what happens tomorrow?'

'Have a think about what I've said and then let me know if you're going to stay.'

'Well, I'm here now.' Henrik looked like he was chewing something unpleasant. 'What do I have to do tomorrow?'

CHAPTER 8

Hazel was sitting on her red swivel chair in the upstairs production office surrounded by her shivering team. As wind blasted the black windowpane her eyes roved the graffiti on the peeling walls. The Glenlivet bottle was nearly drained. She'd only drunk a couple of fingers to warm her but, having missed the pizza slices, the alcohol had taken advantage of her empty stomach.

She was eager to get Henrik Fossen in front of the camera the following morning. He was the individual who tied the deaths together. The victims' friends and family were starting to fly in tomorrow afternoon. His responses to them would make for some interesting viewing, but clearing them as suspects was her priority before she could begin to focus on the lone tourist theory and why Broomfield and Meredith became targets.

She took out her iPhone and opened the crew's 'Turkey Shoot' WhatsApp group. They were on it, sniggering over suggestions of how they'd provoke the killer. Hazel wasn't amused but knew it was only because they were nervous and distracting themselves from their surroundings.

You don't have any balls.

'Very creative, Sweeting.' Hazel didn't have a handle on the new assistant soundman yet, although his default seemed to be muted sarcasm. He was probably the oldest of the crew. Bar Rena, everyone was early thirties. Sweeting looked to be early forties.

He was hunched low in his parka in a telescopic chair. 'I imagine he could be pretty creative with balls.' His fingers rearranged the strands of hair over his baldness.

Hazel examined Rena's contribution to the discussion.

Choke on it, loser.

'Good to see the associate producer setting an example.'

Rena looked briefly contrite but had already drunk way too much. Hazel was going to have to keep an eye on her. She was clearly more naïve than she made out. Her pink hair was messily tucked into her black woolly hat, and she was stroking Keeler's beard. The two of them were seated on the empty equipment boxes and had got very cosy. Keeler was a hairy beast and completely dwarfed her. He was killing time before he had another production gig and had offered to be a runner for Rena while he waited for the call. Now Hazel could see why.

Come get some, fuckface!

'Nice, Keeler.'

'I notice you haven't chipped in yet, Haze.' Cox drained his paper cup.

'I'm good.'

'Come on,' he insisted, 'if we're all condemning ourselves to death for this gig you certainly can.'

Hazel didn't want to rain on the camaraderie but felt distinctly uncomfortable. It had probably seemed like a harmless joke when the victims had done the same. She visualised Meredith heedlessly typing in her message. 'OK, if I could I'd put Joel Patterson's name forward… '

'Who's Joel Patterson?' Cox asked.

'CEO at Riker. They're the eleventh distributor to turn me down.' Hazel typed:

Spineless bitch.

Hazel noticed Lucas hadn't participated either. He was sitting on the desk, and she could tell he was thinking about a cigarette, even though he'd just put one out. But something had been different since she'd arrived. She wondered if she should ask Weiss what.

The blonde-haired soundman was seated next to Lucas, slowly rubbing his hands to keep warm. He and Lucas always worked closely together.

Cox got to his feet. 'What about mine?'

She scrolled back and located Cox's.

Blow me!

'Succinct.'

He tucked his long auburn hair behind his ears and picked up his bag and orange motorcycle helmet.

'You heading off now?' Lucas said incredulously.

Cox nodded. 'I've only been drinking coffee, and twenty cups is my limit. And now I've given up my deluxe penthouse to Henrik Fossen…'

Hazel pocketed her phone. 'We can find you somewhere else to sleep for tonight.'

'I'd rather travel while the roads are empty. Look, any problems, call me.'

Much as she enjoyed Cox's presence, Hazel couldn't afford to pay her location manager to stick around. He'd negotiated their occupation of Fun Central and had been there to give them keys and a tour the previous day but now he was going to spend a few days driving to his next paying gig. He had two ex-wives to support.

'You know where to drop the keys when you're done.' Cox leaned down and kissed Hazel on the cheek.

Hazel nodded. 'I owe you big time.'

'You already did.'

He was about to slip on his helmet but paused when they heard a clatter in the corridor. 'Henrik?'

The crew turned to the door but he didn't enter.

Cox walked over and opened it. Hazel followed him. There was nobody outside. Hazel's head darted to the source of the sound. A draught rolled an old beer can to the wall.

Cox zipped up his leather jacket. 'Yep. One night in this freezing shithole was more than enough for me.'

CHAPTER 9

Keeler's cold hands slid up from Rena's waist and lightly gripped her breasts from behind. For such a stocky guy he had a gentle touch, and she felt a little disappointed by that.

'Jesus, this is a toxic little oasis you've brought me to.' His beer breath was warm on the side of her face as she led him down the path from Fun Central through the birches and to the pond. Plastic bottles and other detritus were motionless on its surface, and the inky water barely reflected the smudged moon. The toe of his boot hit a thick root, and he staggered and released her. 'Shit.'

A few crows lazily complained from the branches above them.

He was drunker than she thought, drunker than she was. Did she want to get a reputation as the crew slut? As the associate producer, Rena knew she should be behaving more professionally. But, having broken it off with her boyfriend just before New Year's Eve, she knew exactly what would happen when Keeler topped up her paper cup for the third time. She should be asleep in her bunk. Now she'd be exhausted for the first interview day of the shoot.

But she was twenty-three and had been faithful to one guy for two and a half years. Working the internship for Hazel Salter hadn't exactly put her in the middle of a media social scene so she was determined to capitalise on any attention she got.

Plus Keeler wasn't going to be around for the whole week so things wouldn't have to be awkward for too long. And that gave her scope if there was anyone else she was interested in. Sweeting was the only other guy who had tried to hit on her but he was married and had bad teeth and that told Rena all she needed to know about how he looked after the rest of himself.

She'd assessed the dynamic of the remaining crew. Lucas was the cutest in a moody, unavailable way but, even though she'd gleaned he was living with his partner, she could tell there was something between him and Hazel. There was a familiarity but also a diplomatic distance that spoke volumes. They'd worked tightly on the Syrian shoot so she guessed they might have been an item at some point. Blonde-haired Weiss was very reserved, maybe even gay. Henrik Fossen creeped her out. Even though his father was loaded, she knew nothing good was going to come from hooking up with him. Fortunately, he'd stayed up in his room the entire evening.

Rena took Keeler's icy palm, led him to the mini jetty and sat down, cross-legged.

'Hope you're not thinking about a swim.' Keeler dropped heavily beside her and pulled out a pack of menthol cigarettes.

Rena shivered. The water smelt of soil and paint. 'No, I don't need to grow an extra head.'

'Nothing wrong with extra head.' Keeler grinned, put two cigarettes in his mouth, lit both and passed one to Rena.

She'd lost count of how many she'd accepted from him that night, even though she was meant to have given up. She inhaled heavily and blew the smoke out through a tight hole in her lips. They were lights and she could barely taste the tobacco. 'Pity, I've got a great bod for skinny-dipping.'

'Well, let's not rule anything out. We could just skip the dipping part.'

'Sure about that?' Rena put her hand out and touched his wiry beard. She'd already found plenty of excuses to stroke it that evening but now she didn't need any.

Keeler smiled as her fingers explored it and pecked the tips of her fingers when they brushed his lips. He exhaled smoke.

She nodded at the black water. 'You first then.'

His bushy eyebrows bounced against the brim of his beanie.

'I'll show you my skinny if you show me your dipping part.'

Keeler laughed. 'It must be three below.'

'You've got all your hair to keep you warm. Bet you're covered from head to toe.'

He smirked, and they both leaned in to kiss.

His bristles tickled her mouth. Her ex had never wanted to grow a beard so this was a new one on her. She felt his arms lightly encircle her, tasted the beer and tobacco on his lips. But they were hot and she sucked on the bottom one. Bit into it a little.

He attempted to undo her wax coat.

'It's Velcro.'

'Relax. I can work with Velcro.'

The noise of it ripping seemed deafening around the pond, and they both giggled as he removed it.

Rena lay back, and Keeler grunted as he positioned himself over her. She could see nervousness briefly register in his features but then his lips were back on hers. She closed her eyes as his prickly face ground at her chin. She was going to have a rash in the morning.

Briefly, she fell asleep. It was the booze and the long trip to the location the day before. But the chill of his hands moving up inside her blouse roused her again. She reached down and felt how awake he was. 'Have you got a condom?'

'There might be one lying around here somewhere.'

'Don't joke. Have you got one?'

He shook his head and waited for her approval.

She sighed. 'OK.'

Keeler pulled away so she could drop her jeans and panties and was ready for her when she lay back again. He nudged the head around her labia, and she realised he was doing it on purpose. He teased her a bit more, and when he slid inside Rena wrapped her legs around his back and pulled him in tighter.

Now he wasn't being so gentle.

Rena sighed in his ear to encourage him, and he pumped his buttocks harder. He wasn't as big as she'd thought, and she tried not to giggle as he gyrated his hips. It was obviously his Saturday night special, and she didn't want to dampen his spirit.

Maybe she'd just made the job of being taken seriously as the AP a lot more difficult. It was very likely the rest of the crew would soon know about this so she told herself to enjoy it. Keeler licked her neck and, she had to admit, his gyrations were starting to touch her just where she needed it.

As they both found a rhythm and began to lose control neither of them noticed somebody step out of the trees three feet away to watch more closely.

CHAPTER 10

Hazel woke, fingered her hair behind her ears, located her iPhone and flipped the cover: 5:53 a.m. Her cot creaked as she swung her legs off it and looked over to Lucas who was still sleeping. The room stank of his boozy breath but it was a familiar and bizarrely comforting aroma.

She winced as the bare soles of her feet touched the freezing concrete floor and quickly tugged on her thick woollen socks. Hazel watched his shuttered eyelids as she removed her padded nightshirt and quickly pulled on a bra, two sweatshirts and a pair of jeans.

Her coyness was seriously misplaced. They'd slept together during the nights of the Syrian shoot but neither had contacted each other since the awards. She knew he was living with someone else now – Carrie. But that was OK with Hazel. They'd started to get too close and that was always when she backed away.

After she'd told the crew about sleeping two to an office they'd organised themselves and automatically assumed she would be sharing with Lucas. He'd come in a few hours after her, and she'd listened to him shivering as he got undressed and sat on the edge of his cot. She'd had her back to him and hadn't moved. A few minutes later she'd heard the springs of his mattress squeaking and his instantaneous snoring.

The air hissed through the crack in his lips. The barrier was back up between them. Not just because of their incomplete history. This was the familiar one between crew and producer. It was always there because she stood to enjoy a bigger slice of any success their collaboration earned. You could find it on any indie shoot. Amongst the comradeship there was always a vague mistrust that their contribution would never be properly rewarded.

Hazel slipped on her boots, crept out of the room and into the corridor. She checked Henrik's door at the far end, which was slightly ajar. Before he'd retired, he'd informed her his meds had turned him into an insomniac. Maybe there were other reasons he couldn't sleep.

Despite Veracity Media hanging in the balance, Meredith Hickman's death had compelled her to initiate the project but she knew its whole success hinged on Henrik's participation. His involvement was the hook to hang it on because the central emotion of the piece would come from the remorse he felt about creating the @BeMyKiller account. But she had yet to see any evidence of that. Even though Henrik Fossen had no alibi during the time the killings had taken place, the spotlight of the official investigation had shifted quickly away from him. He hadn't left Saratoga and outwardly, at least, appeared to be just a rich kid with too much spare time to devote to online mischief. Hazel wasn't about to subscribe to any FBI presumptions, however; from their FaceTime conversations, she too suspected Henrik was entirely innocent.

She stole past the production office and briefly inspected the wreckage. The guys had been playing Midnight Train, Keeler's six dice game, when she'd come to bed. She'd told them she wanted an early start but none of them had responded. But as they were supplying their skill sets unpaid Hazel knew exactly to what degree she could wrangle them and had left them huddled around the heater steadily emptying the cool box.

Keeler had been all over Rena, and her associate producer hadn't appeared averse to the attention. Rena was learning on the job and seemed inordinately proud of her schedule, which she imperiously enforced, and the trolley she'd brought along to ferry coffee and equipment around on. Hazel hoped she was going to be capable and not curled up in Keeler's sleeping bag until noon.

It was the catch-22 of her shoots. Alcohol was a cheap perk to provide but it always impacted the productivity, hence her assembling everyone an hour earlier than necessary. Coffee and painkillers had to be administered and then she'd begin her performance about how much time they were losing. They'd enjoy her getting agitated for a while but then Hazel would have them all corralled by the time she really wanted to start.

She padded down the stairs from the admin level and pushed the stiff door at the bottom. The concourse was even more glacial than upstairs. The draught on her face felt like the raw wind was blowing directly in from outside.

Unlike their previous shoot, it was a controllable location and she had the golden keys to the kingdom. She'd secured the sliding doors the night before but the crew didn't trust her security measures and hid their equipment.

Lucas had showed her the independent spy cams he'd brought along and offered to dot them around the complex. Hazel hadn't thought it necessary. They hadn't seen anyone else on the lot. Surely it was too damn cold.

Before she'd arrived the previous day, she'd taken a lone drive out to her old neighbourhood. The family house was gone, replaced by a private dental clinic. It was the place she remembered being happy. As carefree as it was possible to be. Then her father had lost his battle against fibrosarcoma. She'd left the town with her mother soon after. His ashes had gone with them, and her mother had gradually disintegrated. She'd been cremated in 2012. Hazel's memory was her only connection to her childhood here.

Blue Grove Park hadn't changed. Even though the new swings were fenced off on a square of bark chips they were in exactly the same position with the condemned tyre factory looming over them. A couple of kids had been playing under the grimy clouds, and Hazel felt like she'd been slotted right back into her past. She'd instinctively turned to the left corner of the adventure area, almost expecting to see Meredith awkwardly lingering, watching the others and waiting to be invited in.

Gusts flapped the aluminium cladding of Fun Central and sounded like a plane in turbulence. Hazel folded her arms tightly to her chest and surveyed the derelict fun zones as her breath loitered mistily around her face.

The murder of Meredith Hickman had acted like a cancer; her brutal slaying swiftly blighting what had once been a family destination. Nobody had wanted to bring their children back here after what happened.

Another squall blasted the roof but a different sound turned her head towards the shrine. A candleholder rolled across the tiles, and Henrik emerged from behind the pillar.

CHAPTER 11

The breeze buffeting the panels above had concealed the noise of her entrance onto the concourse, and Henrik was engrossed by the images of Meredith taped to the shrine.

Hazel guessed he was going to be more self-conscious about the lens than the average subject, so capturing genuine emotion would be a real challenge. Maybe Lucas had been right about using his remote spy cams.

She observed Henrik lean forward and extract one of the photos. He stuffed it into his pocket and straightened again. Was he stealing a trophy?

'Insomnia?' Her voice sounded clamorous in the vast space.

He spun his head in her direction and waited for her echoing boots to reach him before he responded. If she'd taken him by surprise, he didn't show it. 'I got about half an hour, which is a miracle… considering.'

'Considering where you are?'

'Considering how freezing it is up there.'

His goatee partially concealed a pout but Hazel sensed he was using the complaint to deflect his presence at the shrine.

'It's certainly warmer up there than down here.' She tried not to glance at his hand, which was still inside his pocket.

'Nobody going to sweep these up?' He kicked at the leaves under his spotless white Reeboks.

'We want to show this place as it really is.'

Henrik scanned their surroundings. 'I didn't really understand why you wanted to drag me all the way here to do the interview. But now I think I do.'

Hazel rubbed some warmth into the tops of her arms. 'Death makes a big impression in small places.'

'I mean, location and accommodation all rolled into one. That's some creative budgeting.' Before Hazel could respond, his attention was drawn back to the pillar. 'Can't believe this could be the result of something I did.'

It was the first time she'd detected a hint of egotism in his voice, and Hazel registered how captivated he was by the Meredith pictures. 'I thought we agreed to have the camera present for this.'

'I just needed some time alone here. This is the first time it's felt real to me. Ever since I set up the @BeMyKiller Twitter account, I've been completely disengaged from everything that happened. That's what's fucked me up. Trying to estimate the guilt I should feel for the lives of four people I've never met. But none of what I've seen online or on TV prepared me for this.'

Hazel studied his rapt features closely. But she couldn't work out if the shrine repelled or attracted him. 'And does that make you afraid of meeting the others?'

'Take a wild guess.'

'I've told you how difficult this might be for you.'

'Time and time again.' His gaze dropped to the dead flowers. 'Before I do go on camera, though, I need to know exactly how you intend to portray me.'

'That can only come from you.'

'Don't insult my intelligence.' He didn't look up at her. 'I know about selective editing. You can manipulate everything I say.'

Hazel had been prepared for this. Now he'd committed to the project she had to make him feel firmly in her confidence; not just a participant but someone who could influence its direction as much as her. 'I'd like you to watch the security footage of Meredith Hickman's death.'

'You have that?' He turned to her and was suddenly whispering.

'I've watched it and can vouch it's a hundred times more persuasive than this.' She nodded at the shrine.

'How come the police released it to you?' he asked suspiciously.

'They didn't. The owners of Fun Central had it backed up on their security system.'

'But it's evidence in an ongoing investigation, right?'

'Are you prepared to view it?'

'Do I have a choice?'

'It may give you clarity.'

'Clarity? I'm being accused of instigating the deaths of four people. You don't think maybe I have a strong sense of clarity already?'

'No, you've just admitted you've felt completely removed from what happened.'

Henrik opened his mouth but thought better of it. He pulled his fingers from his pocket, and Hazel noticed they were empty.

'Look, I can't even begin to contemplate how the footage will affect you. It's sickening but I'm hoping that seeing it will make you differentiate between what you did at a keyboard and the cold, premeditated way Meredith was killed. I want to make it real to you, Henrik, and to the audience. This is about her life – and three others – being viciously cut short and whether it was really because of something you unwittingly put online.'

'You believe that? Was I unwitting?'

Hazel wondered how many times a day he asked himself that. 'Help me make sense of what happened between the moment you conceived @BeMyKiller and when it became this.'

Henrik contemplated the curled up and yellowing photos.

'And we both know this wasn't what you intended. Was it?'

He didn't reply.

CHAPTER 12

Lucas quickly assembled his kit and tried the run-and-gun DSLR rig on his shoulder for comfort. His trusty Lumix camera was the one he'd shot *Isil Brides* with, and he adjusted the familiar grip, put his eye to the viewer and panned along the shabby fun zones. What an eerie place. It was crazy but he felt more threatened here than he did in Syria.

As they'd shared a joint the night before, Weiss had told Lucas about the tweakers who hung about in the vast forest and waste site behind them. Hazel said they could lock the place down every night but, judging by the graffiti, there were plenty of other ways in.

He framed Hazel pep-talking Henrik Fossen outside the ball pit. Neither of them was going to be able to brush off the intimacy they'd shared on the last shoot.

That's why he'd decided to bide his time before hitting the sack the previous night. He couldn't afford to let her think they could pick up where they'd left off. Not now. It was going to be awkward but, if the schedule were anything to go by, they'd both be exhausted before they got to their cots.

'Lucas.' Weiss beckoned him over. He had his headphones on and was preparing the mics for the interior interviews while Sweeting unravelled the patch cords.

Lucas moved to where they were setting up by the shrine.

Weiss finished tightening the legs and stood. 'Had a word out of our star yet?'

Lucas zoomed in on Henrik Fossen's pensive expression. 'I was taking a piss and he walked into the bathroom. Asked me a lot of questions.'

'About what?' Weiss asked.

'Expenses mainly. He's so intense. Quite freaked me. I almost zipped up before I'd finished.'

'I heard him talking in his sleep last night,' Sweeting chimed in.

Lucas swung the camera back to them but one of Weiss's spectacle lenses filled the shot. He zoomed out until the heads and shoulders of the sound department were both in frame. 'What was he talking about?'

'Couldn't understand a word. Sounded pretty heated though.'

'Maybe it was Lucas and Hazel.' Weiss raised his eyebrow.

Lucas didn't respond to that. Weiss was a son of a bitch.

Weiss blew Lucas a playful kiss.

Lucas darted the camera to Sweeting.

But he was too busy surveying the grubby concourse while he unwound the cable. 'Christ, this place is like Disneyland with rigor mortis.'

CHAPTER 13

When Cox regained consciousness he smelt solvent. Something solid nudged the back of his throat and made him gag. His retching had a strange hollow echo.

Where was he? As he panicked and stirred his body, blood surged into his knees. It was daylight and he was crouching in the dirt surrounded by birch trees. His last memory was of the night before – driving his bike down the ramp and out of Fun Central.

His molars scraped and squeaked on something metallic. Cox attempted to expel the object but couldn't draw air in or around its sides. He inhaled through his nostrils as he struggled to move his head away. The exertion tugged at his cheeks. Whatever he was biting on, his mouth was stuck to it.

Above him was the license plate of his beloved vintage Triumph Bonneville. He was positioned behind it doggie style, and the insides of his lips were glued around one of the twin exhaust pipes at the right-hand side of the back bike tyre, his teeth clenched against it. His feet weren't tied but his wrists crackled at his back. Sounded like they'd been secured by tape.

'Help!' His misshapen cry vibrated through the cylinder. Cox shouted again and coughed as pungent petrol fumes burnt his chest.

The tendons in his neck tautened as he drew back from the exhaust, and his face stretched tight. If he couldn't get free, he was going to choke to death.

Now he recalled somebody had been waiting at the bottom of the ramp. Had swung something heavy at him out of the darkness – a bat or metal bar. This was no prank.

He detected movement behind him. Someone was a few feet away but he couldn't turn to see who it was.

A figure walked past him to the bike. He was wearing Cox's leather jacket. He couldn't see his features, however, because he was also wearing his orange motorcycle helmet.

The figure cocked their leg over the seat.

Cox tilted to the left as the side stand was kicked in and the Triumph straightened up. The stranger dropped hard into the seat. Keys jingled; they braced on the handlebars and lifted their boot from the mud to kick-start the bike.

'No!' His lips resisted his body's recoil.

The figure slammed their heel on the pedal, and Cox felt the exhaust stab the roof of his mouth.

The engine didn't fire up but Cox knew if he didn't release himself, his lungs would be blown apart. Closing his eyes he used his guttural scream down the exhaust to cover the agony of beginning to tear his flesh away. He trembled and the skin ruptured. Better he was left disfigured than what would happen if he stayed where he was. But whatever had been used to stick him to the carbon steel was holding him fast.

'Answer the fucking phone.'

He froze and bit down on the exhaust to stem the hot fizzing pain.

'I said answer the fucking phone, asshole.'

It was Cox's comedy ringtone. He'd had it for some years, and it drove his friends nuts.

'Pull your thumb out your ass and answer the fucking phone.'

The stranger straightened and plucked the phone out of Cox's jacket pocket.

Now Cox remembered briefly gaining consciousness when it had still been dark and a hand pressing his fingertip to the iPhone's button to access it.

'If you don't pick up the fucking—'

Cox heard his visor snap up and discerned a voice asking for him. Sounded like the producer of his next gig. He howled at it and churned his hands in the tape.

The figure hung up and put the phone back into his pocket.

Cox stiffened the muscles in his jowls and prepared to violently jerk back.

The stranger lifted his boot off the leaves.

Cox snorted three times as he girded himself then bellowed and yanked with both shoulders. He felt the tissue rip but still wasn't free.

The Triumph revved six times before the heat blasted through him; his eyeballs rolled up to his license plate and Cox no longer saw the numbers there.

Blow me!

His suggestion to the crew chat group the previous night was already wiped from his brain.

CHAPTER 14

Hazel leaned over Henrik and hit the keyboard to activate the black-and-white footage of the pillar in Fun Central the day before it became a memorial.

A hooded figure was finishing securing Meredith Hickman there. The barbed wire encircled her body from head to toe and, as she tried to move her lips against one of the tight steel coils, the soundless clip couldn't convey her moans for help. The figure exited left of shot.

The security camera was looking directly down at the bleach blonde, almost as if the person who had bound her there had deliberately chosen the pillar to allow the lens to capture the killing.

As he watched the recording, Henrik's chin rested on his balled hands, his elbows on the small table he was seated at. Hazel and the crew were assembled around him in front of the shrine. The main entrance had been darkened with drapes, and the overhead bulbs were switched off. Lucas was going to capture his reactions in the guttering light from the candles they'd lit around the pillar as well as the glow from the screen.

Normally, the crew banter was right up to the take but, as they'd set up for the shot, nobody had spoken. They'd known exactly what Henrik was about to sit through. Everyone but Henrik had seen it. Everyone but Henrik and Hazel looked away from the laptop.

The hooded figure appeared behind the pillar and turned the rotten wooden fence post the razor wire was still attached to, increasing the tension and making Meredith bite down harder on the cable as it cut deeper into the corners of her mouth. Hazel shuddered as blood trickled from the wounds to Meredith's chest.

As he hovered the camera around Henrik's expression, she directed Lucas by lightly touching his shoulder.

Henrik gulped. 'How much longer does this last?'

'Another four minutes,' she replied.

'I know what happens.' He jigged his leg nervously. 'I saw the news. Do I really need to see any more?'

'Yes.' Hazel anticipated his horrified reaction. Would he be as appalled as she'd been?

Meredith's captor walked around the pillar and entered shot from the right. They applied glue to her eyes, and she pleaded as much as she could, her lips working against the wire. The hood spoke to her, head moving and then slipped out of view of the lens.

Meredith's lips moved faster.

A car slammed into Meredith, crushing her lower half against the pillar. Her features froze on impact but her chest heaved as the dark Nissan immediately reversed away.

'Jesus wept… '

Meredith's shattered legs were revealed.

The vehicle came back into shot and battered the pillar again, slotting back into the first indentation.

Henrik rigidly observed the car silently strike Meredith another eight times, her torso slipping further down the cage of wires until her thighs were a pulp and her pelvic area hung in shreds. The ninth blow made the camera image flicker. Meredith's mouth was still.

Her captor reversed the Nissan out of shot and returned to examine what was left of her. Turning, the figure removed the hood and ran his hand through his dark, collar-length hair. His impassive, slender features betrayed nothing of what he'd just done.

The footage froze.

As Lucas tightened on his revulsion, Henrik leaned back in his chair. 'Could I get a glass of water?' His voice trembled.

Hazel stepped into shot. '"Hit me up". That was Meredith's tweet into the @BeMyKiller Twitter stream only a few hours before she died.'

'Think I don't know that?'

'Know who that man is?' She pointed to the composed face. 'He's about your age, wouldn't you say? Twenties?'

He swallowed and shook his head.

'You're positive?'

Henrik stood and made swiftly for the doors. 'I need some air.'

CHAPTER 15

Hazel found Henrik staring at a mini twister of leaves weaving across the empty parking zone. 'You OK?'

He stood up from his leaning position beside the main entrance. 'What d'you think?'

'You knew how Meredith died.'

'Yeah but that was fucking brutal.'

'Henrik, I want to shoot at a pace you're comfortable with but I do have a finite number of days before the crew have to go off and do other things.'

'Paying jobs?'

'Exactly.' Even though it actually felt a little warmer outside, Hazel wrapped her black puffer jacket tighter around her.

'I've been speaking to some of them. They seem very loyal to you.'

'They are but not indefinitely. They're great guys but they all have bills to pay. So you can understand the pressure I'm under. That's why we have to start interviewing the others tomorrow.'

'Tomorrow?'

'They'll be flying in this afternoon.'

'Jesus. "A pace I'm comfortable with"?'

'Don't worry. They're staying in town tonight. I want to focus on you today.'

'I really don't think I'm ready for this.' His head turned briefly to the forest as several crows noisily took flight. 'Particularly after watching that clip. I thought you said it was just me for the first couple of days.'

'That was my original intention. But I've had to condense the whole schedule because of everyone's availabilities.'

'So tomorrow… you want me face-to-face with all of them?' There was panic in his eyes.

'Of course not,' Hazel placated. 'We'll be calling them up here one at a time to begin with and interviewing them separately. You can watch the monitor in the production office. If you don't feel up to it, we can pick up those interviews later.'

'IF I want to be part of them.'

'Of course. Although we have discussed this.'

'That was before you sat me in front of that laptop. How can I look her parents in the eye after that?'

'Nobody holds you directly responsible.' But Hazel couldn't deny she'd felt a tiny satisfaction from making him experience Meredith's suffering.

'We both know that's not true… Hazel.' Again, his use of her name sounded awkward.

'I've FaceTimed everyone at length. Spent as much time with them as I have with you. They're all taking part for the same reason. They want answers.'

'And that's just what you're going to give them, right?'

Hazel opened her mouth to reply but sealed her lips again. That was a conversation she didn't want to have off-camera. But the lone tourist theory relied on first proving all of her interview subjects were innocent, and she wasn't yet a hundred per cent positive they were. 'We'll be showing the same clip to everyone. It's not you on the screen.'

Henrik gauged her reaction for a few moments. 'What about Eve Huber?'

'How many times do we have to go over this?'

'Until I feel a hundred per cent secure. She has threatened to kill me. Or, at least, threatened to get someone else to do it.'

'That was directly after her brother had been murdered.'

'And what has she said to you since, specifically?'

'D'you think I'd put you in any sort of danger?'

'I repeat, what has she said to you?'

The puddles in the concrete suddenly went black as dark clouds passed across the sun.

'She's not a threat. And I'm here to protect you.'

'That makes me feel so much better. If you can't give her the person who killed her brother, don't you think I'm going to be the next best thing?'

'I've asked you to trust me.'

He slitted his eyes. 'Are you holding something back?'

'Should I be asking you the same question?' she dodged.

'What the hell does that mean?'

But Hazel knew his mortification was a deflection. She'd found out about his six-figure book deal. 'I just want to remind you that you've promised me exclusive access to your side of events.'

'And you have it.' He studied her chin. 'But if you're stringing me along and there's no more to this than you pushing me forward as a punchbag to give you conflict for your movie, I'm out of here.'

'Believe me, I understand how distressed you must be after what you've seen. But I'm not going to put you in any situation you haven't given your blessing to. I just think once we start talking you're going to be driving this more than me.'

He nodded and watched the leaves settle.

'Today, it's just you.'

Henrik tugged his goatee a few times and then a new thought soured his features. 'So… you're actually paying for the others to stay in town?'

CHAPTER 16

'Henrik, why don't you just begin by telling us something about your-self.' Hazel settled back in her red swivel chair, which was positioned in front of his. Lucas had the camera on the legs beside her and had set up the monitor on a stand to her right. She looked down at it and could see the votives on the shrine flickering behind Henrik.

Weiss tapped his headphones. 'Wait.'

Henrik shot a nettled glance at him.

They'd been waiting for the breeze to die down, but the roof of Fun Central was still shuddering. After a few seconds it ceased.

'There's got to be a way around this.' Weiss took off his spectacles and cleaned them. It was his way of thinking. Eventually he put them back on, checked his sound rig and nodded at Hazel.

She did the same to Henrik.

'My name's Henrik Fossen. Uh, I'm a mature student studying for a distance education degree in global ecology.'

'Don't look directly at the camera and be more conversational. Just relax. I may use snippets of this. If you're not happy with what you've said, just pause and repeat it. I can cut around it.' Hazel tucked her hair behind her ears.

Henrik straightened in his chair.

'You're not making a clip for a dating site. Just tell me about what you like to do.'

'So you can paint me as a loner, right?'

'I'm not painting you as anything. Give me something that will dispel people's preconceptions about you. Just be honest and take your time. If you want a few minutes to think, we can cut.'

Henrik considered that. 'No, I'm good.'

The wind glanced the complex again, and Weiss held one finger in the air until the rattling had died away. A chorus of crows took a brief shift before he indicated it was OK to proceed.

'My name's Henrik Fossen, and you've asked me to be honest. So, honestly, the one thing I can tell you about myself is that I'm terrified.'

Hazel looked down at his fidgeting hands. 'Of what?'

'You, this crew, being here, the people you're going to make me talk to.'

'Nobody's making you do this, Henrik. You must have your own motives for being here.'

Henrik wiped at his beard. 'And what happened to Meredith. That terrifies the shit out of me now. Whoever murdered her is probably still around here. Somebody capable of that is out there going about their daily routine while they have the memory of that inside their head. I wonder what they're doing right now. This second.' He folded his arms.

Hazel opened her mouth to respond but could see he was turning something over in his head.

'When I was a teenager, I had obsessions with different celebrities. And at certain specific times during the day I used to wonder what they were doing at that exact moment – sleeping, being bored, drinking coffee, masturbating. I felt an odd connection with them then because I was probably the only person thinking about them in those terms. Most people perceive others' lives, especially celebrities, as abstract entities. It's like when you're a kid; you believe everyone else orbits your existence; that they're just there to furnish it and nobody else has the same feelings or emotions.'

'Was that how you felt when you were a child?'

'My parents were good at making me feel isolated.'

'And do they now?' Hazel knew how sensitive a question it was.

'What do you think?' he replied testily.

'You father's Theodore Fossen—'

'I know who my father is.'

'I'm doing it for the benefit of viewers who don't. Tell us about him.'

'Maybe you know more about him than I do. Why don't you go ahead?' He tightened his arms across his chest.

'Theo Fossen, founder of TechFlex, the second largest multinational technology company on the planet, and Republican election candidate, although his political ambitions have recently been stymied by your online activities.'

'He already has enough power.' He grinned scornfully.

'So was @BeMyKiller a deliberate attempt to sabotage that? Because it seems to be working.'

'My parents, particularly my father, don't care about me and I don't give two shits about them.'

Hazel changed tack. 'You were talking about childhood. As an adult do you still feel other people's lives are inconsequential?'

He knew where she was going with that and sighed. 'Of course not. But online we all wilfully strip away reality. We deliberately emulate celebrities because they're so removed from it. On Facebook we all try to make our lives seem perfect to the people who know us, as well as people who don't.'

'So the serial killer account you created, you never once thought people would believe it was real?'

'Millions of people didn't. They just saw it as it was intended – for shits and giggles.'

'But some didn't.'

He scuffed some leaves on the floor. 'No.'

'Do you regret creating it?'

Henrik shook his head a few times before answering. 'Of course. It probably took me less than twenty minutes to germinate the idea and activate the @BeMyKiller account. Then I used a cluster of others to get the hashtag #BeMyKiller trending. I was bored, and it was a whim. A fucking stupid whim. I do vividly remember asking myself what I'd do if it led to someone actually being killed.'

'And what was your response?'

'Truthfully?'

Hazel nodded.

'I don't think I had one. I just went ahead and did it.'

'"For shits and giggles"?'

'When I'm online I question everything I come into contact with. If someone I don't know tries to communicate with me I know it's probably a troll, a bot or a paedophile. When @BeMyKiller's followers kept racking up it all seemed unreal.'

'Nearly eight million people had used the #BeMyKiller hashtag while it was trending, briefly, before the @BeMyKiller account was suspended, and Twitter and Instagram started blocking accounts of anyone using it. After four people had been murdered, you dropped the comment "Burn me in hell" into your own Twitter timeline. Is that because you thought you were responsible for their deaths?'

'No. I wasn't thinking straight.'

'In our other conversations, you've given me the impression you had doubts about that. So why didn't you just immediately close the account yourself? Or were you enjoying the attention?'

Henrik shifted uncomfortably in his chair. 'You really think I want the public profile I have now?'

'If you didn't, you'd have deactivated the account before Twitter did. Or are you saying shutting it down was like an admission of guilt?'

'It's the advice I was given.'

'By your lawyers?'

'Yes,' he said truculently but his leg jigged.

Hazel held his gaze. 'Particularly as you have no alibi for the time period when all of the victims died.'

Henrik exhaled. 'Really? Is this going to be the thrust of the interview?'

'So accusing you of murdering four people… '

'Is fucking preposterous.'

'Of course it is.' Hazel kept her voice as level as his. 'But again, although we've talked about this, I still need to have this conversation with you on camera. I don't want to make any suppositions on the audience's behalf. We agreed you wouldn't hold anything back.'

'I'm not.'

'Just indulge me then.'

'You know I was dealing with some personal issues.'

'You were on meth.'

'Yes.' His green eyes hardened.

'So why not say that?'

'Because that was between us.'

'Or is it more to do with the fact you're writing in-depth about that particular episode for a major publisher?'

Henrik tried not to look surprised but failed spectacularly.

'This movie experience would also be great for the book. After your suicide attempt, are you looking for enough material to fill the last chapters?'

Henrik chewed the hairs of his goatee as he considered his reply. 'Can we stop recording?'

'I'd prefer it if we continued on camera.' Hazel watched his chest expand but he didn't breathe out.

'Who told you about the deal?' he asked petulantly. 'I'm meant to keep it under wraps till May.'

'The book is likely to be out before my movie. Anything you're holding back from me for your readers?'

'I thought you said you were here to protect me.'

'And everyone else who participates. That's why we can't conceal anything from each other. I need to know why you failed to tell me you were writing a book.'

'I told you; I was gagged.'

'I take it the advance is commensurate with the size of the publisher. And they're a pretty big one, from what I understand.'

'You're not paying me, Hazel. And I still have to earn a living.'

'So you've decided you want to live now?'

He narrowed his eyes at her. 'I suck at suicide – is that the same thing?'

'It was your brother that found you when you OD'd?'

'Yes.'

'Hadn't you asked him to swing by that afternoon?'

'You're saying it was a showboat suicide?'

'You tell me. Did you want to be found?'

'Yeah, I also planned to have seizures for the rest of my life. I need daily meds now. Oh, fuck this.' Henrik ripped off his mic and strode to the door leading to the upstairs offices.

The crew watched him tug it and walk through.

As it sluggishly closed behind him Hazel didn't move from her chair.

CHAPTER 17

'You going after him?' Weiss cut sound.

'I will.' Rena took a few paces towards the door.

'Don't. Let him go.'

Rena obeyed Hazel but pouted.

'Nice, Haze. Just put them at their ease.' Lucas stood and arched his spine.

'He has to know this won't be an easy ride. And his publisher deliberately leaked the deal so he needs to take that up with them.' But Hazel knew she'd pushed too hard. She was angry about the book – at the notion of him profiting from the deaths of Meredith and the others. But couldn't she make the same accusation about herself?

'If he walks, you don't have a documentary.' It sounded as if the prospect pleased Lucas.

Up until then Lucas had been stand-offish but this was the first time Hazel had detected any antipathy. Was it because she hadn't waited up for him the previous night?

He fished out his smokes. 'Maybe you should call this one and go back to the project we were talking about in Syria. Online radicalisation is much more relevant than indulging this spoilt little fuck up. Don't you think he's just doing this to piss off his daddy?'

'Maybe.'

'If he is throwing his toys out of the pram, can we talk about doing something more worthwhile?' His cigarette bounced between his lips.

'If he's gone to pack his bag, he has to come back this way.'

'What a cock.' Lucas stepped away to light up with his Zippo.

Hazel addressed the rest of the crew. 'He'll be back. He needs to go on record and put things straight.'

Weiss cleaned his spectacles. 'Sounds like he's doing that already. There's probably a ghostwriter on it now. Maybe he doesn't need us.'

'If he doesn't, we'll know soon enough.'

'Caffeine?'

Everyone nodded at Rena, and she headed for her trolley.

'I'll give you a hand.' Keeler trailed after her.

'Should I hold fire on charging the batteries?' Sweeting was tying the long split ends of the dark hair that encircled his bald pate into a measly ponytail.

Hazel wondered if his wife really went for the look. 'Let's give him a few minutes.'

Lucas pocketed his lighter. 'Are you buying any of that stuff he said earlier?' he asked through blue fumes.

Hazel waved them away. 'About being removed from what he was doing? No. Too rehearsed.'

'What's his game plan then?'

'This performance? To remind us he's indispensable.'

'You sure about that? Maybe it's because he *is* shit scared of Eve Huber.'

Hazel prodded her chest. '*I'm* shit scared of Eve Huber.'

'What time's she in tomorrow morning?' He stamped on his cigarette.

Hazel knew he was still trying to give up and only allowed himself three puffs per smoke. 'It's in the schedule.'

'That's OK. It might be obsolete at this rate.'

He followed Weiss and Sweeting over to Rena's trolley and left Hazel wondering if he was right.

CHAPTER 18

'Miss Salter.' Detective Bennett sounded like he was in a busy diner. 'Do you never get tired of hearing the same answer?'

Hazel closed the production office door. 'Just thought I'd update you about my progress here.' It was a hollow claim. Henrik Fossen's interview had yielded nothing more than she expected, and she'd only been able to prevent him from walking by divulging her ultimate aim was proving the lone tourist theory.

'Progress? And to think I'd wasted all those man hours when I could have come straight to you.'

She detected a tremor of uncertainty in his voice though. 'The Hubers are in Broomfield.' Momentarily there was nothing but the buzz of the other tables around Bennett.

'Trying to provoke a reaction from me?'

'No, just thought I'd let you know who's in town.'

'If there's any sign of trouble, I'll be closing you down.'

'Why don't you drive out here? Keep an eye on things.'

'I'm not giving an interview.'

She heard a coarse noise against Bennett's mouthpiece. She guessed he was cleaning his lips with a napkin.

'You paying to fly everyone in?' He sounded amused.

'Everyone that's relevant.'

'What about Kristian O'Connell's sister? Sheenagh getting a vacation in Broomfield as well? I see she's been doing the rounds of the TV shows.'

'Why?'

'Maybe save yourself some money.'

'Is that a tip?'

'You won't get any of those from me. But if your journalistic expertise extends to watching the TV news, maybe you can catch one there.' He hung up.

CHAPTER 19

Eve Huber's mud-spattered black Acura SUV arrived at Fun Central dead on 8 a.m., and Hazel and Rena were waiting outside the main entrance to greet it. The car came to a halt in the nearest space, and she switched off the engine. Her door swung open but Eve didn't climb out.

'Somebody get my scooter from the trunk!' a piercing voice yelled before they even reached her.

'Eve, Hazel. Good to see you face-to-face at last.' She extended her hand inside.

Eve didn't take it and tried to swivel in her seat but her considerable body mass only allowed a slight turn of her head. 'The door's unlocked. Careful when you lift it.'

Hazel joined Rena as she opened the hatch, and they both struggled out the mobility vehicle.

'Just wheel it here. I'll do the rest.'

The two women positioned it, and Eve bounced her body to the edge of the seat, reached down to the handlebars and used them to shakily lift her bulk and swing it onto the scooter. She tucked her aquamarine dress back over her knees. 'There.' Wiping the few strands of hair poking from her camouflage print headscarf out of her red, perspiring features she passed the keys to Rena. 'Lock it up for me. It's sticky. Press hard for the alarm.' Her scooter jerked forward. 'I didn't sleep at all last night.'

Hazel tried to keep up alongside but its speed was too fast for walking and too slow for trotting. 'Sorry to hear that.'

They reached the open entrance doors, and Eve paused. 'He's here?'

'Henrik Fossen?'

Eve looked up at Hazel through heavy lids. 'Who else?'

'He's on-site.'

'Jacob's back at the motel. He was going to drive me, but I told him to stay put. Good thing as well. Wants to pull Fossen's arms out of their sockets. Can't guarantee I can control him either.'

'Eve, you promised.'

'Yeah, I did. But Jacob didn't. He was Caleb's twin brother, and the two of them were real tight.' She accelerated her scooter towards the doors but Hazel stepped past her and stood in her way.

The wheel nudged her boot.

Eve glared and raised her pencilled-on eyebrows.

'I need your word there won't be any trouble. I know Jacob has a history.'

'He wants to know why you don't want to interview him same time as me.'

'Because we need some assurances.'

Eve smirked and dimples deepened either side of her mouth. 'Or because you want to keep us apart so you can see we get our stories straight?'

CHAPTER 20

'Mind not smoking that in here?' Eve grinned humourlessly at Lucas.

Lucas met Hazel's eye. He'd only just lit up. She nodded.

'Am I the first?' Eve asked before the cigarette had been extinguished. ''Cept for Fossen?'

Hazel seated herself in the swivel chair opposite Eve's scooter. It was the same interview set-up as Henrik. 'Yes.'

'You gonna be talking to *her* parents?' She jabbed her thumb at the shrine.

'In good time.'

'Not like they'd have to travel far as I have.' Despite the cold, Eve activated a small handheld fan and held it to her flushed complexion. It agitated the dark ringlets protruding from her headscarf.

Hazel knew they weren't real. 'How's the chemo?'

'Lost a third of my weight so far.'

Hazel tried not to look surprised. It was difficult to believe Eve hadn't yet hit her mid-twenties.

'Last year sucked and swallowed – fibromyalgia then leukaemia, then Caleb's murder. Both my brothers have always looked out for me but Caleb was more a carer than Jacob. You filming now?'

Hazel turned to Lucas to acknowledge this. He'd knelt to his Lumix, which was positioned low on the tripod.

'Let me see the screen.' Eve pointed at the monitor.

Hazel turned it in her direction.

'No good. Six chins. Shoot me from above.'

'Sure. Lucas?'

Lucas didn't reply but extended the legs.

'OK.' Hazel swivelled the monitor back. 'We're set.'

'Still haven't told me why I'm first.'

'Because you're the only person to have given a description of the perpetrator to the police.'

Eve smiled slyly, as if it were the answer she expected.

'Wait,' said Weiss adjusting his headphones. 'Can we just kill the fan?'

She looked sharply at him and switched it off.

'Speak to me and not the camera. Take a breath and tell me what happened in your own time.'

Eve played with the plastic blades. 'If I'd been sleeping properly, Caleb would have died twenty feet from me and I wouldn't have known.'

'You'd already heard of the @BeMyKiller account?'

She scowled at Hazel. 'You know it was me that put his name on Twitter along with the hashtag.'

'Forget the conversations we've already had. Imagine you're talking to me for the first time.'

Eve puffed her cheeks and filled out the dimples. 'Caleb wasn't very smart. Had an iPhone but didn't know how to use it. I set up his Facebook and Twitter accounts for him but he was nervous about putting stuff out there.'

'So you did it for him?'

Eve's expression became increasingly sullen. 'We all baited the killers. It was Halloween, and we were bored. Jacob wrote "you ain't got the guts". I wrote "bite me". As a joke,' she mitigated.

'And what did you write on Caleb's behalf?'

'"Want a piece of me?" Eve paused. 'When I told him what I'd done he blew a fuse. Caleb wasn't very good at managing his temper. Jacob had to lock him in the ute room till he'd calmed down.'

'So you did it for fun and forgot all about it?'

Eve shuffled her buttocks in her seat, straightened but quickly sagged again. 'Everyone was doing it,' she said sulkily.

Hazel let Eve take a faltering breath. 'So three nights later… '

'Three nights later I wake to hear Caleb. I was taking new meds and not getting a lot of sleep. Caleb was on one of his drinking jags, and I'd left him and Jacob downstairs in the den.'

'And when did you realise something was wrong?'

'I could hear him shouting for Jacob but I couldn't work out why he sounded so weird. I told him to shut up, and that's when he started hollering for me. I got out of bed and headed for his room, but my door was locked. Thought Jacob and him were playing a trick on me and told them to open it. When I stopped banging on it, Caleb was screaming. That's when I realised his voice was coming from the backyard. I went to the window and lifted the blind.' Eve focussed on an area beyond Hazel's shoulder as if she were looking out of it.

'What could you see?'

'Caleb, first of all, lying there. Thought he'd fallen over drunk. Then I saw the black tape around his wrists and across his mouth. Opened the window and yelled down at him.' Eve switched on her mini fan and played it around her face.

Weiss held his hand up to Hazel to complain about the noise of the tiny motor, but she quickly shook her head.

'I tried to wake Jacob.'

'Where was he?'

'Out cold, downstairs. Skull fractured by whoever slugged him with his own tyre iron. I see a stranger coming out the shed. I thought he was carrying a flamethrower in his hand. It was too much of a drop down to the yard. I would never have gotten out of the window.'

'You didn't call the police?'

'They couldn't have stopped it in time,' she snapped. 'Then I see whatever he's carrying is plugged into the socket in the shed.

He pulled the trigger and a blast of water came out. I thought it was just a hose. But it was one of those high-power jet hoses for blasting meat off bones they use in slaughterhouses. I freaked out, and the guy with the hose stared right up at me. It was dark but I could just make out his scrawny face. I looked straight into his eyes and begged him to stop. Then he started blasting chunks off Caleb with the hose. He'd stripped his ribcage clean by the time I got to him.'

'You'd know him if you saw him again?'

'The police did a drawing for me but it was all wrong. I can still see him in my mind though: him with one eyebrow up like he was pissed for being interrupted.' Eve swallowed and played the fan around her neck.

'Do you still blame Henrik Fossen for Caleb's death?'

'That asshole in the yard murdered Caleb.' Her expression was blank.

'But do you blame Henrik Fossen?'

'He was in a different state.'

'That still doesn't answer my question. Both you and your brother made threats against his life.'

'We were all upset,' she said flatly.

'There have been stories about your association with a local hitman.'

'Do I look like I could afford to pay a hitman?'

'How do you think Henrik felt about that?'

'Couldn't say. Hope it makes him understand his actions will have repercussions though.'

'So they're still to come?'

'It's a figure of speech.' Eve sniffed. 'We're human. He needs to be made accountable. Fossen's just walked away from everything.'

'You heard about his suicide attempt?'

Eve turned off her fan. 'I heard his story.'

'And that's not sufficient?'

She peered around the concourse as if he might be hiding nearby. 'He can't duck out that easy,' Eve said loud enough, in case he was.

'So, what would you say to him, if he was sitting where I am?'

'It's not what I'd say. More what I'd do.'

'Would you listen to what he had to say?'

Eve pursed her lips and nodded. 'Sure.'

'So, if Henrik is guilty for something you believe he triggered remotely, does you putting your brother's name and the #BeMyKiller hashtag in the Twitter timeline make you equally responsible?'

Aggression bulged in Eve's eyes.

CHAPTER 21

'Like I said… we all thought it was a game.'

'Don't you think Henrik felt the same?'

'I don't care what he feels.'

Henrik allowed the door to shut slowly, and quietly climbed the stairs. He'd read the reports about what had happened to Caleb Huber. Seen myriad interviews with Eve before. But hearing her reliving the experience, her words echoing around the space where Meredith Hickman took her last breath, churned up the sediment of dread that had been sitting in the pit of his stomach ever since he'd first been told about the shooting of Denise Needham.

He crept back to the monitor in the production office and closed the door behind him.

Henrik slammed a few pills then took his phone out and found the number he'd recently stored in his contacts. It rang for a long time before it was answered. 'It's me,' he said when they eventually picked up and knew it would be sufficient. 'Eve Huber's just arrived, and Hazel Salter's interviewing her. Huber's brother's here but he's back at the motel.' They asked the inevitable question. 'Rifkin Lodge, just on the edge of town. She's putting all of them up there and then calling them out here to do their piece.' He heard footsteps outside the door. 'Gotta go.' Henrik hung up.

Somebody knocked.

'Yes?'

Hazel leaned in. 'You watching?'

He nodded.

She didn't seem convinced. 'Eve Huber has agreed to talk to you on camera.'

'I'm really not ready for that.'

'She flies back to Clearwater on Wednesday morning. It's today or tomorrow.'

Henrik turned his phone over in his sweaty palms.

Hazel eyed it. 'I don't think you're in any danger.'

'And that's meant to reassure me, right?'

'I've asked her brother to stay away. It's just her.'

He shook his head.

Hazel pushed the door fully open. 'Henrik, you've already achieved so much by just coming here. I know I've already put you through a lot but this is probably the hardest thing I'm going to ask you to do.'

'I thought I did that yesterday.'

'Come downstairs. She's outside getting some air. We'll only bring her in when you're ready.'

Henrik didn't budge. 'Have you told her what you've told me?'

'Not yet.'

'Why not?'

'She hasn't tried to walk out.' Hazel folded her arms.

'Yet. So when are you going to? I want you to brief her. Before I go down there.'

'I'd prefer to record it. The camera is your insurance.'

'Or maybe you want to see her physically attack me. That would be even better, right?'

'Henrik, she's in a mobility scooter. I promise, you'll be fine. Let's do this.'

CHAPTER 22

Hazel registered how white Henrik's knuckles were as he gripped the edge of the ball pit. Had he requested his meeting with Eve Huber be played out in here so he could dive into the pool between them if things got ugly?

Lucas rehearsed panning the lens from Henrik to the closed smoked glass door without getting Sweeting crouching with the mic in shot. 'Running.'

'OK.' Weiss put on his headphones.

'You ready, Henrik?'

Henrik chewed his goatee then nodded at Hazel.

She paused. Was this wise? He was visibly terrified. But Hazel's instincts told her to precipitate the confrontation as soon as possible. 'Send her in.'

Rena disappeared through the door. A few seconds later she held it open from the other side, and the whirr of Eve's mobility scooter announced her arrival.

On entering she halted the other side of the pool, looked first at Hazel then rolled her eyes slowly to Henrik. She absorbed him as he regarded her from under his eyebrows. 'You look older than I thought.' He remained silent. Eve switched on her handheld fan. 'Caleb had started growing a beard. Didn't suit him neither.'

'What d'you need me to say?' Henrik's voice trembled as he released the edge of the pit. He momentarily wobbled before settling on his heels.

'Nothing that's going to make a difference.'

'You've said you want me dead. That still true?'

Eve waved her hand dismissively. 'That'd be making it too easy. Plus I hear you nearly did the job yourself.'

'But my death would make things right in your eyes?'

'Certainly in Jacob's eyes. He misses his brother. Wonder if you thought about that before you invented your little game.'

Henrik plucked a blue ball out of the pit and squeezed it tight in his palm.

'If Jacob were here he'd tear you limb from limb. Me, I want you to suffer as long as possible, and I hope every time you throw one of your fits you remember Caleb and the other people you sentenced to death.'

Henrik kept staring at his hand pumping the rubber there. 'But you played the game as well.'

'I know what you're going to say.' Eve turned off her fan. 'I know how you're going to try and make this my fault.'

'Not your fault. But, like me, you couldn't have envisaged what happened.'

'I'm not you.' Eve's voice quavered. 'I don't set traps for people. You weren't the guy I watched from my window but the thing you did appealed to whatever sickness was in his mind.'

'And what if he was standing beside me? Who would you be talking to then? Would I even be relevant?'

Eve shook her head and blinked away a tear. 'I want him crucified along with you.'

Hazel felt her fingernails in her palms. Was it in Henrik to say sorry, even if it was just for Eve's loss? But it was clear he couldn't begin to empathise with her grief.

'But the police haven't caught him so I'm in the frame now.' Henrik stopped squashing the ball and met her eye. 'It's got to be better than blaming yourself, right?'

A shadow of something passed over Eve's features, and Hazel watched Henrik's gaze shrink from it.

CHAPTER 23

Henrik flattened the ball again. 'None of us can predict the consequences of what we put online. I couldn't. You couldn't.'

'I'm done here.' Eve sniffed and reversed her scooter. 'Open the door.'

Hazel held up her hands. 'Please, Eve, keep talking,' she whispered.

Henrik stood upright. 'No, it's time you started talking, Hazel. Tell Eve why we're here.'

Eve turned, rolled forward and butted the doorframe with her front wheel. She backed up again.

Henrik hurled the ball at Eve.

It bounced harmlessly off her shoulder but she immediately halted.

There was a collective intake of breath from the crew.

'Just listen to what she has to say.' He put his hands in his pockets, as if he hadn't thrown it.

After a few seconds, Eve arced around so they could see her incandescent features.

'Tell her, Hazel,' Henrik demanded.

'Tell me what?'

Lucas swung the lens to Hazel.

'My intention here isn't just to point a camera at emotional consequences. I'm looking to answer questions the police have failed to.' It was part of the rehearsed speech she'd given Henrik when he'd threatened to leave.

Eve glowered at Hazel. 'And what makes you think you have an edge on the FBI?'

'Because they're looking for different perpetrators.'

Eve sighed. 'Jesus, you're not going to tell me you believe that lone tourist theory.'

'The police have asserted that, of the eight million people using the #BeMyKiller hashtag, a tiny percentage of them would have been murdered in any case. There was a 'BeMyKiller' victim in Europe, where it was categorically proven that the perp had never accessed social media. It's why the investigation refuses to give the lone tourist theory any credence.'

'They didn't give it credence because it's bullshit,' Eve spat.

'You don't believe Caleb's death was just a coincidence?'

'Of course not.'

'It's already been established that homicides in the US were linked to the actual words the victims made in the timeline alongside the #BeMyKiller hashtag.'

'And?'

'So if we believe the murders were direct results of #BeMyKiller, why can't we believe it was one person?'

'Because it wasn't fucking possible.'

But Hazel was more than prepared for Eve's rebuttal. 'The lone tourist theory was dismissed because the timescale made it impossible for one person to travel to each state and murder all four victims.'

'So what's changed?'

'Kristian O'Connell.'

'The junkie?'

'It's now looking increasingly likely his murder was drug related.'

'That hasn't been confirmed.'

'Yesterday, Cheyenne PD said they were now looking for O'Connell's dealer in connection with his murder. The police only investigated his death as far as they did because of its possible link to a high-profile case. And he was the only victim who didn't bait the killer when he tweeted @BeMyKiller.'

'So?'

'If you take O'Connell out of the equation, it would have been possible for one person to have travelled to each US location to kill the other victims.'

Eve shot Henrik a poisonous glance. 'Of course, this would make life easier for you. Convince people there's one man out there, not that you planted ideas in the heads of nutjobs far and wide.'

Hazel knew she needed to keep them both in the room. 'Someone could have comfortably achieved it.'

'A sick fuck killed Caleb because of something *that* sick fuck put on the Internet.' Eve jabbed her finger at Henrik.

'Henrik didn't kill your brother, Eve. Or the others. Don't you want to find the man who did?'

Eve raised a pencilled eyebrow. 'So, you've already decided it's one man.'

CHAPTER 24

Hazel sent Henrik back upstairs while Eve took a break outside. The crew made only muted exchanges as they shifted the gear out of the ball pit. It was Eve's turn to watch the clip of Meredith.

Hazel had told her she was welcome to return to the motel for an hour to compose herself. Eve had said she wanted to get it over with. But it was clear Eve wasn't as thick-skinned as she made out, and Hazel was concerned about her health and emotional state. She was obviously still raw about Caleb's murder but were she and her brother, Jacob, really a threat to Henrik?

Hazel decided to keep Henrik out of sight for the rest of Eve's visit.

Eve had dismissed the lone tourist theory out of hand. But even though it made her job easier, Hazel wasn't ready to dismiss Kristian O'Connell's death and was keen to interview his sister, Sheenagh. She was meant to be on a flight tomorrow and Hazel certainly wasn't going to cancel it, despite what Bennett and the Cheyenne PD had said.

Hazel was to interview Griff Needham after Eve. The stepbrother of the nanny who had been shot with a high-powered rifle had landed and was at the motel. She opened her iPhone and found his Facebook page.

He updated it nearly every hour and from the image of his latest meal, posted only six minutes previously, she wondered where he would find such fine cuisine in Broomfield. But having spoken to him via FaceTime she knew the person whose life appeared so cultivated online was very different to the one that existed in reality.

She looked over to the shrine and happy expressions of Meredith stared back. What reality did her innocuous smile conceal?

Hazel observed Rena emerge from the bathroom and hold the door open while Eve rolled out on her scooter. It was time for her to view Meredith's last moments.

CHAPTER 25

'That's him.' Eve Huber put the tips of her fingers against her throat.

Hazel didn't speak and allowed her to take in the frozen last frame of the Meredith Hickman footage.

Eve looked up from the screen. 'It's the guy I saw from my bedroom window.'

'Are you sure?' Hazel studied her reaction. Any guilt she'd felt about exposing her to the clip had been mitigated by Eve's enthralled expression. Hazel hadn't been able to watch again.

Likewise, the crew were all looking anywhere but at the laptop. They were set up on the edge of the track in Speed Zone, which was a cavernous go-kart arena. Weiss said it was partially soundproofed. A row of four feet high tyres demarcated the winding course, and there was a shuttered coffee stand positioned at the rear where the adults used to score their hits of caffeine.

'Is that as clear as this gets?' Eve squinted at the face.

'Yes. Sure it's the same man?'

Eve nodded. 'Positive.'

'The quality of the image has been enhanced as much as it can but it's still pretty low-grade.'

'It's him.'

'Plus it was night when Caleb was attacked.'

'I saw him clear as I see you.'

'But surely it would be difficult for you to identify anyone if their face was in darkness.'

'Saying I'm lying?' Eve pouted.

'Of course not. I just want you to be a hundred per cent about this.'

'Isn't this what you want to hear?' she said with exasperation.

'I only want the truth, Eve.'

'I'm telling you, that's the guy who was in my backyard.'

'OK, thanks, Eve. And sorry to have put you through that. OK, guys.' Hazel lightly gripped Lucas by his elbow. It was her signal to keep recording. She nodded at Weiss, and he took off his headphones but only for show. He knew the drill. So did Sweeting. He stood but left the mic directed at Eve.

'I hope you didn't feel I was leading you with this.'

Eve glanced back to the laptop. 'I speak my own mind, not anybody else's.'

Hazel walked into shot. 'Some interview differently on camera than they do off.'

Eve fingered a dark ringlet back under her camouflage headscarf. 'That doesn't make sense.'

'It's human nature. If they hit it off with me they start to play the part they think I want them to.'

'Who says I hit it off with you?'

'It's why I didn't want to immediately tell you the objective of this documentary.'

'But you did.'

'Henrik forced my hand.'

'And I would have said you were nuts. Now, I'm changing my mind. Looks as if the same guy who murdered Caleb at least killed this Hickman girl.'

CHAPTER 26

On my way to top secret movie location!

Griff Needham took a photo of an empty Broomfield grain silo through the front window of the cab with his iPhone, attached it to the update and swiftly posted it to Facebook.

That he was actually doing something worthy of posting to Facebook was a rarity, although his friends had never realised this. From their perspective, he met interesting people, dined on the finest cuisine and was constantly globetrotting. How did Griff find the time, energy and money to do the many things they 'liked', commented on and were so insanely jealous of?

The reality was that Griff had become addicted to perpetuating a life he didn't lead. It was his full-time occupation. Having been dismissed from a marketing strategy training post in 2014, at the age of nineteen, it had begun as a way to fill up the surfeit of hours he suddenly had on his hands. Now there weren't enough in the day.

The lies had started small. Desperate to say something of interest, Griff had copied an image of some sushi rolls and posted it, implying he'd snapped them, and said he was trying out a new eatery. He'd done it half as a joke and waited for somebody to get wise. Instead, it had prompted a number of comments asking him about the restaurant.

Initially he was bemused but had been chary with his responses, hastily finding a local Japanese place online and convincing his interested new friends that he was sitting inside it while he communicated with them. He found that lying once meant he had to lie again. And again. But he was interacting with people who, up until that point, would never have given him the time of day.

His life of travel began. Regular trips to sunny climes with more images filched to reinforce the deceit. But, as he gradually discovered, he had to stay permanently on his toes to sustain his online lifestyle – from making sure he allowed for the time difference of wherever he was meant to be (and not post instant daytime images when it should have been night) to concocting spats and temporary break-ups with his fabricated girlfriend.

But Griff relished the challenge it presented and, because of the running commentary he provided about his exploits, began to partially believe it. He told himself that what he did was harmless. Griff had so much debt it was unlikely he'd ever visit the places he did in his fictional world so what was the harm in sharing his fantasy with others? He wasn't using his lies to extract money or snare a partner. Besides, he could never meet the women he impressed. His cover would immediately be blown.

Griff was more comfortable with his unreality than the alternative, and why should he stop something that brought him and others so much amusement, education and pleasure? As long as he never tried dovetailing his Facebook life with his actual one he could continue to enjoy the prestige he accumulated from the security of his bedroom.

But his bogus existence had been thrown into turmoil the morning a sniper shot his stepsister. The outpouring of sympathy had completely blindsided him. Not because the compassion had been in any way a surprise but because his online friends had reacted to an event that had genuinely happened.

Denise had been all over the news and presented him with the sort of platform he'd always craved. That was why he'd agreed to do Hazel Salter's documentary. Griff had decided it was time to put his real self out there. Perhaps the spotlight of celebrity might bleach out his defects. Plus documenting his experience was another way to maintain and maybe multiply his Facebook friends.

He'd signed a non-disclosure agreement but told himself he would only be sharing images with his intimate Facebook community. It's not as if he would be leaking material for financial gain. He just wanted to record his involvement and use it as a teaser for the rush of interest that was bound to follow the release of the movie. It was unofficial publicity, and how could that be a bad thing for Hazel?

The car climbed the ramp into Fun Central, and Griff snapped a picture. He examined the faces of the three people outside. Was one of them Henrik Fossen? He was the guy Griff most wanted to meet. He certainly didn't blame him for the death of his stepsister and actually felt an affinity with a man who had become a victim of his own online creativity.

A woman with short blonde hair wearing a black puffer jacket and jeans approached the car as he got out. It was Hazel. He immediately recognised her from their online chats. He remembered how much he'd panicked when she'd asked him to speak face-to-face.

'Griff?'

He paid the driver then shook the warm hand she offered.

'Settled in OK at the motel?'

'All good, thanks.'

'We're just finishing lunch. Have you eaten?'

Griff nodded. He'd gobbled down a meatball sub but it had been ahi tuna with nappa cabbage salad – image cut and pasted courtesy of a gourmet web page – according to his recent Facebook post.

'I'll introduce you to everyone in a minute. This is Rena. She'll be looking after you.'

'Hi.' The hot girl with the pink hair and clipboard showed him the chunks of pizza crust in her teeth. 'I'm the AP.'

'AP?' His question caused her smile to falter.

'Associate producer.'

Mental note: she was obviously very important. He shook Rena's hand and established eye contact, which made her look uncomfortable. He let go and told himself to dial it back.

'Coffee?' She'd seen him stare and sucked at her teeth.

He was desperate for one. 'No. I'm good thanks.' Meeting two women had already been exhausting. 'Can you tell me where the bathroom is?'

'Sure, I'll take you there.'

'That's OK. Just point me. I'll find it.'

As Rena jabbed her finger and explained, he tried not to fixate on the cold sore at the edge of her glossy lips. 'Thanks.' He headed off, having only half-listened to her directions.

CHAPTER 27

Hazel observed Griff Needham's oatmeal hoody-clad frame amble uncertainly into Fun Central and slow as he spotted the shrine. She nudged Rena. He took a photo with his iPhone then darted his unkempt head of mousy curls around to check if he'd been spotted. 'Get that phone off him.'

'How am I supposed to do that?'

'Say you're taking them from everyone.'

Rena glanced over to Weiss, Sweeting and Keeler who were standing to the left of Griff speaking on theirs.

'Say all the interviewees are being asked to give them up,' Hazel pre-empted. 'They can have them back at the end of each day.'

'You don't trust him?'

Hazel watched him stroll out of view to the bathrooms. 'I don't want any of our content to be compromised.'

'So… you *don't* trust him.'

'No. Or Henrik. Confiscate his next. He may have a book deal but he's signed an agreement not to disclose production details until post release date.'

'Which would be fine if we had one.'

'I'm in the middle of negotiating distribution with Criteria.'

'Jesus. That's awesome.' But Rena's brow quickly hardened. 'You didn't tell me.'

Hazel internally chided herself and lowered her voice. 'I wasn't going to until I knew for sure. I've got a conference call with them tomorrow morning.'

'Criteria? They're hardball players. Is that why you brought the schedule forward?'

Hazel nodded. 'They want delivery by late April.'

'Including post?'

'All signed off by the twenty-seventh.'

'Shit. Is that even possible?'

'It has to be because they'll fund the post-production facility with pre-sales and everyone here will get paid. Criteria have got the clout.'

'Mob clout?' Rena whispered.

'These days it's all corporate and legit.'

'Not what I heard. Sounds like it's in the bag though.'

'Not quite, so you and I are the only ones who know about this at the moment, understand?'

'Of course.'

'Get those phones. They can have them back when they leave. Needham's a Facebook abuser.'

'I'm on it.' Rena strode determinedly into the complex.

Hazel was about to head inside herself when she noticed another vehicle mounting the ramp as Griff's cab left. It was a police car.

'Don't tell me we don't have official permission to be here.'

She turned and found Lucas standing behind her puffing smoke and rubbing the prickles on his scalp. She ignored him, opened her mouth to call Rena but decided it would be easier to handle the situation herself.

CHAPTER 28

The patrol car took its time crawling over to them before the doors opened and two overweight, uniformed male officers got out. One of them sported a wispy, carrot moustache.

Hazel guessed they were both near retirement age. 'Afternoon,' she greeted them warily.

Neither of them uttered a word until they'd done the leisurely, looking around stroll cops do and were standing a few feet in front of her.

'We heard you guys were out here,' the officer without the moustache said.

Hazel noticed he had a broken nose. 'Can we help you?'

'Making a movie about Meredith Hickman?' Carrot Moustache nonchalantly tucked the protruding ends of his tight shirt inside his belt.

Hazel registered he had a cleft lip that his orange hairs barely concealed. 'Did you know her?'

He glanced at Broken Nose as if seeking permission to answer, but his colleague was peering beyond Hazel and Lucas to the activity inside Fun Central. 'Well enough.'

Hazel wondered if Detective Bennett had tipped them off or if it was just a slow day in town. 'Look, we're really up against it here.'

Lucas stepped in. 'If it's OK with you guys, we have to close these doors now. For sound.' He was always good at dealing with unwanted spectators.

Carrot Moustache fixed him indifferently. 'If you could just spare us a moment of your time.'

'I've got permits to be here, if that's what you need to see.'

Carrot Moustache met Hazel's eye. 'Sure they're all in order. Just wanted to advise you to watch your equipment. This place is quickly becoming a hang-out for junkies and drifters.'

'That's why we're right at home,' Lucas joked and stamped on his cigarette.

Broken Nose wasn't amused. 'A dealer was shot by a rival gang in Holtwood Forest last spring.'

'We haven't seen any trespassers yet,' Hazel assured them.

'You sleeping here?' Carrot Moustache gazed over their shoulders to the complex.

Hazel nodded. 'Most of us. Got some people staying at Rifkin Lodge in town.'

'Just stay alert and don't be afraid to call us if you see any undesirables.' Broken Nose reached past Hazel to hand Lucas his card. 'My direct line.'

'Appreciate that, officers. We will. This is the lady in charge though.' Lucas passed it to her.

They both regarded Hazel uncertainly and started meandering back to the patrol car.

A thought struck her and she called after them. 'Would either of you be prepared to give an interview about Meredith Hickman?'

They halted and turned.

'Neither of us was on duty that night,' said Carrot Moustache.

'I promise it'll take ten minutes max.'

CHAPTER 29

'No make-up?' Broken Nose, or Officer Soles, was leaning on the patrol car in the parking zone, where they'd set up for the interview.

'Not necessary.' Hazel positioned herself behind Lucas. 'Just handheld for this.' As he'd agreed to be on camera she assumed Soles wasn't there as Detective Bennett's envoy. She would love to hear his reaction when he knew a Broomfield officer had been unable to resist a screen test.

Weiss and Sweeting knelt and adjusted the wind muffler mic under Soles.

'OK.' Weiss put on his headphones.

Carrot Moustache, or Officer Drake, hung back looking bemused.

'Ignore the camera and talk directly to me. Just introduce yourself for level.'

'Officer Gene Soles, Broomfield PD.'

Weiss held his thumb up.

'OK, what can you tell me about Meredith?' Hazel felt Drake's warm breath on the back of her neck as he leaned in to watch.

'She was a loner,' Soles replied grim-faced.

That was no surprise to Hazel.

'She had a lot of issues but she was a good kid… from what I know. Her older brothers had already set low standards for her long before she dropped out of high school. Every town has a family like the Hickmans. Petty theft for the boys to begin with, then dealing crank. Both of them are serving time now. The parents are always having domestics in the street. One day I had to haul Wade

Hickman in for slamming his wife's head against a manhole cover outside Stooky's bar.'

Hazel hadn't expected the officer to be quite so forthcoming. 'So you're more than familiar with Mr and Mrs Hickman?'

'Yeah. My fellow officers get called out to their old turkey farm to crowbar them apart from time to time.'

'We're due to interview them here tomorrow.'

'Well… ', he pinched something invisible from the end of his tongue, 'careful as you go.'

'What was your experience of Meredith?'

Drake chimed in. 'We picked her up after a security camera recorded her stealing grass.'

Hazel turned to him and frowned.

Drake continued. 'Actual grass. Rolled up a newly laid lawn. Caught her with it in her car. She gave us a big sob story, said she was selling it to pay the bills because her brothers weren't bringing any money into the house.'

Hazel returned her attention to Soles. 'Anything else?'

Soles looked daggers at Drake. 'No. That's the one time she had any trouble.'

'And that was your only involvement with her?'

Soles wiped at his tongue before he answered. 'I saw her in the street on a couple of occasions but that was the only time I really spoke to Meredith. Can't recall any other episodes.'

'Who do you think killed her?'

'That investigation is still ongoing,' he said, like it had been programmed into him.

Shit. Hazel knew she wasn't going to get any further. 'I know, but who do *you* think killed her?'

'She grew up surrounded by bad people. Couldn't be protected from that.'

She wondered if Soles's remorseful tone was just for the benefit of the camera and remembered Meredith's elated expression when she handed her the rainbow friendship bracelet. 'And would her death be lower priority if she hadn't been tied in with BeMyKiller?'

Soles thought carefully about his answer. 'That investigation is still ongoing.'

CHAPTER 30

'What's happening out there?'

Griff Needham was looking through the open entrance doors and turned to the stooped man who had joined him and asked the question. He immediately recognised his face. 'Henrik Fossen…'

'You say that like it's a good thing.'

'Griff.' He extended his hand.

Henrik regarded his fingers as if they held something dead.

'Griff Needham,' he added but dropped his palm.

'I know who you are. I've been told to stay upstairs out of your way till they call me. Like they're my parents. Have you seen a woman on a mobility scooter?'

Griff shook his head.

'Her car's still parked up so I know she's here somewhere.' Henrik darted his eyes around.

'Cool tee shirt.'

Henrik glanced briefly down at his yellow *Sons of Anarchy* print as if he needed reminding what it was. 'So, what *is* happening out there?'

'The cops arrived and now they're making them part of the documentary.'

'Everyone loves to be on camera.'

'Except the guy who murdered my stepsister.'

Henrik tightened his lips but didn't give Griff the reaction he expected. 'You're up next then?'

'They're meant to be doing me now but then these guys showed up.'

'Hazel paying for you to stay in town?'

Griff nodded. 'For a couple of days.'

'I've been on your Facebook page, Griff. Quite a lifestyle you've got going for yourself. Ever have any moments of clarity?'

Griff was euphoric. Henrik had been on his Facebook page. But he didn't let it show. 'Some say delusional, I say aspirational.'

Henrik snorted. 'So you inspire the people you deceive?'

'You inspired a lot of people.'

'And what about your sister?'

'Stepsister.'

'Think I inspired someone to kill her?'

'If you turned her into psychobait, I'm cool with that.'

'You do know you shouldn't be, right?'

'Everyone makes their own choices. You said that. Denise willingly put her name in the timeline.'

'Yeah… *but*… that's not to excuse the person who killed her. Didn't pan out so bad for you though. You were a nobody before she died.'

'Doesn't the same apply to you?'

'Difference is, I don't want any of this.' Henrik gestured towards the crew.

'Really? Suicide attempt not timed to swing the spotlight back to you then?'

'Jesus, if I knew people were going to think that was a career move…'

'You would've made a better job? But here you are still alive with the ink drying on a six-figure book deal.'

Henrik's expression froze.

'It's all online. And you've got at least one Amazon pre-order. I'm desperate to read how you're going to paint yourself better than me. And see how Denise fares.'

'You do remember her then?'

'It's true. She's done more for me dead than alive. That'll tell you how close we were.'

'Heart-warming,' Henrik said disdainfully.

'Look, I don't know how this went south so fast. I'm probably the only bereaved family member who's going to give you an easy ride.'

'And I should be grateful for that, right?'

Griff made a weighing action with his hands.

'Based on this conversation, I'd probably be more comfortable having a one-to-one with the maniac who shot your stepsister.'

'And to think I was so looking forward to meeting you.'

'Speak to Hazel. She might want us to do it again on camera and, perhaps, that time around, I'll let you suck my cock.' Henrik turned on his heel and walked back towards the stairwell.

Grinning, Griff watched him disappear through the door. He took out his e-cigarette, shifted his attention back outside and observed the officers get in their patrol car and drive off.

CHAPTER 31

'Running.' Lucas had set the camera on the legs in the production office.

'Come and join us then.' Hazel wasn't about to let him off the hook.

Lucas reluctantly came to stand with Hazel, Sweeting, Rena and Keeler in front of the closed door so they were all in shot.

'You too, Weiss.'

He nodded and ditched his headphones on the sound rig before crouching in front of the group and readjusting the mic that Sweeting had positioned on the stand below them.

'Are we sure Fossen's out of earshot?' Sweeting whispered.

'He wanted some exercise so he's checking out the pond.' Rena was squinting at the monitor and angling her body so she didn't appear too wide.

'Where is this pond?' Sweeting rearranged his strands of hair.

'Down a dirt track through the trees.' Rena looked sideways at Keeler. 'I've been stretching my legs around there the last couple of nights.'

Keeler cast his eyes to the floor and tried to keep a straight face.

Hazel checked her watch. 'It's eight sixteen p.m.,' she addressed the lens. 'Our participants have gone back to the motel so we're taking this opportunity to tell you about the figure in the Meredith Hickman clip. His name is Shaun Stirling, and he's an actor. Meredith was played by Mia Todd. On day one we undressed the shrine downstairs so I hope Meredith's family and friends will forgive us. This is Rod Keeler.'

Keeler nodded awkwardly at the camera.

'As far as anyone is concerned he's our general dogsbody, but Rod actually works in Hollywood for Radical FX. He sculpted a prosthetic mask of Meredith Hickman, which was worn by Mia. Both actors were released after we completed the sequence, and we redressed the shrine exactly as it was.'

A muffled bump came from the corridor. They all turned to the door.

Weiss opened it and peered out. 'Nobody.' He waited a few seconds, closed it again then re-joined the others.

Hazel continued. 'In the actual Fun Central security footage of the murder, Meredith's real killer was unrecognisable. So we spliced our end shot onto the original camera clip. The quality was too low-grade to apply CGI. Now we're showing our participants the edited version. The reason we've done this is to gauge their reactions to the face of our actor. Tomorrow we'll be showing it to Meredith's parents.'

Lucas took his Zippo lighter out of his top pocket. 'We still haven't agreed to that.'

Rena sighed. 'Shall we cut?'

'No.' Hazel didn't shift her attention from the lens. 'We need to discuss this on camera. I completely understand why all the crew except myself and my associate producer have reservations about what we're doing but I need to introduce a fail-safe.'

'A fail-safe?' Lucas said scornfully. 'I signed up to work on a documentary. So did everybody else.'

Hazel hadn't realised Lucas felt so strongly. Was that why he'd been so remote? 'But Eve Huber is already convinced our actor was the same man she saw murder her brother.'

Lucas left the group and turned off the camera. 'Yes, because now she's had time to think about it she's realised if she helps you shoot the movie you want to make, there's going to be renewed interest in her part of the story and she can keep the dollars flowing.'

'We should be recording this.' But Hazel could see he was uncomfortable talking about Eve on camera. 'What if her incentive isn't for financial gain?'

'Of course it is. All those stories about a hitman for Henrik were bullshit. She was just trying to wring more cash out of her brother's murder by selling her interviews to the highest bidder.'

'We have nothing to substantiate that. Maybe she said she recognised him to distract us from something else. It's our responsibility to exhaust every possibility.'

'By concocting evidence?' It was Weiss who spoke up now. He took off his specs to clean them. 'And by introducing a decoy there's no way we can possibly claim to be objective.'

'Our intention is to prove one person committed these crimes, and using our actor's face will demonstrate if any of the victims' friends and relatives is hiding anything. If the Hubers have motives beyond lining their pockets then I need to know exactly what they are. I want to make disproving the lone tourist theory as difficult as possible.'

Weiss put his specs back on. 'But we're soliciting responses that'll taint the testament of everybody who views it.'

Sweeting raised his hand. 'I have serious issues with showing the footage to Meredith's parents.'

'Then you should have said something earlier,' Rena huffed.

But Hazel shared his misgivings. 'They may not agree but, if they do, I really only want them to view the last frame. I just need to get their reaction to our actor.'

Lucas folded his arms. 'Haven't they been through enough already?'

'After interviewing those police officers today, we've learned more about Meredith's parents. There's violence in the family. They may even know who killed their daughter. If they watch the clip and see someone they're not expecting, their faces will tell us for sure.'

CHAPTER 32

Sitting cross-legged on the edge of the small, rotting fishing jetty, Henrik looked over the pond and past the dumpsite to Fun Central's rear storage building. In the stark moonlight he could see large patches of plaster had fallen away from the façade exposing the black cinder blocks beneath. But he guessed it had been that way long before the place had been abandoned.

It was always the same story when you peered behind the gaudy frontage. He'd briefly worked for a fried chicken chain to piss off his father and knew the division was paper-thin. If you showed the customers a glimpse of what was drawing the flies in the backyard, they'd run screaming. Everyone knew what was there though; they just didn't like to think about it.

Being willingly oblivious to what couldn't be seen was a human talent. When he'd set up @BeMyKiller he hadn't perceived the millions of followers he'd attracted as actual people. They'd just been a quantity represented by a counter number on his screen. It seemed inconceivable that moving his fingertips over a keyboard could impact so many lives.

He recalled his dialogue with Griff Needham. The guy was so in denial about the real world he was surprised he could function out in the open but, no matter how much he repulsed him, Henrik wondered if they really were that different.

A fist slammed into the top of his spine. Momentarily stunned, he rocked forward and back on his interlaced legs. Then the arm of the figure behind him locked tight around his larynx and he was being dragged backwards towards the brush.

The pressure on his windpipe increased and his buttocks scraped across sharp stones. Henrik put both his hands on the arm holding him and dug his nails into the taut flesh, but the muscle clenched harder and completely cut off his oxygen. He couldn't make a sound.

Henrik managed to unfold his legs and kicked them in different directions to try and slow the progress of whoever held him. A rope was tightened across his Adam's apple, harshly jerking his head up. He felt the bark of a tree against his scalp.

He put his fingers around the rope but both ends were already being tensed from the other side of the trunk. Henrik dug into his throat to try and get a grip underneath it. He felt the vessels of his eyeballs quickly reach bursting point and wondered if he would asphyxiate before the rope started to cut through his flesh.

It slightly slackened, however, just enough for him to breathe. Somebody seized both his wrists and twisted his arms behind his back. He heard a pair of cuffs snap in place.

His vision was bleached white. Was he passing out? But the change in the sound of his choking told him something had been put over his head.

At first he thought it was a white polythene bag but as he looked upwards he could see the night sky above him through a circular aperture. Henrik could hear someone moving around him. 'Please.' The word barely emerged.

Henrik moved his face from side to side to try and shake what had been slipped over it and realised what he was wearing. It was a conical dog collar, the type used to prevent wound licking after an operation.

He went into overdrive, thrashing and shaking his head violently to try and displace the collar; the rope sawing into his neck with each movement.

The kick to his balls halted him but the solid chunk of pain in his abdomen barely registered as his assailant stretched the rope again.

A few moments later, Henrik saw the Shell logo on the canister as it was tipped against the rim of the collar. The cold liquid splashed against his face, soaking into his goatee until the level was just above his top lip. It was in his mouth; the fuel burning his taste buds.

He tried to spit the mouthful out of the collar but the flow didn't stop. Henrik spat more upwards as the canister kept glugging. His eyes stung and were then immersed.

Henrik didn't hear the scrape of the lighter but, as the flame ignited him, his limbs acted out the torture his voice couldn't. His eyelashes and lids were seared away.

His face bubbled and spat, the heat blinding him, and his arms and legs dancing against the agony. The fire cooked his tongue and the inside of his mouth, and Henrik could hear his skin hiss before it was muffled as both ears sealed closed.

The flesh was stripped quickly from his skull but, after his struggling ceased, Henrik's brain cooked long before the collar had collapsed and melted over his smoking shoulders.

CHAPTER 33

'April nineteenth? That's physically impossible.' Hazel seated herself on one of the red plastic tables in the vacant District Burger restaurant and tried to keep her voice down so the rest of the crew couldn't hear. 'I've brought the schedule forward by three weeks as it is.'

'I'm sorry, Hazel; Wesley says there's no wriggle room on this one. It's that slot or none at all.'

The status of her movie was very unstable. The majors had passed and Criteria Distribution still weren't all in. They didn't have the best reputation but they had the engine and platform the project needed. If they said no, Hazel knew her remaining options were slim to non-existent.

She was meant to be speaking to Wesley Park directly so it was a bad sign they'd put his minion, Rick Bloom, onto her. 'Even if I can wrap a few days early, that doesn't give me nearly enough time in the edit. Can't we be looking at this for summer?'

'Sorry, you know there's no crawl space there.'

'Perhaps I should be examining other options.'

But Rick knew she didn't have any. 'Look, we're all very excited about this project, Hazel, but Wesley has others that have to take precedence.'

Which meant she had to accept whichever deal they put forward while it was still on the table. 'But I can't jeopardise what we're trying to achieve here by putting us under that sort of pressure.'

Rick didn't say anything and waited for her to fill the silence.

Hazel sighed. 'But let me review the schedule and see if I can square some circles.'

'Excellent. I'll brief Wesley. I'm sure he'll be stoked.'

Rena ducked under the half-closed shutter of the restaurant and hovered beside Hazel.

'Call me if there's even a tiny chance of some leeway, Rick. Even an extra day would be a luxury.'

'I'll let Wesley know this afternoon.'

Which meant there wouldn't be. 'Thanks a bunch, Rick.' But he'd already rung off.

'Criteria?' Rena raised both eyebrows expectantly.

She knew Rena had been loitering outside since she'd seen her sneak off to make the call. 'They want us to deliver eight days earlier.'

'But they're still in?' Rena smirked.

Hazel didn't share her enthusiasm. 'You'd better forget sleep for the foreseeable future. Something you wanted?'

'I don't want to panic you but I can't find Henrik.'

Hazel nodded absently and then the sentence sunk in. 'Since when?'

'He's not in his room and nobody's seen him this morning.'

Hazel slid off the table. 'But he came back last night?'

'I assumed he'd gone up to his room when I locked the doors.'

Hazel took out her phone and speed-dialled his number.

'I confiscated his cell, remember?' Rena pulled it out of her pocket.

Hazel hung up and briefly closed her eyes.

'On your instructions,' she added, crisply.

'You're sure he's not upstairs?' She hadn't seen Henrik since she'd wrapped him.

'Doesn't look as if his bed has been slept in.'

'Shit…' But Hazel was mystified. 'Why the hell would he split now? He's already had his confrontation with Eve Huber.'

'Maybe the pressure got to him. I saw him popping pills yesterday.'

'Where was he heading when he left?'

'He went for a walk around the pond.' Rena followed Hazel back under the shutter onto the concourse.

Lucas, Weiss and Sweeting were setting up the equipment there, and Keeler was helping out.

Lucas stood. 'Any sign?'

Hazel shook her head as they breezed quickly past and headed for the doors.

CHAPTER 34

'Henrik!' Rena bellowed from the fishing jetty.

His name bounced back at them from Fun Central but both women were looking into the murkiness of the pond.

'D'you think? … ' Rena dipped her head towards it, as if it would help her see through the pollution.

Hazel scanned the water's edge the other side. 'Maybe. He could be lying on the bottom but more likely he's on a plane heading home.' As Henrik appeared so eager to exploit his brief window of celebrity, however, it seemed odd he would bail on the project now. 'Why would he leave his phone behind though?'

'He wouldn't exactly want to clue me in on his escape plan.'

'If that's what this is. You circle around to the other side, and I'll take a look here.'

Hazel scoured the bank but only found several used syringes. She recalled how scared she used to be of the big sprawling forest beyond. She'd dared to go out to the old well at Third Base on a few occasions though. It wasn't a name that was on any map. It was the secluded glade couples visited to light fires and get some privacy. A group of them often ventured there in daytime to find out what the older kids got up to, and Meredith sometimes came along. All they'd ever seen were used rubbers.

No sign of Henrik. Maybe his publisher had convinced him to leave. She figured that's whom he'd been having his surreptitious phone conversation with the day before. They'd probably paid him the first tranche of his fat advance, and Hazel had only given him his cab fare.

She'd pushed him too hard and been just as guilty as the rest of berating him in the absence of the real killer. He was just a messed-up guy who had done something stupid and got in way, way over his head, and she'd allowed her own anger about Meredith to impinge on the interview. Henrik wasn't her main suspect but, after the conversation she'd just had with Criteria, his timing couldn't have been worse. She was now without a central narrative for the documentary. And if she couldn't deliver to Criteria, her crew wouldn't get paid. Her intention had been to shoot his confrontation with each subject she summoned to Fun Central but that was yielding less compelling results than she'd thought. Parts of the Eve Huber segment were usable but when he'd met Griff Needham it actually appeared as if he, perversely, hero-worshipped Henrik.

She returned to the jetty and was about to call Rena when she spotted something nestling in the weeds beside it. It was a brown plastic pill canister. Hazel scooped it up and examined the handful of capsules behind the label.

Flunitrazepam.

'What's that?' Rena appeared from the trees.

Hazel held it up. 'You mentioned he was popping pills yesterday.'

'There's a lot of recreational medication lying around here.'

Hazel slid the canister into the pocket of her puffer jacket.

'Just a lot of smashed bottles over there. Looks like somebody uses this place for target practice. Should we call the cops?'

'Not yet. He's got to be missing twenty-four hours before we can report it.'

Rena shivered. 'But Henrik's a celebrity.'

'Whose fame is built on deception. We still don't know if his suicide attempt was a performance. And I don't want to give Bennett an excuse to shut us down. Let's just hope he's OK and has second thoughts before the end of the day.'

'We'd better get back. The Hickmans are due on-site.' Rena took three steps and halted.

Hazel looked around again, momentarily lost in thought.

'We are going to carry on?'

Hazel refocussed. 'We don't have much choice.'

'Maybe he's getting his head together. At least the Hickmans live locally. If we need to do a pickup with Henrik when he comes back, it shouldn't be a problem.'

'*If* he comes back. We'll just have to stick to the schedule in the meantime. Come on.' Hazel followed Rena out of the forest, the pills gently rattling in her jacket pocket.

CHAPTER 35

Hazel watched the recording of her interview with Henrik Fossen and Griff Needham the previous day.

Hunched forward, Henrik shifted in his swivel chair and examined his new Reeboks.

'Like I say, I'm not putting it on you.' Griff Needham was seated beside him and waited for Henrik to look up but continued when he didn't. 'I'm not out for your blood like the others.'

Henrik nodded. 'So why come all this way then?' He chewed his goatee.

Griff shrugged. 'Fight your corner.'

'You don't even know me. Why would you do that?'

'Jesus.' Griff reclined in his chair so a wall of children's smiling features became visible. 'If this is the thanks I get.'

Hazel had shot the stilted exchange in the Face Painting Zone. The fading sample photos of kids' dyed and grinning expressions offered a discomfiting contrast to their conversation.

'I don't blame you for Denise's death,' Griff stated dramatically, as if he were on a white trash talk show.

'I appreciate you saying that but don't you think you should be more concerned that whoever killed Denise hasn't been caught? Or had you forgotten about them?'

'Of course not but the cops have reached a dead end. Why are you giving me such a hard time?'

'I've read some of your Facebook posts. You're a fantasist. Just want to attach yourself to anything that will yank you out of obscurity, even if it's your dead sister.'

'Stepsister.'

'Hazel showed you the footage of Meredith Hickman, right?'

Griff looked off-camera in her direction and then back at Henrik. 'Yeah.'

'You think that was the man that murdered your stepsister?'

'I don't know.'

'You mean you don't care.'

Griff leaned forward and lowered his voice. 'Are you busting my balls for real?'

'Yeah, so now you finally know we're not going to be big buddies or anything.'

Griff looked genuinely hurt.

'Somebody assassinated your stepsister but you seem more interested in meeting me than finding whoever it was that pumped those bullets into her.'

Griff's face started to glow.

'You and I don't share a connection, Griff. Neither of us has any special talent. We're only sitting here now because of a tenuous link to some people who are dead, and yours is even flimsier than mine. But I bet you're wishing your stepsister had died long ago so you wouldn't have had to wait so long for your big moment.'

Hazel paused the footage, waggled in her swivel chair and wondered if she really needed to call Griff again before he flew back to Wilmington. He was clearly freeloading on Denise's death.

It repulsed her. Griff was treating the whole thing as an amusement. Did he really not care about his stepsister or was it just an act for the camera? But looking at his Facebook posts there was little evidence of any grief. How much mourning had there been for Meredith? Or was her death nothing more than an opportunity for others? She couldn't deny it had been the trigger for her project.

'They're here.' Rena was at her shoulder.

Hazel's stomach fluttered. She hadn't been able to eat breakfast because of the interview ahead. It was her first face-to-face with

Meredith's parents. She'd spoken to Meredith's father online but now she had to look them both in the eye. Would they be as cold and attention-grabbing as Griff? She knew they'd neglected their daughter during her childhood but had to resist any urge to censure them. Hazel was still concealing the fact she'd known Meredith, and it had to stay that way. She wouldn't be able to cajole the truth if she told them.

She closed the interview window and selected the Meredith clip. Hazel glanced over at the crew, set up and in a tense huddle by the shrine.

They were distinctly uncomfortable with what they were about to do and so was she. How could she put Meredith's mother and father through the ordeal of even watching one frame that wasn't real? But from what Officer Soles had said, it sounded like the Hickmans were still 'persons of interest' and she needed to determine if that was justified. She'd tried contacting Detective Bennett to get the low-down on the couple, but his deputy categorically said he would no longer take her calls.

Hazel stood from her chair at the small table. 'Don't bring them in just yet. Give me half a minute.'

Rena trotted back to the main entrance.

Hazel followed but forked away to speak with Lucas. 'Can you move the crew away from the monitor? I don't want the Hickmans to know you're shooting them. Use the zoom. Weiss, can you quickly put a mic behind the laptop?'

Weiss looked at Lucas for his approval.

Lucas nodded and Weiss trotted over to the table.

'Think you still have a project without Henrik?' Lucas said when Weiss was out of earshot.

'We're carrying on until he shows up.'

'Maybe he's not coming back.'

'Just keep the faith.'

'Faith in what? That showing bereaved parents the little horror show we put together will give us something we can use in the edit?'

'I promise I'm only showing them the end frame. Just start shooting as soon as I've brought them in.'

'You're the boss.' Lucas nudged past her to get his Lumix.

CHAPTER 36

'First time I seen it close up,' Wade Hickman said to his wife, as they both halted in front of the shrine.

'You haven't been up here?' Hazel couldn't disguise her surprise.

Tamara Hickman examined the dog-eared photographs. She was an elegant and compact fifty-something woman in a slate-grey shawl, tight jeans and spiked heels. Her long, jet-black hair had blue neon streaks, and it looked like she'd had Botox because the smooth top half of her face was betrayed by the smoker's fatigue around her lips. 'Too upsetting.'

Wade Hickman moved his mouth while he read the tributes and gently shook his head and ponytail. He obviously shared the same hair dye as Tamara. He was a similar age and shorter than his wife but his muscular frame was too big for the indigo cheesecloth shirt he was wearing. A leather necklace clung tight to his throat. 'We do our grieving in private.' He scraped his tongue around the inside of his cheek, as if he'd found a morsel of food there.

Hazel recalled what Officer Soles had told her about Wade trying to bust Tamara's head open on a manhole cover. She nervously glimpsed Lucas. He had the camera rested on the cool box and was pretending to go through his battery bag while he recorded them. 'I'm so sorry for your loss. Would you like a few moments here?'

Wade's eyes darted around the crew, a flash inventory of everyone there. 'We're good. Let's get this thing underway.'

Hazel noticed him furtively wipe away a tear, as if he didn't want his wife to see. The small action touched her. How private did his grieving really have to be? 'First, would you mind taking a look at the clip we discussed?' She didn't want to delay the deceit any longer.

'So how come the cops only showed us a still of it?' Wade scratched his stubbly throat, and it rasped under his nails. 'Couldn't see shit in that.'

'It is very upsetting. If you're not happy to do this now... ' But she needed them to. Had to see their reaction to the actor.

'Those assholes have left us out of the loop this far. May be our only chance to see it. You say there's actually a face?'

'I'd like you to view it in private then we can talk about it on camera. I'd rather you examine it alone beforehand though. I'm sure seeing it for the first time is going to evoke some powerful emotions.'

Wade put his arm protectively around Tamara.

'I'll leave you to it. All you have to do is sit yourself at that table over there and touch the keyboard. It's just that last frame I'd like you to see.'

Wade nodded a little too earnestly.

'We'll set up for the interview afterwards. I'll wait here until you're done.'

But the couple had already turned from Hazel and were approaching the table. She could see Wade leaning into his wife to speak with her and willed them to reach the laptop so she could hear via Weiss's mic.

Hazel made her way over to where the crew were assembled. Weiss was crouching at his rig behind the equipment cases and had slipped on his headphones. 'Are they in range?' she whispered.

'Just picking them up.' Weiss blinked as he listened.

Hazel angled her body so she was completely concealing him.

'Want me to break out the directional mic?' Sweeting said, loudly.

Weiss held up his hand for silence.

Hazel glanced back to the Hickmans. After they'd seated themselves in the swivel chairs, Wade leaned down to the laptop and hit the keyboard.

'This has got to be our finest hour,' Lucas murmured.

But Hazel knew she had to be tough to get to the truth. This was her job. And she had to remember how many times she'd taken care of Meredith in Blue Grove Park because Wade and Tamara hadn't been around. She didn't shift her eyes from the couple. They would be seeing the actor's face now.

Wade and Tamara looked at each other then back to the screen.

'What are they saying, Weiss?'

'Nothing yet.'

She observed Wade's head move as he spoke. Hazel returned her attention to Weiss and tried to read his expression.

CHAPTER 37

April's father had told her never to hang out at the junkyard or in the old building behind it because of CFCs. She didn't know what they were but did know there was nowhere more exciting to play.

Some grown-ups occasionally visited. They usually sneaked inside Fun Central. April wasn't brave enough to venture in there. Knew something bad had happened inside. The grown-ups could have that place; she was more interested in the things they'd thrown away. April had decided that, as nobody else used the junkyard as much as she did, it more or less belonged to her.

She called it Apriltown and was familiar with every nook and crevice of her domain. If grown-ups ever came, she knew exactly which old freezers and ovens to use as cover until the coast was clear.

It was much safer than in Blue Grove Park. The kids who acted like they owned the swings and slides there were a lot older than April and never friendly. She was seven but her next birthday seemed a lifetime away. The grown-ups who sat on the broken benches were the ones who frightened her the most though. Sometimes their gaze followed April, as if they needed something from her.

This was where April felt safe and could be whatever character she wanted without anyone spoiling her fun. She invented stories, populated them with creatures who lived inside the machines.

Wandering the rows of dilapidated and corroded kitchen equipment, she liked to sniff their interiors. It was the same as the damp metallic aroma April had smelt when she'd played in the broken-down car that had been parked in the garage before her father had it towed.

Most of the time she was quite happy on her own. Sometimes though, after spending hours alone, April panicked that she was the only person left in the world. That's when she ran all the way home through Holtwood Forest, craning to see her mother at the kitchen window and not feeling safe until she had.

Her father poked fun at her; said it wasn't normal for April to spend so much time in her own company. But she knew it was because he didn't have any imagination.

Just as she was thinking of heading back for lunch, someone else visited Apriltown. She immediately ducked down the side of the old industrial kitchen dishwasher that had the heavy glass door and a huge metal basket inside that slid out on rusty runners.

She listened to their feet treading the jagged stones in the channel the other side of the scrap wall and peered through a gap. April missed them but it sounded like a heavy grown-up. She wondered if they'd turn the corner at the end of her row.

They did, and April shut her eyes, believing that would make her even more invisible. She put both her thumbs in her mouth and bit down on them. The grown-up's shadow passed in front of her, and the footsteps slowed before they reached the end.

The stones crackled under their shoes, as if they were standing still but considering which direction to go. A door squeaked, something rustled and then it slammed.

They tramped away, and the junkyard was silent again. She still didn't budge but counted backwards from twenty before opening her eyes and emerging.

April crept in the direction the grown-up had gone and examined the area they'd stopped at.

Gripping the long handle of the large microwave oven, she swung it partially open. It squealed loudly, and she wondered if the grown-up were still nearby and had heard. She scurried back to her hiding place and remained there until she was sure nobody was coming back.

Eventually, April returned to the microwave door and dropped it carefully the rest of the way, tensing her tummy until it was firmly down.

Tucked inside was a black leather sports bag.

CHAPTER 38

The Hickmans didn't want to be interviewed in front of Meredith's shrine. Wade insisted being around it would be too distressing for Tamara. Hazel asked where they'd be comfortable, and Tamara chose Neptune's Party Zone. It was where families used to host their kids' birthdays. Tamara said she'd held Meredith's party in the venue when she'd been a child. Hazel was curious which friends had attended. After opening its shutter, Weiss complained it wasn't as soundproofed as Speed Zone but Hazel was keen to accommodate them.

Chairs in the shape of pink oyster shells had been stacked away but the tables that resembled yellow coral were fixed to the floor and nets of dusty plastic sea creatures were still hanging down from the ceiling. When they switched it on, the filtered green and blue lighting projected fish shapes against the wall that shimmered as if the room was underwater.

While the couple wandered around, Hazel asked if they minded having the camera running. Neither of them objected so Lucas walked with them while they surveyed the cartoon murals of seahorses and jellyfish. She noticed both of them became visibly crestfallen as soon as he was recording. Seemed like a perfectly timed performance for the lens. Or was it what she'd seen so many times before – subjects more open with a camera and a faceless audience than they would ever be with the people standing right next to them.

Initially, Hazel thought she hadn't detected any physical likeness between mother and daughter but, from a distance, she definitely glimpsed Meredith in Tamara's profile. She tried to imagine what it had been like growing up in the Hickman home. Meredith had made every excuse not to return there. When a ten-year-old Hazel had asked her why, Meredith had always bitten her bottom lip so hard she left an indentation, as if she was afraid of what would happen if her answer was allowed to escape.

After the crew were content with sound and lighting, Hazel invited the Hickmans over to the table they'd selected where Rena had set the chairs.

'You had happy times here?'

Wade nodded slowly and didn't unglue his arm from his wife's shoulder, even though it looked uncomfortable. 'Meredith's birthday was May nineteenth.' He paused, allowing his successful recollection of the date to register. 'Meredith brought all her friends up and we had her a little party for her eighth.'

'Seventh.'

Wade didn't turn to Tamara. 'Sure it was her eighth.'

'No, Meredith's—'

'Seems like yesterday,' he trampled over her contradiction.

'What sort of child was she?' Hazel wondered if they would really remember.

'A real firecracker.' Wade approximated an expression of misty-eyed nostalgia.

That certainly didn't tally with Hazel's memory of her: scared of and detached from the other kids in Blue Grove Park. 'So how old was Meredith when she started getting into trouble?'

His features hardened.

'I understand she had a few issues with the local police.'

Tamara sighed. 'This is a small town. Growing up here, most kids have a run-in with law enforcement.'

'Boredom?'

'Yeah, on the part of the cops,' Wade sneered.

'You think Meredith was victimised?'

He grimaced. 'Her name was Hickman.'

She recalled her interview with Soles. 'And d'you believe the police have investigated Meredith's death as thoroughly as they should have?'

Wade snorted. 'Only reason they got interested is because it was all over the news and people like you were in town. They gotta make themselves look good. Cover up their involvement.'

'Involvement?'

'I don't know who that was you showed me and Tam on the laptop but I know Meredith was told by Officer Soles exactly what would happen if he caught her dealing out here again.'

'Soles is all piss and wind,' Tamara interjected.

'Just telling her what he said.' Wade still didn't look at his wife.

'Meredith sold drugs here?' Hazel didn't know if she was more perturbed by the revelation or the casual way it had slipped out.

'Knew a lot of the kids who worked here,' Wade said defensively. 'If she wasn't supplying, somebody else would've been.'

Hazel attempted to keep her expression neutral. 'And Officer Soles threatened to take her in?'

'He'd done that already. Plenty of times.' Wade stroked the spiky grey hairs his razor had missed around his lips. 'Soles had a very unofficial conversation with her. Said not even *we* would recognise her.'

But Soles had told Hazel he'd only spoken to Meredith once. 'You're blaming Officer Soles directly?'

Wade shrugged. 'It's not Officer Soles on the security camera.'

But that wasn't an answer. And Hazel knew the fake footage was immaterial.

'Why have you never said this before?'

'To the police?' Wade said contemptuously.

'There was a media frenzy. Someone would have listened.'

'They were only interested in her being part of the story you want to tell. Nobody wants to hear Meredith died any other way. Including you.' Wade wet his bottom lip with his tongue.

'I just want to tell the truth, Mr Hickman.'

'That right? Well, Soles was always going after Meredith.' He nodded at Hazel's reaction. 'Always sniffing around her. Since she was a child.' Wade awkwardly unhooked his arm from Tamara and leaned forward in confidence. 'Soles often called around. Checking on our eldest. But I knew he was always keeping an eye out for Meredith. She hated him. Nobody wanted to do business with her because he was always buzzing around her, looking for an excuse to haul her in.' He licked his fingertip and wiped at a white stain on the leg of his jeans. 'His wife was sick for years. Committed suicide by drinking weedkiller.'

'How long ago?'

'In 2014.' Wade didn't need to think about it. 'Soles was the one who found her body, and it wouldn't surprise me if he was the one who filed the report.'

Tamara suddenly put her hand flat on the yellow coral table top. 'I chose this one because it's where we sat when we came here for Meredith's birthday.' There was a pause for effect. 'Blew out her candles right where you're sitting.' She fixed Hazel with glacial blue eyes.

A cool current passed through Hazel, and she barely restrained herself from revealing to Tamara that she'd known Meredith. That she wasn't just a stranger only interested in her daughter now she was dead, and that she'd shared more of her life than the location she was sitting in.

'We might not be liked in this town but we had a right to watch our girl bring her own kids here.' Tightening her lips she sniffed loudly but there were no tears.

'And what about Meredith using the #BeMyKiller hashtag?'

Wade looked disinterestedly at a black blood blister on his nail. 'Didn't know about all that till the reporters started calling the farm. When something like this happens, there's usually somebody closer to home responsible.'

'So you don't think Meredith tweeting the hashtag made her a target?'

Tamara opened her mouth to speak.

Wade cut her off for the second time. 'The girl had a target on her chest the day she met Officer Soles.'

'Sir!'

Hazel turned to find Rena trying to keep up with a hulking man in sweatpants and a tatty brown leather bomber jacket striding aggressively into the Party Zone. She recognised him by the tattoos either side of his neck.

CHAPTER 39

'I told him we were recording.' Rena kept her distance.

'Where's Fossen?' Jacob Huber's bleached yellow hair seemed stranded on the top of his craggy flushed complexion.

Lucas panned the camera to him. 'If you could just step outside until we're done here—'

'Fuck that. Just tell me where Fossen is.'

Hazel nodded at Lucas to keep recording. 'Eve said you were going to stay put at the motel.'

'My sister's taking a nap,' he barked, as if it were explanation enough.

'And you're drunk.'

'What of it?'

Hazel hadn't been sure, but knew, from her conversations with Eve, that it was a fairly good bet. 'So why don't you let us get you a cup of coffee before you do something you regret?'

'Just tell me where he is.'

Again, Hazel regarded the angel tattoo he had at one ear and the devil at his other and guessed which one he was listening to.

Wade remained seated in his pink oyster chair and didn't seem at all fazed by the situation. 'Think you should just take a breath there, friend.'

Jacob appraised Wade with bemusement.

'Maybe your business is more urgent than ours but, fact is, this lady's conducting an interview.'

'Somebody here point me in Fossen's direction.'

The crew studiously avoided Jacob's gaze.

Hazel stood. 'What you gonna do, Jacob, beat it out of somebody here? I know you don't want to violate your parole.' She could see the scar on his scalp where he'd been struck with the tyre iron that Eve had told her about.

He returned his attention to Hazel, and his eyeballs caught up with his head a second later.

'What would Eve say if she knew you were here?'

'She'd get over it.'

'Well, you can tear this whole place apart if you want. Fossen's gone.'

'Bullshit.'

'It's not,' Rena weighed in. 'We don't know where he is.'

Jacob didn't acknowledge her; his eyes had started an audit of Hazel's.

'Maybe *you* know something about it.' Hazel swallowed but tried not to let it show.

'Of course, I came all the way up here because I've already seen him.' He scowled.

'Certainly would make sense, if you wanted to make it look like you had nothing to do with it.'

'Or is this just a bluff to get me out of here?'

'I can't lie. I don't want you within five miles of here. But you can take it from me, we'd like to know where he is as much as you.'

Jacob glanced at the camera then lunged at it.

Lucas took a few steps back.

He chuckled. 'This whole thing's a joke.'

Wade tried to stand, but Tamara put her hand across his lap.

'A joke?' Hazel folded her arms.

'You've made the guy who killed my brother a fucking celebrity.'

'All I'm asking is you let us finish up here.' Hazel's mouth had dried. 'We're on a tight schedule but, if you want the opportunity to have your say, we can interview you right after.'

'I've told you; I'm not interested in any of this crap. I'm just here for Fossen.'

Wade took Tamara's hand off his lap, stood and strolled to Jacob so he was contemplating his colossal chest. He looked up to meet his glare. 'And both these ladies have already told you he's not here. Time you split.'

Jacob snorted hard in his face but Wade didn't blink.

'Jacob… ' Hazel took a pace towards them.

Jacob thrust his meaty fist within an inch of Wade's nose.

Wade still didn't flinch. 'You do that again and it won't be me that cripples you for life. Twenty-seven years I've been married to that woman over there… ', he jerked his thumb at Tamara, 'and I've never seen her lose a dirty fight yet. Now fuck off.'

Jacob eventually grinned. 'Maybe I'll just take a look around while I'm here.'

Hazel gestured towards the door. 'Be our guest. But if you're not out of here in ten minutes, we'll get a police officer to escort you.'

Jacob unclenched his fist and clapped Wade on the shoulder. 'Nice to meet you, pussywhipped. Maybe we can pick this up when I'm through with Fossen.'

'Ten minutes, Jacob.' Hazel signalled Rena to watch him.

He turned unsteadily and reeled out.

CHAPTER 40

Hazel squirted some shampoo into her palm while she waited for the weak and lukewarm jets of the shower to dampen her hair. The pipes in the wall complained as the water pumped sluggishly through them, and Hazel shivered in the cheap plastic cubicle.

'Looks like Soles got somebody else to do his dirty work.'

The recording of Wade's private comment to Tamara, courtesy of the mic Weiss had hidden behind the laptop, seemed to bear out everything he'd told Hazel about the officer in the interview.

She massaged the shampoo into her scalp.

It was evident Soles had more to do with Meredith than he wanted to let on. Why would he lie? Sounded like he had a fixation on her that went beyond his desire to bust her for dealing.

Meredith selling drugs at Fun Central confirmed the girl she'd played with had become a woman that severely contradicted the innocence of Hazel's memories. Wade and Tamara's appeared to be just for show.

MEREDITH SUCKED DICK FOR CHANGE

The graffiti on the pillar was a clear indication Meredith had probably got mixed up in every bad choice she could have possibly made. Maybe Soles was trying to cover up his own sordid transactions with her.

But her death was an interpretation of the specific words she'd used alongside the #BeMyKiller hashtag. If she'd died at the hands of local drug dealers would they have even cared about disguising their involvement, when sending a message about their ruthlessness was usually the aim?

Unlike the other victims, Meredith had died only a few hours after tweeting. If it was a single killer who had abused geotagging, could Hazel accept they had just happened to be nearby? But it was too much of a coincidence that she would have been murdered in an unconnected attack and in a way her tweet suggested. Hazel still wanted to persevere with the lone tourist theory and was sure her interview with Kristian O'Connell's sister the following day would give her the basis for pursuing it further.

She hadn't found a trace of Wade's allegations about the police's involvement in Meredith's death online so either nobody in the media had been interested or he'd never made them. She'd tried to speak to Detective Bennett about Soles, but he still wasn't picking the phone up. Was he stonewalling because he wanted to prevent his department being involved? Soles had been pretty candid in his interview but it could all have been a deflection. She needed to get him back in front of the lens.

But her session with the Hickmans also troubled her, and the crew seemed to be of the same mind. Did they want to resemble responsible parents for the camera because they had something more significant than their neglect of Meredith to hide?

Hazel recalled Meredith telling her how she used to accompany her mother into Holtwood Forest for secret target practice. Blowing apart bottles with guns was a popular pastime in Broomfield but had Tamara had other motives for learning how to handle a firearm?

The door squealed and Hazel's fingers froze. She swiped her hand across the mildewed screen. 'Occupied!' she yelled for the benefit of whoever wanted to use the bathroom. She thought the crew were all out shooting exterior cutaways.

Hazel stopped shivering and squinted through the burn of the shampoo but the door gently closed again.

CHAPTER 41

Keeler regained consciousness and wondered why Meredith Hickman was watching him. His eyelids felt heavy, like somebody was resting their fingertips against them. But as Meredith's face trembled he realised he was peering at his own reflection in a small square mirror.

He was hanging upside down wearing the latex mask of Meredith he'd made for Hazel, minus its wig. His breath heated his clammy skin beneath the rubber, and as his nostrils and mouth strained at the small slits cut for the actor, he could smell the talcum powder of the interior.

The blood thudded in his brain. Had he gotten drunk with Rena? This was some hardcore kinky shit. But he'd had sex with Rena for the last time by the pond the previous night and told her then that he had to fly out to his next FX gig.

Keeler recalled Wade and Tamara Hickman leaving Fun Central. That had been the afternoon. What had happened immediately afterwards? As the crew had headed off to shoot exteriors he'd said his goodbyes and gone upstairs to take a leak…

He'd been peeing when he'd become aware of someone in the bathroom behind him. His last memory was of being on his back listening to wheels trundling and helplessly staring up at strip lights above him.

Keeler tried to pull off the mask but his hands wouldn't respond. He couldn't turn his head either. His eyes swivelled left and right and found his arms hanging uselessly beside him. Their muscles were dead. He attempted to bend his inverted body but it was paralysed.

Someone passed by the slits of the mask.

Keeler couldn't call out to them. Whatever had incapacitated him had numbed him from the soles of his feet to the top of his gullet.

'Ssshhh.'

He glanced back in the mirror and saw their legs to the right of the Meredith mask. Then they bent down and met his eyes in his reflection.

Keeler's surprise at the face emerged only as a grunt, his exclamation restrained by the constriction of his vocal cords.

They unwound some duct tape and wrapped it around the neck of the mask so it was sealed tightly to his. They'd positioned the small mirror in front of him so he could see exactly what was about to happen.

A length of tape was ripped off and fixed over his nostril slits so he could only breathe through his mouth. Then a strip was stuck over that opening as well. The last air holes were his eyes. Keeler's panic tightened the mask to his face.

His captor looked into the terror of his reflected gaze before they applied the last strip, blocking his vision. He was about to suffocate inside his own handiwork.

Keeler knew he had to slow his panting but the alarm stampeding through him was quickly draining the last of the oxygen from the mask.

How long would he have? A minute? His bulk swung gently and at odds with how it needed to react.

A sharp jab just below his jawbone briefly halted his wheezing, and Keeler felt warmth trickling down his chin inside the mask. It percolated through his beard, ran into his eyes, down his forehead and spread across his scalp. The skullcap of the mask was filling up. He wasn't going to die from the knife wound or asphyxiation. Keeler would drown in his own blood.

He clenched his lips but, as the warm level rose steadily up his face, he couldn't close his nostrils. Keeler gagged as he felt it run inside them and tasted its salty tang coating the top of his throat.

Come get some, fuckface!

As he choked motionlessly, Keeler didn't even consider why his specific words had hung him there.

CHAPTER 42

Hazel grabbed the roll-on from her cot, lifted the edges of her two sweatshirts and quickly slid its cold ball around her armpit.

Hazel was to interview Kristian O'Connell's sister tomorrow morning but Sheenagh hadn't called to say she'd landed. She shared some of the same vices as her brother, however, so Hazel was going to be surprised if she made it onto her flight from Cheyenne at all. There was a contingency plan if Sheenagh didn't show but her testimony was crucial to underpinning the lone tourist theory.

Kristian O'Connell was the one victim who looked like an unconnected killing. If she could eliminate him, it made her theory about the perpetrator travelling from Belle Meade to Clearwater then Broomfield entirely plausible.

The door swung inwards and Lucas walked in holding his phone.

'Hey.' She didn't know how to speak to him alone now. As they'd been so intimate in the past, were they now doomed to be awkwardly polite?

He brushed past her and bent down to plug into the charger. 'Keeler gone?'

'Yeah, Rena's at a loose end.'

Lucas stood. 'About Rena…'

'I know.'

'She's pissing the guys off. We all have jobs to do but there are ways and means. It's just her manner. And as for that trolley of hers…'

'I'll speak to her.' Hazel rolled the wet deodorant head with her thumb.

Lucas dodged around her then halted. He sealed the door and turned. 'Listen, I know things are tight but the others are far from happy about the way this shoot's panning out.'

The bathroom door opened and slammed in the corridor.

Lucas took another step towards Hazel and lowered his voice. 'It's not the money. You know they're all solid but they're uncomfortable with showing that fake footage and so am I. Are you really happy to be churning out sensationalist bullshit for Criteria?'

So, Rena's tongue had been wagging. 'You know I'm fully committed to this project.' She considered taking Lucas into her confidence and telling him exactly why it meant so much to her.

'But you can't make the whole thing on your own and soon that might be your only option.'

She dumped the deodorant on her cot. 'So, is this a mutiny?' Her gaze dropped to his mouth.

Whatever Lucas was about to say evaporated. Before Hazel could meet his eye, he'd angled his head and dipped his lips to hers. He inhaled but didn't withdraw.

Hazel could see his eyelids were closed and briefly shut hers before detaching herself. 'No.' She put her fingers against his chest.

He slid his warm palm over her hand and trapped it there so she couldn't break contact. He leaned in again.

Hazel craned her neck away but made it tense enough for him to press firmly back to her. She kept her lips tight shut and felt his fingertips brush her cheek. Hazel said his name as a warning but it only emerged as a muffled gag. She yanked her hand out from under his and shook her head free.

His expression anticipated her reaction.

Slapping Lucas seemed like such a cliché. Perhaps she should just knee him in the balls.

'Haze—'

She seized him by the belt and considered how easily she could pull his crotch against her kneecap but jerked Lucas forward and returned the kiss.

Lucas gripped her waist before coasting a hand up to hold her face again. The aroma of his breath evoked all the intimate moments they'd already shared, like a trigger that wiped out the intervening months.

The leather of the belt creaked as Hazel clenched it harder and held him in place. She needed his weight against her, wanted Lucas to make her forget to breathe like he had when they'd been together before.

Lucas glided to her neck, and Hazel knew it would be academic if he touched her there. His bristles scratched and then the gentle suction moved downwards. She stiffened against it, knowing if she could resist now she'd always be able to.

The crew and tomorrow's schedule momentarily deserted her thoughts, and her hands grazed the shaved sides of his head. As he locked himself closer Hazel knew the barrier was as easily removable as it had been the first time they'd slept together. That had been after months of tension living in each other's pockets during *Isil Brides*.

But they hadn't known each other then as they did now. Hazel was acquainted with every inch of his body. There was no clumsiness as there'd been the first time. Now there was only yearning for what had been good. But her instincts told her it was a mistake to start the cycle again.

'No.' She released Lucas and turned her back to him.

CHAPTER 43

Keeler was silent but the Meredith mask, inflated by blood, creaked under the liquid's weight. Droplets beaded at the tiny gaps in the duct tape around his neck.

Meredith's features were unrecognisable, contorted like a black Halloween pumpkin. As her face had warped and darkened, the piece of tape that had been fixed over the mouth had gradually come unstuck.

It finally lost adhesion; the dead fluid exiting the bladder in a harsh spray, hosing the tiny mirror in the baby changing room and spattering the cartoon animal characters on the walls.

The tension was slowly released, Keeler's ten pints steadily draining down his body and into the mask to maintain the flow.

CHAPTER 44

Fearing the grown-up could have still been watching her, April had been too scared to rummage in the black sports bag. She'd closed the microwave door and raced home just in time for lunch. But returning to an empty Apriltown the following morning, she decided it must be safe to look.

Dumping the bag on the ground, she seized the zip. But something still restrained her from immediately opening it. This was a grown-up's bag and probably held grown-up things. And even though them concealing it in the microwave had her imagining it might contain treasure, a voice reminded her there was a lot she didn't understand and maybe shouldn't see. After all, her mother and teachers at school had repeatedly warned her never to have anything to do with strangers.

April told herself she would unzip the bag, quickly peek at its contents and put it right back where she found it. Except if it was full of money. That would please her mother. Her parents were always talking about not having enough of it. They'd be so pleased and grateful if she took that home. It seemed heavy enough.

She put her hand to her face to brush away a strand of yellow hair, and her cheek was burning hot.

'Don't touch what isn't yours,' her mother often cautioned.

'Finders keepers,' her father had said about a wallet he'd found in a sports jacket that somebody had left on the park wall.

April tugged the zipper back and peered inside.

A long length of thick rope filled most of the bag, and she lifted it out so she could see what was underneath. A folded sack covered a huge knife. Not the kitchen sort. It was like the one her father used to hack bushes in their garden. She picked the blade up and it weighed heavily on her tiny wrist.

There was a polythene bag of silver handles. She put her fingers in, trying not to make it crinkle too loudly. There were also some thin pieces of foil. She peeled one open to reveal a tiny sharp blade. She guessed you attached the blade to the handle. Wasn't that like the knives the surgeons used on TV? Next she took out a big roll of black tape, some police handcuffs and a tube of glue.

Then she extracted the last object she didn't recognise. Initially it looked like a red ball but, as she withdrew it, realised there was a strap attached to it that had a buckle.

April examined it. Perhaps it was a toy. Or did it fit around a dog's neck? April knew; it was a grown-up's watch. She tried to fix it to her arm but there weren't enough holes along the length of the strap to secure it there. April tried twisting the ball. Maybe the watch was hidden inside. But it was solid. It had little dents in it as well, like bite marks, so that got her thinking about it being a dog's toy.

She sniffed it and it had an odd smell. Like her mother's mouth did when she kissed her first thing in the morning. April decided to keep it. She'd put everything else back so the grown-up probably wouldn't even notice it was gone.

April zipped the bag up and was just about to return it to the microwave when she noticed the pocket at the front. She set it down again and searched that as well. She discovered some pieces of paper and unfolded one. It was a printout from a computer, a photo of a man's face.

CHAPTER 45

'OK?' Hazel watched Sheenagh's yellowed fingers shakily rolling a cigarette paper around a sprinkle of tobacco.

She didn't look up. 'It's the camera.' There was a strong Irish lilt to her voice.

Hazel had seen Sheenagh on TV plenty of times. 'Want us to cut while you finish that?'

Sheenagh raised her burned-out brown eyes. 'Finished.' She ran the tip of her tongue along the edge of the paper and deftly sealed the cigarette, twisted the end and lit it with the Zippo Lucas let her borrow.

Hazel could still smell Lucas and his cologne. She had to focus. 'Just relax.'

'I'm not used to all this opulence.' Sheenagh gestured around the mini go-kart track.

Weiss had insisted they return to the semi-soundproofed zone, and a wall of low tyres now surrounded them.

'You've been on the circuit before… ' Hazel smiled.

Sheenagh hissed smoke and wiped a fragment of glowing ash from the knee of her black jeans. She had angular and handsome good looks but seemed a decade older than her twenty-seven years.

Hazel knew that behind her battered exterior was an intelligence that had been squandered. She took in her undernourished frame. Her knitted canary-yellow halter-top exposed her tight, grey midriff but it didn't look like the cold bothered her at all. She'd taken off her denim jacket as soon as they were seated.

Sheenagh quickly flicked the curtain of dyed lilac split ends from her face and arranged it on both shoulders with her free hand before leaning back. 'Shoot.'

'You know why I want to talk to you.'

'Same reason as the others: everyone loves to see the rich kids fucked up.'

But Hazel sensed Sheenagh was being defensive to conceal her feelings. 'You have the same addiction issues as your brother?'

Sheenagh made the end of her roll-up glow a long time as she shook her head. 'Kristian was wrestling with bigger issues. But our privileged upbringing allowed us both access to things we shouldn't have had in such plentiful supply. At least, that's what they say.'

'And who are "they"?'

'Anyone who doesn't take a shot at me to my face.'

'You're in a programme at the moment?'

'Sixth one. Three step, twelve step, two steps back.' The blue smoke clouded her expression but she let it hang there.

'You miss Kristian?'

Momentarily, it looked like she was going to chastise Hazel for the banality of the question but her eyes softened. 'I still wait for him to call me.'

'Who do you blame?'

'Somebody like him. I don't know who he was hanging with at the time. He moved in his own circles. Brothers and sisters do that. Do you have a sibling?'

'No. You don't think Kristian putting himself up as bait by tweeting with the #BeMyKiller hashtag was the cause of his death?'

Sheenagh rolled her eyes. 'But that's what he's going to be remembered for.'

'I've explained to you, that *is* the focus of this interview.'

'And I want to put the record straight. My brother probably knew his murderer long before he dropped his name into that Twitter stream.'

'What makes you so sure?' But Hazel had already seen Sheenagh's response to this question.

'He owed money. Much more than I ever thought he did. When he came to me, I couldn't help him any more.'

'What about your parents?'

'They'd already disowned him. Told me I'd get the same treatment if I stayed in contact with him. I don't resent them for that. Kristian didn't exist by then. His addiction had eaten him up. He'd stolen from all of us; assaulted my father so badly he had to have seven stitches in his face. Plus he'd been interviewed by the cops about a mugging in the park where he hung out. They didn't have enough evidence but we all knew it was a matter of time.'

'So why didn't you give this version of events when the police first interviewed you?'

Sheenagh's features sagged. 'I was protecting him. It was naïve but I thought I could hide what he'd become. Everyone wanted to make his death more sensational than it was. That's why I kept quiet when people connected his death to him using the #BeMyKiller hashtag; even though I knew it was bullshit. Better that distracted people than his habit. But the media wanted to keep squeezing out every detail.'

'So you really don't believe Henrik Fossen was responsible for Kristian's death?'

'We all tried so hard to save Kristian but *he* was the only one responsible for his own death. Last year he was becoming capable of the same desperate acts as the person who killed him. But people don't want to hear that.'

'I promise, I'll feature what you say in this interview in its entirety.'

Sheenagh lifted a cynical eyebrow. 'But only because it reinforces the idea that the others were murdered by one person.'

'D'you think it's possible?'

'If that's what you're using to sell this to your viewers, I think it's a cheap shot.'

'So you don't believe the lone tourist theory?'

'I've no interest in it.' She flicked her roll-up but the ash had already fallen to the floor. 'Probably none of the people spending their time discussing it online had to identify their brother's body after he'd been stabbed so many times his ribcage was caved in. That's the reality of it. It's not fodder for entertainment; it's a chunk of me gone. It's just pain and emptiness, and there's nothing remotely sensational about it.'

'And what about the person who did that to Kristian?'

'Like I say, the thought that frightens me more is that it could have been Kristian who did that to somebody else. Whoever stabbed him was probably as far gone as my brother and could have suffered the same fate by now.'

'Does that comfort you?'

'Nothing comforts me. Fact is, Kristian was dead the moment he got hooked on junk.'

'And how's your recovery?'

'I take it a day at a time, blah, blah, blah.' Sheenagh angled her roll-up in her fingers and watched the straight column of smoke. 'What d'you want me to tell you? Kristian was my wake-up call but I may not be here in a couple of months' time.'

'You have the will to recover, the support of your family. You haven't done the things Kristian did.'

'You don't know me or what I'm capable of.' Sheenagh's gaze seemed to align with a moment of whatever poisoned history had dulled it.

Hazel nodded at her remote expression and waited.

After a few seconds Sheenagh took a last toke on the roll-up, dropped it between her legs and crushed it with the rubber sole of her pink All Star. 'Am I the only one to notice that?' She pointed beyond the crew.

Hazel turned in their direction. They were looking as puzzled as she was but behind them she could see the smoke pouring from the door to the main concourse.

CHAPTER 46

Hazel was the first to run. 'It's the shrine.' Beyond the rolling clouds she could just make out the pillar of flame.

Lucas was close behind. 'But no candles were left burning.' He coughed and waved smoke from his eyes.

Hazel couldn't recall noticing an extinguisher mounted on any of the walls. Vandals had probably ripped them all down.

'Need any help?' Sheenagh was beside her.

'You'd better head to the main entrance. I'm sure we can get this under control but I don't want you breathing this in. Rena, take her outside!'

'How the fuck did it catch light?' Sweeting had joined them.

'I'll see if there's an extinguisher in the production office.' Hazel was already feeling her way to the stairwell door.

'I'll get the emergency services.' Sweeting produced his phone.

'No!' Hazel snapped. 'We can handle this.'

Nobody responded. They knew why she didn't want Sweeting to make the call. If the fire team were summoned, they'd condemn the location.

Hazel found the door and pounded up the stairs two at a time. She bolted for the office but couldn't find an extinguisher. Darting to the sleeping quarters, she stripped the sleeping bags from the cots before heading into the bathroom. She dumped them in the shower cubicle and wrenched the dial.

She watched the jets soaking into the nylon. Jesus, what next? Perhaps the whole project had been jinxed from the beginning. She attempted to lift the soaked sleeping bags but they were double the weight. Dragging them to the other end of the corridor she yanked them down the stairs and back into the wall of smoke the other side of the door.

Hazel made a beeline for the conflagration and joined Lucas, Sweeting and Weiss there.

Lucas whacked the column with his jacket. 'I smell petrol.'

'Take one of these.' Hefting one of the sleeping bags, she swung it at the middle of the shrine. It adhered and briefly the flames abated. Then it slid down, and the blaze intensified.

Lucas slung his, and Sweeting quickly followed. They both stuck so only half the pillar was on fire.

Hazel seized hers again and it was scorched and hissing. She could feel the heat tightening her face.

Lucas and Sweeting's dropped but Weiss hurled his. Hazel heaved and this time hers wrapped around the column. 'Keep them coming!'

A few moments later, the flames had been suffocated but they still had to retreat outside.

'Put it out?' Sheenagh had rolled herself another cigarette and lit it.

Hazel took a few breaths and gagged. 'It must have been deliberate.' She straightened.

Lucas wiped the moisture from his eyes. 'Whoever started it, we've just lost our central icon.'

'Did you get enough cutaways?'

He sighed. 'Jesus, Haze. Fossen's split; the delivery date is yesterday, and our location has nearly burnt to the ground. D'you really need a GPS to locate the clusterfuck?'

'Whatever you've been told about the schedule… ', Hazel shot a glance at Rena, 'is my problem not yours.'

Weiss swiped a burning fragment of a Meredith photograph from his arm. 'When were you going to level with us?'

'Have you finished with me?' Sheenagh exhaled smoke at them. 'I'm getting dizzy from this little brush with Hollywood.'

'I've got her cab waiting.' Rena was eager to placate Hazel.

'I'm at the motel just tonight?'

Hazel nodded. 'We'll call you.'

Sheenagh swung on her denim jacket, handed Lucas his Zippo lighter then followed Rena to the top of the ramp, where a cab driver had got out of his Chrysler and was watching the smoke being sucked out of the doorway.

'Tell him not to raise the alarm and that everything's under control!'

Rena nodded emphatically at Hazel, clearly relieved she was still being spoken to.

CHAPTER 47

Sweeting readjusted the strands of hair on his baldness. 'You're really expecting us to go back in there now?' He nodded at the open main entrance as another cloud belched out.

It wafted over Hazel, and she restrained a coughing fit. 'Once the air's cleared, there's no reason we shouldn't carry on.'

He frowned hard at Lucas, as if passing a baton.

He seized it. 'Look, Haze, we know you've got a lot invested in this project… '

It was the last thing she needed to hear. 'D'you have somewhere else to be?' She fixed him coldly, any afterglow of their fleeting intimacy gone.

'Matter of fact, I've put another gig on ice for this.'

'So what are you saying? You wanna leave?'

He puffed his cheeks and rolled his eyes. 'Look, just take a breath for fuck's sake.'

'That's exactly what I can't do.'

'You'll find another distributor.'

'No, Lucas, I won't.'

'After *Isil Brides*, there's going to be no end of open doors.'

'I've already given up on that delusion. Criteria's it and there's no latitude with the delivery. I'm already way behind.'

Anticipating fireworks, Weiss clapped his hand on Sweeting's shoulder. 'Come on, let's rescue the equipment.' He dragged him back through the entrance.

Hazel reacted a second too late. 'Wait for the smoke to clear… '

But they'd disappeared back inside.

She shook her head and watched Sheenagh getting into the cab. 'So that's it: you've all discussed this?'

'Nobody's got it in for you. Maybe the schedule's impairing your judgement.'

'Don't you trust me?'

'Of course I do. I just think you're under a lot of stress, and that's not good for thinking straight.'

'I won't close this down, Lucas.'

'If you don't have a crew, you might have to.'

CHAPTER 48

April had returned the black sports bag to the microwave but had
kept hold of the red ball on the strap and the folded pieces of paper
she'd found in the front zipper. As soon as she'd seen the top photo
she knew the other two would be of things she wasn't meant to see
so had walked out of Apriltown and into the cover of the trees.

How long had she been wandering? She felt tempted to keep
going, further and further into the forest, until she was positive the
grown-up who had left the bag couldn't possibly have followed her.
Or was it because she wanted to put off inspecting the pictures?

They were in the back pocket of her jeans, which were made of
her dad's old ones that her mother had cut up and adapted when
he said he was throwing them away. They smelt of him, and the
pockets were deep, even though her mother had shortened those
as well. Wearing them made her feel like a grown-up.

April didn't feel like a grown-up now. Being alone with the
photos made her think she might be sick. Was it because she'd taken
the printouts without asking and feared being caught with them?
Or was it because she knew they'd been hidden away for a reason?
But even though she was frightened, April still wanted to look.

There was no wind in the trees, only the sound of her circulation bumping her ears. April slid them out of her pocket and sat
cross-legged on a cut trunk.

The top one was of a man's face. He had red hair, and his eyes
were closed. He was her dad's sort of age, maybe younger. The red
ball was in his mouth. It was held in place by the strap, and his
teeth were half-closed over it. That explained the dents and the

strange smell. Was this a sport? Why wear something that made him so uncomfortable?

But April knew she was studying something like her parents watched when she'd been put to bed. She lay awake sometimes, trying to work out what was making the sounds coming from the TV. Taking a deep breath, she unfolded the next one.

It was the same man. His eyes were rolled in his head like one of the boys did at school to frighten her. And now he was wearing black lipstick. Was he sleeping? April examined his mouth closer. It wasn't lipstick. His mouth was ragged and burnt. A tiny alarm sounded in her head.

She opened the third. She knew she was seeing things that would give her nightmares. It was a skull, and it was burnt as well. And there were frazzled bits still clinging to the bone.

April put the three images down beside her and gazed up at the still trees. Everything was the same. Maybe if she stopped now the pictures couldn't do her any harm. She got to her feet and walked around them, keeping her gaze locked on the image of the man with the red hair. April ignored the skull.

She needed to go now. Wanted to hear her parents' voices, even if they were arguing. April picked up the photos and carefully folded them. Hiding them beneath the overhang of a bush with the ball and strap, she memorised their position. She broke two of the branches for good measure and, even though she still had hours of playtime left, headed for home.

CHAPTER 49

Hazel surveyed the blackened shrine. 'So, we're agreed: this didn't start by itself.'

Lucas waved away one of the embers floating about. 'I can still smell petrol.'

The dead flowers and happy photographs had been scorched from the pillar. Cracked votive holders and pools of dirty set wax were the only remnants of it ever being a memorial. The sight chilled Hazel. It was a final violation of Meredith.

Weiss circled the column. 'Could it have been tweakers?'

'I haven't seen a sign of them yet,' Sweeting replied.

Weiss nodded. 'Maybe Henrik? Or Jacob?'

'So, we're looking at arson and we're still not calling the cops?' Sweeting kicked a smouldering vase. 'What about Sheenagh?'

Hazel picked up a blackened teddy. 'Didn't see her within six feet of it. Look, I know you guys aren't comfortable with everything we're doing here but we only need a couple of days before we're done.'

'A couple of days?' Weiss sounded sceptical.

Sweeting gestured around. 'And this is a crime scene we're walking all over.'

'Look, it's your call.' Hazel knew she had no leverage and had to make it their decision. 'We can pull out now, regroup in the edit and see what's left to shoot.' She didn't want to leave that option in the air too long.

'We still have to come back here though.' Sweeting sighed.

Hazel nodded. 'And whether or not I'll be able to recall our interviewees is another matter.'

'Aren't we done with most of them?' Lucas peeled a fragment of sleeping bag from the pillar.

'We'll still need their reactions when we reveal the face we showed them was our actor.'

'And when were you planning to do that?' he asked warily.

'When they've all seen it. The responses so far certainly throw doubt on some of them.'

'You mean Eve Huber? She's just happily performing for you because she wants to keep exploiting her involvement. Henrik reacted as anyone would; Needham didn't care; the Hickmans think it's the police, and Sheenagh O'Connell had to be evacuated before she'd even seen it.'

'I'd still like her to view the clip.'

'What the hell for? She's convinced her brother was killed by another junkie.'

'Which reinforces the lone tourist theory. If I can confront the others about the fake footage and eliminate them I can focus on who really killed Meredith, Denise and Caleb.'

Weiss halted. 'But Henrik is still missing. And how are you aiming to find this lone tourist?'

'I can already prove one individual could have flown between each of the remaining three states. An FBI flight manifest search for fake ID could be narrowed down.'

'Simple as that,' Lucas snorted. 'What if they drove?'

'Unlikely over those distances.'

'And what if it really is more than one individual?' Weiss slid his hands in his pockets.

'I still don't buy the idea that Henrik Fossen could have motivated three people to kill in one week.' Hazel rubbed soot from her fingers.

'Four. If you scratch O'Connell there's still the European victim,' Sweeting reminded her.

'He's already been dismissed because his killer never accessed social media.'

Lucas took out a cigarette and slid it behind his ear. 'But one of our participants could still be hiding something.'

'Exactly, which is why we need to do our follow-up interviews. We have to exonerate them all.'

'Think you can exonerate Eve Huber and the Hickmans?' Weiss asked dubiously.

'They'll have to justify their reactions to the doctored clip.'

'But the Hickmans didn't know I'd concealed a mic. They genuinely believe Officer Soles was to blame.'

'And I intend to get him on camera again, which we can't do if we split now. Like I said, I want to make proving the theory as difficult as possible, and I'm keeping an open mind about everyone.'

'But if we do carry on, are we comfortable working with an arsonist about?'

Weiss had a point but at least he'd put it in the context of them continuing. It was the tiny opening Hazel needed. 'Why did we stop shooting?'

Lucas shook his head but the others shifted uncomfortably.

'Whoever did it, this is a reaction to what we're doing here. We should've kept recording.'

Sweeting chimed in. 'Has anybody considered that it could be this lone tourist Hazel's talking about?'

That had occurred to Hazel. Maybe it wasn't Henrik Fossen or Jacob Huber at all. If so, she had to consider that somebody else didn't like what she was doing at Fun Central. And she couldn't think of a better reason to continue.

'Just calm down, Sweeting. Nobody knows we're here,' Weiss placated.

'Except Criteria, the local police and our interviewees,' Hazel reassured. 'And they've signed non-disclosure agreements. Despite Griff Needham's attempts, we've kept a lid on it.' Sweeting was getting paranoid but, she had to admit, Fossen's disappearance and the fire were starting to put her on edge as well.

Lucas blew air into his fist. 'As Weiss says, it could have been Henrik or, more likely, Jacob Huber. We did kick him out of here, and he clearly has an axe to grind with us.'

The crew looked nervously about the concourse.

'After what we all experienced shooting *Isil Brides*, I assume none of us are going to be intimidated by him.' Hazel searched their expressions.

Sweeting put up his hand. 'I wasn't on that shoot and I am intimidated by him.'

'Duly noted.' She indicated the shrine. 'But this has now become part of our investigation. We can talk further but, for the moment, can we please get some footage?'

Nobody responded to Hazel's attempts at marshalling them.

'There's barely enough smoke left. If we hurry, I can do a piece in front of it.'

Lucas folded his arms. 'What do you want to do? Set it on fire again?'

Before she could respond, Rena trotted into the concourse from outside.

'Eve Huber's just rolled up. Says it's urgent.'

CHAPTER 50

Hazel followed Rena to the main entrance. 'What does she want?'

'She won't tell me,' Rena replied, peeved. 'Says she only wants to speak to you.'

They hurried outside, and there was a taxi idling in the parking zone, leaves circling it as if readying for attack.

Eve had the back window rolled down. 'What the hell's happened here?' She looked beyond them to the last wisps of smoke drifting out of the doorway.

'Amateur pyromaniac; nothing we can't handle.'

'I'm looking for Jacob. He headed out yesterday morning, and I haven't seen him since.'

'He was here yesterday morning. Came looking for Fossen. We had to ask him to leave.'

Eve's expression curdled. 'That skunk.'

'We haven't seen him since he walked out of here drunk. Could still be hanging around though.' Hazel waited for the significance of that to sink in.

'He's always drunk. Had so many hairs of the dog it's completely bald. But he's always around to help me take my meds. Took my car, so this cab's going to cost me a fortune.'

'He was pretty aggressive to the Hickmans and my crew. And now we've had our mini inferno… '

The penny dropped, and Eve nodded with resignation. 'Well, I'd like to say he isn't capable, but I'd be lying.'

'He's set fires before?'

'He's damaged property in the past.'

'What about his phone?'

'Only getting his answering service.'

'Rena, can you take a good look around for him?'

She gaped. 'Now?'

'He could be sleeping it off somewhere. Maybe check the pond.'

'Is this a punishment?'

'Rena – no time.' Hazel turned back to Eve. 'We're in the middle of a set-up. D'you mind waiting here while Rena scouts around?'

'This isn't like him,' Eve said to herself and distractedly tucked a ringlet under her headscarf.

'Can you do that for me, Rena?'

Rena sighed heavily, swivelled and strutted off.

Hazel ignored her tantrum. 'Give me ten minutes, Eve. That'll give Rena time to search for him. Have you taken your meds?'

'Of course I have. I'm not brain-dead.'

'OK. Ten minutes.' Hazel strode quickly back to the crew.

CHAPTER 51

Hazel paced slowly around the sooty pillar while Lucas walked backwards in front of her with the camera. Weiss and Sweeting were crouching out of shot.

'Someone resents our presence here. Two seconds, I've still got to catch my breath.' She did so and composed herself. 'It appears our presence in Broomfield has provoked an extreme reaction. Midway through recording an interview, the crew had to quickly exit because of a sudden fire. Thankfully, everybody was in a different location when this memorial was set ablaze but we're convinced it was no accident. Now, this is all that remains of the place where Meredith Hickman lost her life, the place her friends left their messages and tributes.' Hazel looked down at the debris, and Lucas followed with the lens.

'The place we stripped down and redressed for the sake of a deal with Criteria.'

Hazel looked up sharply at him.

'It's OK, I've cut.' He lowered the Lumix. 'We don't know for sure that somebody wants us out of here. It really could have been kids.'

'I hope you're right. Have to get back to Eve.' Hazel sidestepped him and could feel his eyes on her back. If she was right, they had the piece on camera they needed. If she was wrong, Hazel had got him to dismiss the fire as the work of vandals and made the rest of the crew more comfortable about continuing. But Hazel believed somebody had sent them a pretty potent message.

* * *

Reaching the main entrance she ran into Rena. 'Any sign?'

Rena glanced back over her shoulder. 'Not of Jacob.'

'What d'you mean?'

'Wait.'

The cab was just swerving at the doors. As the vehicle accelerated past them, Eve studied them both through her open window.

'I thought she was going to hang fire until we'd finished.'

'The taxi was getting too expensive. She's going back to the motel to wait for him. Said we should call her if we see any sign.'

Hazel watched the car turn and head for the top of the ramp.

'She doesn't like me,' Rena sniffed.

'Don't take it personally. I don't think the Hubers do Christmas cards. What did you find?'

Rena waited for the cab to drop down onto the road and pull out. 'This way.'

Hazel followed Rena as she strode back towards the pond.

CHAPTER 52

Eve Huber hung up her phone. 'Shit.' Where was she going to scrape up Jacob from this time? Straightening in her seat, she squinted beyond the cab driver's shoulder to the road ahead for any signs of him.

Since Caleb's death, Eve worried more and more about Jacob's hard-drinking binges, as well as the other abuses she didn't want to know about. He'd never caught a break. After being expelled from high school he'd fallen into the construction industry before the work had all but dried up. He'd applied for other jobs but, on the few occasions somebody had given him a chance, his temper had gotten the better of him and he'd quickly made himself unemployable.

He was lost without his twin. He and Caleb had fought all the time but the pair of them had been so tight they almost squeaked. Now he had nobody to get drunk with but, more importantly, nobody to keep him on a leash. Caleb hadn't been smart but had known right from wrong. Jacob had some weird notions about having fun.

Like a lot of her brother's activities, however, Eve turned a blind eye to them. He worked hard, brought home the bacon, and what he did in his downtime was his business. He'd been on benders before as well. Gone AWOL after slipping out for a few cold ones. But Jacob always checked in and always made it back in time for Eve to take her meds.

She'd lost count of the occasions she'd picked him up naked, bruised and bloody but never asked any questions. Jacob got fucked up; slept it off; life resumed.

But as Eve peered out of the side windows of the cab she couldn't see a trace of him amongst the birch trees that lined the worn-out route back into town.

CHAPTER 53

Rena led Hazel to the burnt tree concealed by the thick brush beside the pond. The bark was scorched about four feet up its trunk.

Hazel inspected the white ash deposits amongst the dark mulch. Was it a campfire that got out of control? It covered a wide irregular area of the forest floor. 'Could be a drifter living here.'

'Look closer.' Rena nudged a sooty heap with the toe of her boot. 'Recognise it?'

Hazel did. It was the blackened scraps of Henrik's yellow *Sons of Anarchy* tee shirt. 'Jesus.'

Burn me in hell.

That was the request Henrik had made after the murders. 'We should call the cops.'

Rena was right. The arson attack they could handle but this was something entirely different.

'I really don't think this is another cry for help...' Rena bent to pick up the material.

'Don't touch it.' Taking the pill canister she'd found the previous morning out of her jacket pocket, Hazel quickly Googled 'flunitrazepam' on her iPhone.

'What are you doing?'

She examined the results. 'These are anticonvulsants. Bet these are what you saw Henrik popping before he vanished.'

'That settles it then. And I'm getting worried about Keeler as well.'

'Keeler? He took off for another FX gig.'

'But he said he'd text me. I've tried his number a gazillion times, but he hasn't responded.'

Hazel bit her tongue. She knew Rena and Keeler had been sneaking down to the pond. 'Wouldn't be the first time that's happened. Just being a guy. Come on, I'll report Henrik and we'll tell the others.'

But when they emerged from the trees there was already a patrol car pulling up the ramp.

Hazel rang off as Officers Soles and Drake got out. 'This is… fortunate timing.' What were they doing here? Hazel warily covered the distance between them.

'We understand you've had a fire issue on-site.' Drake narrowed his eyes at Rena's breasts.

'We have but it's under control now.' Hazel wondered who had called them.

'We have limited fire response in Broomfield,' Soles explained. 'They've had another call-out so we just wanted to assess the situation ourselves.'

If anyone had called them at all. Perhaps Soles was getting nervous about what she'd find out about him and Meredith and was spying on them. 'There is actually a more urgent matter. We're concerned about the safety of one of my interviewees, Henrik Fossen. He went missing yesterday, and we've just found his burnt clothes back there.'

'Burnt?' Drake still hadn't shifted his gaze from Rena's chest.

Rena folded her arms. 'Somebody set a tree on fire.'

'Henrik was meant to be with us for another few days. There's no reason he would have walked out.'

Soles turned to Drake. 'That's two missing people reports today.'

Hazel frowned. 'Two?'

He nodded. 'And both connected to this place. We're also looking for a Jacob Huber.'

So Eve must have called them. Probably told them about the blaze as well. 'To be honest, we weren't as concerned about Jacob. He does have a history.'

'Of?' Drake tucked in his shirt.

'You'll have to speak to his sister about that.'

'So, that makes his disappearance less important?' Drake took off his hat to run a hand through his spikes of red hair.

'No, but he turned up here drunk yesterday morning when I was interviewing the Hickmans.'

Soles smiled wryly. 'Don't tell me, that's when the trouble started.'

Drake turned to his colleague. 'Sounds like textbook Hickmans.'

Hazel noted he was happy to condemn them but not Jacob.

'And somebody else is missing.' Rena produced her phone.

Hazel held up her palm. 'Wait a minute. We know Keeler was off to another job.'

'Who's Keeler?' Soles asked, exasperated.

'Let me call him. I'm sure we can clear this one up.' Hazel took out her phone and speed-dialled. Maybe he was ignoring Rena. Everyone remained silent as she waited, listened and hung up. 'Answering service.'

'I told you.' Rena pouted.

'I really don't think this is anything to worry about, officers.'

'We can't file reports based on people not answering their phones,' Drake said with a pained expression and sucked at his orange moustache.

'We'll try him again but I'm sure he's just busy.'

'And you've tried this Henrik's phone?' Drake jammed his hat back on.

'I confiscated his cell… on-set confidentiality,' Rena added before they asked.

'Seems odd he'd leave it here,' Soles sniffed. 'So, has your Henrik been missing twenty-four hours yet?'

'Yes. Over that now. And I think I found his medication back there.' Hazel took out the pill canister.

Soles sighed. 'OK, one thing at a time; we'll take a look at the damage inside then you can show me this tree.'

CHAPTER 54

Officers Soles and Drake circled the shrine. Lucas was recording, as they'd both said they were happy to be on camera. Weiss and Sweeting weren't but were standing awkwardly in shot after Hazel insisted.

'This wasn't an accident?' Soles narrowed his eyes intensely at Hazel.

She knew he was upping the drama for Lucas and shook her head, more with frustration at the sluggishness of the interrogation. 'Think somebody doused it with petrol but we were all on the go-kart track when the fire started.'

'All of you?' Soles's attention drifted briefly to the lens.

Could her team really trust Soles and Drake? 'Yeah, 'cept for Rena.'

Lucas swung the Lumix to her.

She twisted at her pink hair. 'I was outside but came in when Hazel called me. I would have seen someone going in or out of the main entrance.'

'Are there any other exits?'

Rena answered Soles before Hazel could. 'Fire exits have been sealed but there's another through the burger place.'

'So they could easily have slipped out?'

'Easily.' Rena checked her phone for messages again.

Soles surveyed the charred flowers set in the melted wax. 'And you say Henrik Fossen wasn't present at the time?'

'Not that we were aware of.' Hazel suspected the footage they were shooting would end up being dumped but wanted to keep Soles onside for another interview.

Eventually he zipped up his jacket. 'OK, get me Fossen's phone and then we'll take a look at this tree.'

CHAPTER 55

April was sure the grown-up hadn't gone and remained in her hiding place amongst the branches of the tree. She didn't know how long she'd been up there but it felt like hours.

When she'd heard them behind her on the dirt track, April had frantically scrambled up the trunk. But they still hadn't walked by. Were they crouching somewhere near, waiting for her to climb down?

She'd convinced herself it was the grown-up from Apriltown. Perhaps they'd seen her steal the ball on the strap and pictures and had followed her into the forest. Again she scanned the portions of the muddy ground that were visible through the boughs below but couldn't see anyone.

April didn't enjoy climbing trees, was terrified of heights and had even hated going on the Ferris wheel with her father. Since the time their seat had stopped dead at the top, she'd made him promise never to take her on one again.

She'd been scared of the creaking pin breaking and them plummeting to the grass but had actually been more terrified by another thought that had popped into her head. As they'd waited for it to start turning again, April had been struck by how easy it would have been to release the buckle of her safety belt and jump out.

That's what gave her a funny buzz in the back of her legs when she looked through the window of a high building: the idea of just opening it and allowing herself to fall. And how simple would it be to unhook her armpits from the branch and step from the thicker one below? April imagined the sensation of dropping and the sound she'd make when she hit the earth.

Something rustled to her right, and she craned to see the source of the noise through the leaves. April caught a glimpse of movement. There was definitely somebody passing by. She held her breath and bit down on the ends of both thumbs.

She wished she hadn't hidden the ball on the strap and the pictures. If that's what they wanted from her she could throw them down to make them go away.

Light footfalls right underneath her. As April tensed herself tighter around the bough, her heart thudded against the bark. Could they see her if they looked up? There were several layers of foliage between her and them.

April's teeth pierced her thumb tips; she didn't trust herself to stay quiet.

The footsteps ceased. Had they left or were they still down there?

CHAPTER 56

It was just after one in the afternoon when the crew followed the two police officers out of Fun Central. The low grimy clouds seemed to lie in wait for them over the trees.

Lucas had stopped recording and carried the camera down the track through the forest. Weiss and Sweeting walked either side in silence until Hazel gestured Sweeting to catch up so she could speak with him. He trotted to join her, and Weiss bided his time until he was well out of earshot.

'So what's the situation with Hazel?'

Lucas stepped around a thick root. 'I think we'll all be out of here before nightfall.'

'You know what I mean,' Weiss said sourly but kept his eyes front.

'We're sharing a room but that doesn't make it any easier.'

'You *have* told her about Carrie?'

'I told you I did.'

'But you haven't told Carrie about Hazel.'

'No.'

'And you still haven't told either of them about us?'

Lucas tightened his jaw. 'No, that hasn't changed since I spoke to you this morning.'

'There are three people you owe some honesty to.'

'Two people. I'm already being honest with you. Give me time.'

'And this is where I should say you've had enough time and issue you with an ultimatum.'

'I know I need to man up. And I promise I will.' Lucas still hadn't met his gaze.

They both strode to catch up with Hazel and the others as they reached the pond.

CHAPTER 57

The sound that wrenched Eve Huber from unconsciousness unglued her sticky eyelids.

A cage with a partition separating two dogs was positioned about ten feet away from her. The black-snouted pit bull terriers' hostile barking punctuated the short circuits they made of their confinement before their claws scratched frantically at the metal bars.

Eve inhaled painfully and nausea tingled under her headscarf. How long had she been out?

She took in the considerable dimensions of her dingy surroundings and looked upward at the domed metal ceiling. Eve was inside a grain silo, and the only light came from a doorway on the curved wall opposite. A sliding corrugated panel had been rolled back about three feet to let in the weak slice of sun that illuminated her and the cage.

Eve's breathing faltered as she looked down at the congealed blood on the backs of her hands. What had been done to her? She tried to raise them but they halted and jingled. She was sitting on her mobility scooter, and a pair of metal cuffs secured each wrist to the main trunk of it below the handlebars.

The cage rattled as the dogs became more frenzied. They knew she was awake and started buffeting the bars.

She could feel their barks inside her chest and blinked each time their jaws snapped at the stale atmosphere. Eve noticed her lily print maxi dress was saturated with blood. 'Oh, Jesus.' She could smell it and feel it tacky on her face. Was she bleeding out? She was so weak.

Examining herself for signs of injury she couldn't see any obvious wounds. Her whole body was numb. Maybe it was a cut to her head. But Eve couldn't move her hands to touch her scalp, or lift any of her clothing.

She tried to recall where she'd been before this. Eve had gotten the cab from the motel to Fun Central and spoken to Hazel Salter about Jacob vanishing but couldn't remember anything immediately after that.

Eve cleared her throat. 'Get these off me!' The exertion of shouting made her dizzy.

Her voice bounced off the walls and was swallowed by the canine cacophony. The terriers battered their prison but she could see it was fixed to the floor by an inch thick ridge of cement.

The mobility scooter's power was already switched on and Eve realised she could accelerate, even with her hands fastened to the handlebars. The doorway was about twenty-five feet away. But, although she thought she'd be able to cover the distance in as many seconds, Eve suspected escape wouldn't be that easy.

There was something scattered on the floor around the scooter. Peering down she identified the small chunks. It looked like offal. Pieces of chopped liver in pools of dark coagulated blood. It felt like she'd had a bucket of it poured all over her.

Eve grimly reminded herself what she'd dropped in the @ BeMyKiller Twitter timeline.

Bite me #BeMyKiller

'Ssshhh.' She tried to placate the dogs. 'Nobody to bark at here.' Eve saw the chain. It ran from the rear of the cage and was attached to the back of her scooter. She quickly realised its purpose. It was why her exit seemed too good to be true. If Eve rolled out of there, the chain would lift the hinged door at the front and set the two animals free.

Would the length of chain allow her to reach the doorway? She twisted her head as far as she could to where it was coiled behind her. It was impossible to tell. Eve figured whoever rigged it wouldn't allow her to get there before the dogs were released. And then she was still locked to the scooter by the handcuffs, which also prevented her from unfastening the chain from the back of it or the cage.

Then she spotted the day-glo sign beside the doorway that was about three feet from the floor.

CUFF KEY

There was an arrow below the words pointing downwards. From that distance it was difficult to discern anything underneath it. Perhaps it was hanging there on a hook. Maybe she'd been given a slim chance – grab the key, unlock the cuffs and slam the door shut before the dogs tore her apart.

But when Eve considered what had happened to Caleb, she guessed she was never meant to leave the silo alive.

CHAPTER 58

'You're sure this is his?' Drake crouched, took a pen out of his top pocket and lightly prodded the black remains of Henrik's *Sons of Anarchy* tee shirt.

Rena nodded.

Lucas orbited them with the Lumix but the two cops had already begun to ignore him. Weiss and Sweeting hung back, redundant, as Lucas had opted to use the camera mic.

'Looks too big for a campfire.' Soles inspected the circumference of the scorched earth.

'D'you think?' Rena folded her arms.

Did they really want Soles in charge? Hazel had considered contacting Bennett. It had been made crystal clear she wasn't to do that again though. And having the officer around meant he was available for interview. Persuading him to do that was her next task. She took out her phone and idly tried Jacob Huber.

A distant ringtone. Everyone's head spun in its direction.

She peered into the denser area of the forest. 'I just called Jacob.'

Drake stood and unnecessarily raised his hand for silence.

'Over there.' Soles pointed north through the trunks and crept a few paces forward.

Drake followed and Hazel, Lucas, Weiss, Sweeting and Rena fell in behind him as Soles entered the foliage. Lucas kept shooting.

Soles halted, and Hazel craned to see past him into the darkness. Somebody was moving there.

The melody ceased.

Hazel pocketed her phone and patted Lucas on the shoulder, signalling him to bring the lens to the left of Soles.

'Police officer, stay where you are!' Drake yelled suddenly.

His voice echoed back at them, and they held their breath. The figure fled.

Hazel saw them flit past the gaps in the birches and heard feet stamping over wet ground. She followed their escape with her finger. 'There!'

Soles took off and was surprisingly agile for his age. As he weaved around the trees, Drake tried to keep up with him. Lucas was third to give chase, recording but leaning away from the viewer so he could watch his footing. Hazel caught up and put her hand on his back to guide him. She could hear the others on their heels.

'Police officers, halt!' Soles had already disappeared into the shadows ahead.

As Hazel and Lucas reached the area where the figure had been, the air suddenly became cooler. The pungent fungus there had been crushed and scattered.

Lucas slowed and swung the Lumix around. 'Where the hell have they gone?' He whispered.

Hazel scanned the fingers of daylight beyond them for signs of activity.

Sweeting, Weiss and Rena arrived, already out of breath.

'Quiet.' Hazel took her palm from Lucas' hot spine and inched past him. She could distinguish two voices, a low male mumble.

'I think they went straight on.' Rena gulped.

'Listen.' Hazel hissed. But the conversation had stopped.

Lucas panned the camera around. 'Nothing.'

'Keep shooting.' Hazel strained for sounds again and picked up a set of faltering footsteps. 'Someone's coming.'

It was Drake and he was nursing his shoulder.

'You OK?'

He put his finger to his lips and didn't answer Hazel until he could lean into her ear. 'We'd gotten a hold of him but he broke free.'

'Where's Officer Soles?' Sweeting positioned himself behind Lucas.

'Lost sight of him' Drake bent down and spat on the forest floor.

A rustle of leaves. The six of them tried to pinpoint the noise.

'There.' Weiss jabbed his finger.

Twenty feet away, a silhouette decelerated as it saw the group and jogged sideways. Drake barrelled after them.

'Come on.' Hazel and the crew pounded the mud and just kept the officer in sight.

'Halt! Fuck!' Drake was getting the brunt of each branch that whipped back from the fleeing figure.

Now they were in the thickest part of the forest and there wasn't a chink of daylight.

'Shit!' Lucas took a tumble.

Hazel turned back. She could just make out Weiss and Sweeting reaching him so felt her way forward but couldn't see a trace of Drake or the person he was pursuing.

Rapid footfalls. Coming towards her.

Hazel braced herself. She couldn't work out if they were right, left or about to hit her head on.

CHAPTER 59

Hazel became aware of laboured breathing under her own and then somebody snapping brittle branches ahead. She fumbled for her phone. 'Officer Soles?'

'Did you see somebody come by here?'

She was relieved to recognise his breathless voice. 'Yes, your colleague was right behind him.'

'Not any more.' Drake joined them.

Hazel's phone lit up the three of them.

Soles managed to extricate his jacket from the thicket. 'Listen…'

They all stopped panting but the only sound was the rest of the crew's muted voices behind them.

'I'll call him again.' She speed-dialled Jacob.

The ringtone started a second time. Nearby. Fifty yards ahead of them a small blue screen cast its glow across the forest floor.

'Both of you stay here.' Soles moved off towards the light.

Hazel watched his bulk intermittently blocking the beacon as he tramped towards it.

A motorbike's engine started some way off.

'That's him gone,' Drake said with resignation. He trudged after Soles.

Hazel tapped on the torch of her iPhone and used it to guide her way around the roots of the trees to where they were standing. She hung up the call, and Jacob's ringtone cut off.

'Don't pick it up.' Soles scolded Drake. 'Go get a bag for it. I'll walk along the perimeter and see where he was parked up.' He shuffled away.

Hazel shone her torch down to Jacob's phone.

'Can you stay here until I get back?' Drake's exhausted breath smelt rank.

'Sure.'

'And don't touch it.'

'I got that,' she said stolidly. 'Tell the others to return to base. I'll see them back there.'

Drake didn't reply but she heard him trying to wrangle them soon after and their conversation receding until the forest was silent.

Occasionally there was the hiss of leaves as Soles scoured the area beyond her. She looked down at Jacob's phone.

The screen was still on. It was at forty-three per cent battery. Was it Jacob they'd just been chasing through the forest?

Hazel glanced swiftly up from the screen. She had an overwhelming sensation that somebody was nearby and shone the beam around the trunks. But the torch couldn't penetrate the darkness between.

A soft swipe, hardly discernible but it sounded like the movement of an arm against material.

'Officer?'

Gripping the phone tighter and arcing it around again, the impression heightened but she tried to remain calm. Maybe there was an animal in here with her.

Hazel felt a hard impact in her kneecaps and realised she'd dropped to them before the punch to the back of her neck registered. She lost balance and pitched forward into the leaves. She gritted her teeth as she anticipated another blow. It came harder than she thought, slamming into the bridge of her nose and flashing blue in her eyes. Hazel covered her face with her palms, and the second kick struck the backs of her hands.

She waited for another but could hear their feet pelting away from her.

'Officer Soles!'

Blood pumped hotly against Hazel's fingers.

CHAPTER 60

Eve had spent some time weighing up her options. One of them was doing exactly what her sick fuck captor didn't want and staying right where she was. But, from the lack of traffic noise, it seemed wherever she'd been imprisoned was completely isolated so there was little chance of anyone happening by to hear her cries for help.

Shaking her head to dislodge the blood-soaked weight of her scarf and wig, Eve felt the cool, fresh air on her baldness. Her body still felt so numb. Should she try to reach the key and would it actually open the cuffs? She craned around as far as she could and peered into the shadows behind her. Was someone back there watching Eve and had they expected her to immediately take off for the exit before even spotting the sign?

As much as she wanted to put major distance between herself and the two sets of snapping jaws, Eve surveyed the silo again for anything she might have missed. But as the dogs were driven berserk by the blood scent all around her, she found nothing else that would help her and resigned herself to the fact she had to work with the scant odds available. If Eve didn't act soon, it was likely the terriers would bust out of their prison. But she still felt so feeble.

Gripping both handlebars, she wondered if there was enough battery power in the scooter. Eve had charged it the day before but had gone back and forth to the restaurant a couple of blocks away from Rifkin Lodge for their breakfast special.

She paused to blink away blood before lightly putting her foot on the control pedal.

The animals' barking subsided.

They knew she was about to make a move and monitored her intently. Her ridgeback, Banjo, had always sensed the fear of strangers. He'd been taken from her to be destroyed when he'd attacked a pair of canvassers, and Eve had vowed never to go through the heartache of being a dog owner again. 'That's it; just stay right there. How about I go fix you some food, would you like that?' She couldn't conceal the tremor in her voice.

As Eve depressed the pedal the scooter jerked once and both terriers went rigid, their ears pointing skywards as she came in line with the front of the cage.

'Mummy will be back now. Just lie down and take a nap.'

They remained poised and motionless.

Eve put her weight on the pedal again and juddered forward.

One of the dogs started growling gutturally and the other joined in.

'Stay. Nothing to be afraid of. Stay, now.'

When she heard a rattle behind her, Eve halted and glanced back. The chain had started to uncoil. She had to take it slow, gauge how much ground she could cover before it went taut and started to lift the cage door. There was still some slack though so Eve moved onwards.

The growling lowered until it was an almost indiscernible buzz, their eyes narrowing and heads following her progress.

'Ssshhh.' She could take an hour to cross the floor and they'd still be ready to pounce. Eve just had to avoid any sudden movement and pray the chain would allow her to grab the key.

She could see it now hanging from a hook below the sign. But as Eve neared it and peered beyond the half-open panel, she heard the last coil slacken. Looking back she found the chain had straightened across the concrete floor.

'Help!' Eve shouted through the doorway at the area of dust and flattened dead grass. She waited and listened to the faint echo of her voice. 'Help!'

The terriers started barking again and bouncing around in the cage, their din drowning out hers. How long could Eve wait to see if anyone came? If the door had been left open, whoever kidnapped her must be pretty confident she wasn't going to get any outside help.

Swivelling back to check the chain again, Eve saw it was tight between her scooter and the cage but still lying along the floor. She extended her hand to the key. But because of the cuffs restraining her, it was at least another two feet away. Eve had to negotiate the front wheel flush with the metal wall before she could reach it.

Readying herself, she took a few breaths. The animals went silent again.

'Ssshhh.' Eve turned the handlebars towards the sign and gently nudged the pedal. The scooter surged forward another inch, and the chain started to lift off the floor.

She painstakingly sidled it up to the wall, the end of the left handlebar scraping noisily against the metal. Three inches from the key, Eve heard a creak and looked back to find the cage door had opened a crack.

The motion prompted the dogs to start dementedly yelping as they both tried to scoop the door open with their black snouts.

Eve's lip trembled as she took her foot away from the pedal. The chain was as tense as it could be. 'It's OK. Ssshhh.' Even when she slid her left hand as far along the handlebar as the cuffs would allow, the key was still about four inches ahead of her fingertips. The front scooter wheel was snug against the wall but if she rolled forward she could unhook it. But that meant lifting the door and letting the terriers out.

Eve examined the cuffs, making sure she could quickly locate the lock with the key. She couldn't afford to hesitate.

What was she waiting for? Eve gulped and gradually applied pressure to the pedal. The scooter lurched forward, faster than she intended, and suddenly she was beside the key.

A metallic clap told her the dogs were out. Eve could hear their claws clicking on the concrete as she seized the key with her left hand and rapidly used it to unlock the cuff on her right. She had to block out the sound of the animals' approach and focus on getting free.

To her surprise, the first ring fell effortlessly from her right wrist. She quickly switched the key to her free hand and started unfastening the left cuff. Her sticky red fingers shook as she scraped it around the tiny slot.

The snarls grew louder.

Eve spun to find the terriers two feet from her. She bellowed at them, expelling every ounce of energy she had.

The dogs parted from their trajectory but settled and fiercely jabbed their barking mouths at her from a foot away.

Eve couldn't get the key into the lock. Maybe it didn't fit. Perhaps this was the joke. Let her get close to escape but still bound to the scooter so the dogs could savage her.

She could feel the saliva from their chopping jaws land on her bare arm. Fuck this. Eve could get off with one hand freed, wheel or drag the vehicle over to the door, slip through and use it as a shield. But she was just about to swing her leg off when the second cuff dropped from her left wrist.

'Ssshhh, listen, listen, listen. Stay.' Eve shakily stood, held up her palms and took several steps back towards the doorway, leaving bloody footprints in her wake.

They scampered hesitantly forward, closing the distance.

Eve could feel the cold draught from the open door on the back of her head. 'Stay. You don't want to hurt me, do you?' She reversed another pace, and her shoulder struck the edge of the sliding panel. Sensing there were only seconds before they went for her, Eve turned but then noticed the other restraint.

Eve could see it wasn't metal though and that it was tangled between the two back wheels. It ran from the rear of the scooter and along the floor to where she was standing. She gagged as she realised what it was. The end disappeared under the hem of her bloody dress.

Eve's fingers explored her stomach. There was no sensation there. She'd been anaesthetised, cut open and her intestine extracted and attached to the axle of the scooter. She'd steadily disembowelled herself as she'd driven to the doorway.

Her legs began to buckle. But even though she would still be connected to the scooter and every step she took would eviscerate her, Eve had to get through the doorway and slam it against the dogs. Turning her back to them, she headed into the daylight.

The opening wasn't big enough, however, and Eve jammed half her body into it and pushed on the panel. It was locked in position. She grunted as she rammed herself into the aperture and then yelled as teeth sunk into the soft flesh at the back of her knee.

Eve got her right shoulder through and hooked her arm around the edge. As another set of fangs pierced the top of her leg and sharp claws fought for purchase, she levered herself far enough out to get a look at the other side. At the bottom of the door was a black plastic bulb that had to be kicked up to release the runner.

One of the terriers was at her back now; she could feel its warm solid weight there. But Eve couldn't squeeze herself any further through the gap. A tug below her waist told her the other dog had hold of her intestine and was yanking it in the other direction. Eve's legs gave way and she collapsed to her knees.

She reached for the bulb. 'Help!' Her fingers scraped at the release but she didn't have enough strength to click it up. A snout slid into the crook of her neck, nostrils snorting hot breath while a second set of canine teeth bit deep into the back of her thigh.

Eve recognised the person leaning against the silo. They pushed themselves upright and stepped to the doorway. Looked like they were gripping a car aerial. She tried to grasp the bulb again, and they touched the back of her hand with it. Eve felt a jolt and her muscles went into spasm. It was a cattle prod, and it was obvious they didn't want her letting the animals loose.

Eve couldn't move, closed her eyes, and waited for the dogs to be done with her.

CHAPTER 61

'So, exactly how many bad omens d'you need?' Lucas ripped off some more blue paper napkin from the all-purpose crew roll and handed it to Hazel.

She took it from him, swapped it with the blood-soaked one against her nostrils and tried not to wince. 'You don't believe in omens.'

'No but I do know when to quit.'

'Really?' She made significant eye contact. 'That's not the impression I got.'

The rest of the crew were leaning around the production office and awkwardly waited for the moment to pass.

Who had been out in the forest? Hazel had thought it was Soles and Drake that might have been spying on them before.

The officers finished their muted exchange in the corridor and entered.

'So you think there was more than one of them?' Weiss took a swig from his beer bottle.

'They were talking.' Hazel folded the new swab.

Soles frowned. 'When?'

'When you both chased after them. There was a conversation.'

'Sure it wasn't us?' Drake rotated his arm in its socket and grimaced.

'Positive.'

'Or your crew?' Soles nodded at them.

'No.'

'They were right behind you, and sound can sometimes play tricks.' Soles plucked a few leaves off his shirt.

'I know what I heard; at least two men. You definitely didn't speak to them?'

'No, only to tell them to stop,' Drake said tersely.

'So, did anybody else see more than one of them?' Sweeting darted his eyes around. He was clearly spooked by what had happened in the forest.

'I didn't.' Soles met Hazel's gaze. 'But it was dark in there.'

'There must have been two. The one on the bike and the one who attacked me.' The bridge of her nose pulsated under the napkin.

'You should let us call you a medic.' Weiss restrained a belch.

'I'm fine.' She pinched and waggled it for everyone's benefit and didn't react to the pain as it shot up the middle of her forehead. She wouldn't give the crew a reason to leave. Not after what Lucas had shot in the forest. 'Rena will be back soon.' She'd dispatched her to pick up another bag of ice from town. Hazel examined the napkin in her hand. The spots of blood were smaller. 'Where were the tracks you found?'

Soles watched Lucas examining his camera for damage. 'Edge of the forest; looked like a dirt bike. I followed the flattened ferns all the way to a gap in the perimeter fence.'

'But we don't know where the other one went.' Sweeting glanced at the doorway as if he expected them to appear there.

'Could still be hiding in the forest.' Drake seemed to enjoy topping up his unease until Soles shot him a look.

'And you don't know if it was Jacob Huber that slugged you?' Weiss chugged the last of his beer.

Hazel resisted touching the bruise on her neck again. 'I told you, he came from behind.'

'So who was on the bike?' Weiss nervously clicked his signet ring on his bottle.

'Could have been completely unrelated. Kids hang out here all the time.' But Soles didn't sound convinced.

Lucas puffed his cheeks but didn't say anything.

'Well?' Hazel knew why.

'No damage.'

'You want omens?' She gestured at the intact camera.

Lucas shook his head. 'Really? You've just been assaulted and we've found Henrik's burnt clothes.'

'And that's not enough subject matter for you? Doesn't this look like a ploy to deliberately terrify us?'

'Well, it's fucking working,' Sweeting declared.

'Whose ploy?' Lucas grabbed the last beer.

'Henrik's writing a book. And we know his last attempt to take his own life was pretty media friendly. Hoodwinking a movie crew would be a great last chapter.'

Weiss set his empty bottle down on the desk. 'Come on, Hazel. The burnt clothes, his medication; that's all part of the act? Maybe whoever attacked you attacked him. He could be lying dead out there.'

Hazel knew everybody had to be thinking it. And she was the one who had invited him to Fun Central. Was she unreasonably clinging to the hope that his deceptions in the past were the reason for his absence?

'Do you think we're in danger?' Sweeting asked Soles.

He pursed his lips.

'Then let's pack up and get out of here.' Sweeting fixed Lucas then Weiss.

Nobody answered.

Soles swung on his jacket. 'If I were you, I'd do as he says. Plenty of motels in town. Let me know where you're staying. If you see Henrik Fossen or Jacob Huber or get any more trouble in the meantime, just call me on the direct number I gave you. I don't have enough men to go combing a forest the size of Holtwood, but if there's still no sign by tomorrow I'll call in some local backup.'

'Would you object to me interviewing you again, Officer Soles?' Hazel knew there wasn't going to be an ideal time to ask but she was still determined to question him about his relationship with

Meredith. Wade Hickman was convinced he was involved in her death, and Soles had blatantly lied about the frequency of his dealings with her. Had he really carried out his threat that not even her parents would recognise her if he caught Meredith dealing again?

'Sure.' He regarded her suspiciously. 'But I'll come see you in town.'

CHAPTER 62

Hazel wasn't about to leave Fun Central but knew she had to persuade the others to stick it out. If they all walked, it was unlikely there would be any justice for Meredith or the others. She waited for the officers to hit the bottom of the stairs. 'Sweeting, if you need to go you can. I don't want anyone here that doesn't want to be.'

Sweeting looked to the others for support. 'Even if we're stupid enough to stay, what the hell can we shoot now anyway?'

'It's a fair point.' Lucas turned squarely to Hazel.

'This. I really think you should be running. At least to test the camera.'

Lucas sighed, lifted the Lumix and started recording.

The patrol car's engine started and Hazel paused for the sound to fade before she addressed them. 'The local police are looking for any excuse to get rid of us.'

'Any excuse?' Weiss shook his head.

'The complexion of the shoot is changing. How can we afford to quit now? If there's two of them, there's five of us and we're documenting everything as we go. Let's analyse what's happened and do a risk assessment.'

Everyone was looking at the floor.

'So we all agree that Henrik's shirt didn't set itself on fire either.'

Weiss eventually nodded. 'Eve and Jacob Huber have threatened to kill him in the past. And burning him was what he asked for.'

Hazel responded down the lens. 'Which is why I don't think it's anything to do with them. They'd be the most obvious suspects.'

'But Jacob Huber's got one brain cell.'

'Sweeting…' Lucas cautioned him and pointed at the camera.

Sweeting lowered his voice. 'If he got wasted and ran into Henrik around the pond… It was his phone you found so it was probably him that attacked you, and he's still out there.'

Hazel zipped up her puffer jacket against the chill in the office. 'Doesn't make sense. Means he showed up here to make trouble *after* Henrik went missing.'

'To cover up what he'd done?' Weiss took off his spectacles to clean them.

Sweeting self-consciously fussed his straggles of hair. 'Perhaps Eve Huber's covering for him. She pulled up here unannounced. If Henrik does wind up dead, she's got witnesses to the fact her brother was meant to have gone AWOL.'

Hazel ditched her napkin. 'Hardly a good alibi though. If she was going to lie for him, why not just say Jacob was with her at the motel when Henrik went missing?'

Sweeting fell silent.

Lucas panned to Hazel and waited for her attention to shift to the lens. 'So, what d'you really think's happened to Henrik, Haze?'

She knew Lucas was using his Lumix to make her admit the worst case scenario but she was the one who had insisted on their camera dialogues. Hazel took a breath. 'I don't know but I offered him protection. I haven't even begun to process what that means if he *has* come to any harm.'

'But you have to deliver an online edit to Criteria by April nineteenth… regardless.' Lucas didn't look up from his lens.

Anger spiked, but before Hazel could respond she was distracted by Rena's appearance at the door.

She picked up on the atmosphere. 'What have I missed?' She dumped a bag of ice on the desk.

Hazel dragged it towards her. 'On-camera production meeting.'

Rena bristled. 'Shouldn't you have waited for me?'

Hazel punched a hole harshly in the bag with her thumb. 'Anyone want to leave now? We've certainly been in more dangerous spots.'

Bewildered, Rena waited for the crew to answer.

Hazel hoped there were enough remnants of loyalty to keep them from the door.

After a long silence Lucas shook his head, then Weiss.

Sweeting was last. 'But, like I say, what are we meant to be shooting?'

Rena was eager to make up for her absence and quickly tugged her schedule out of her back pocket. 'OK. Maybe we should bring Eve Huber back. Interview her about Henrik's disappearance.'

Hazel plucked out a cube. 'No. She's focussed on finding Jacob. I'll call her and see if she's heard anything.'

Rena flipped a page. 'What about Griff Needham or Sheenagh O'Connell?'

Hazel tore off another napkin, added the ice and pressed it briefly against the swelling. 'Let's just take a few moments to figure this out.'

Rena rolled her eyes. 'Hazel, we can't afford to lose the rest of the day.'

Hazel bit her lip. 'Perhaps we should let the guys take five then have an emergency production meeting.'

Rena chewed on it a little too long before nodding. 'OK.'

Hazel tried to distract her further. 'And I promise if Keeler hasn't called you by tomorrow, we'll make it official with the police.'

'Don't worry about that. He texted me when I was driving into town.'

'That's something,' Sweeting said.

Hazel felt one of many knots loosen. She noticed Rena was smirking. 'I take it everything's OK?'

'He missed his flight and there's not another till tomorrow.'

'Is he heading back here?'

'Staying in Broomfield.'

From Rena's expression, Hazel guessed there was one more rendezvous planned. 'At least we can cross him off the list.'

CHAPTER 63

April shivered and wondered how much longer she had before hunger and exhaustion made her fall out of the tree. She was sure the grown-up was still down there. Just when April thought they might have gone, she heard boots circling again. Every now and then their progress would halt, as if they were listening for her. They knew she was hiding. It would be getting dark soon, and her thumb tips were wrinkly from sucking them too hard.

She'd considered sliding down the trunk and sprinting as fast as she could but April could never discern exactly where the grown-up was and thought she might run straight into them. But now her mother and father would have missed her and probably called the police.

They didn't know about her secret trips to Apriltown. She always told them she was going to Blue Grove Park to meet friends. They would be looking for her now though. April visualised the whole neighbourhood gathered outside her home; the TV cameras recording everyone as they were arranged into search parties like she'd seen on the news.

Any moment, the forest would be full of people and she craned through the boughs for her first sight of them. April imagined yelling to attract their attention, and her parents rushing forward and being ready to wrap her in a blanket as soon as her feet touched the ground.

April vowed that, as soon as she was safely home, she would never venture out again. She pictured her bedroom with her in it, cosy under her duvet listening to the hot water boiler ticking away like it did first thing in the morning. If she ever got back there April would never leave it, just snuggle into her pillow and be secure and surrounded by her toys and books.

Her stomach gurgled, and she put her hand over it. It seemed so loud. Would the grown-up be able to hear it? April hadn't eaten since breakfast and that had only been a sliced banana. Her father had offered to make eggs, but she hadn't wanted them. April hated the crispy bits that were always on the bottom when he cooked them. Now her mouth watered at the thought.

Why would the grown-up be so interested in her? What was it they wanted to do if they did take her away? But April knew what she'd hidden under the bush might be an answer.

She'd already decided what she'd do if the grown-up found her. Whatever they said to her, she'd refuse to come down. April would tell the grown-up where she'd hidden the ball on the strap and pictures – if that's all they wanted. But if they tried to scale the tree, even though it made her feel sick, she'd climb even higher.

April gazed up at the branches above. They would take her weight, but the grown-up would be too heavy and never get to her.

How long had it been since she'd last heard them? Maybe she should count backwards from twenty and, if there was still no sound of their boots, start to clamber down.

CHAPTER 64

Rena was seated at one of the yellow coral tables in Neptune's Party Zone. It was quiet there but she'd given up on Hazel ever joining her for their emergency meeting. She was still talking to the crew upstairs so Rena was at her laptop seeing what she could shift around in the schedule. Her iPhone buzzed – a text from Keeler.

Want to hook up before I fly out of here?

Rena smiled lopsidedly and replied.

Things getting crazy. Don't think I'll have time to meet you in town.

She waited. The response was the one she was angling for.

I could always meet you in our toxic little oasis…

Rena swallowed while she considered how to say yes without appearing too eager. Jesus, who was she kidding? It was a booty call. After that afternoon, however, she didn't feel safe heading back into the trees. She looked down at her watch and allowed the second hand to do three circuits before typing.

I'll text you when we're done but it might be a late one tonight. Will explain when I see you.

Rena lazily shuffled some papers around in her folder until she got a text back. He took longer than she did.

OK – standing by. What can I bring?

Rena took a swig from her mineral water and thought about it. Eventually she sent him her answer.

Something to keep us warm.

She rolled the phone over in her hand a couple of times before it vibrated again. Keeler had rapidly sent her a selection of emoticons:- a smiling face; a heart and two cocktail glasses. Hazel walked in, and Rena put away her phone. 'So, what's the score? Still got a crew?'

'For the moment.' Hazel pinned her ash-blonde hair behind her ears. 'Looking at the schedule we could finish with our motel guests and send them home early.'

'We might have had word from the police about Henrik or Jacob by then.'

'Just what I'm about to find out; I've had a call from Detective Bennett. Wants to have a face-to-face with me in his office.'

'Because?'

'Wouldn't say.'

'Sounds ominous. D'you think he's going to shut us down?'

'He can try.'

'Shouldn't we all come along with the camera?'

'Don't think that would help our case.'

'What else can I do then?'

'There's not a lot more we can achieve today. Couldn't get Eve on her phone or at the lodge so she's probably still out looking for Jacob.'

'What about Griff and Sheenagh?'

'We'll send for them tomorrow. I don't want to push it. I'll let the crew grab some sleep, and we'll start early in the morning.'

'What time?'

'Let's say six thirty so we're ready to shoot an hour later.'

Shit. Rena couldn't afford to stay out with Keeler as long as she hoped.

'When I get back, I'm going to tuck myself away for the rest of the evening. Have a think and write some notes.' Hazel gingerly touched the bridge of her nose. 'Hopefully, by tomorrow, I'll have more of an idea about a new direction. You should hit the sack as well.'

'OK.' Rena didn't meet her eye.

Hazel turned to leave then halted. 'Rena, I appreciate you rallying the guys like you have been but maybe you should throttle back.'

'Throttle back?'

'Just… you know, give them some breathing space.'

Rena nodded, but her face flushed because she knew Hazel was giving her a dressing-down.

'You're doing a great job of moving everything along but now is probably the time to exercise a little diplomacy. With the current situation, it's something we've both got to be mindful of.'

'Sure.' Rena nodded again.

'Thanks. See you in the morning.' Hazel left.

Rena took a deep breath. It was something she'd learnt to do since the first day she'd worked at Veracity. Didn't Hazel know Rena had the interests of the production at heart as much as she did? She pulled out her phone and sent Keeler a text.

School's out. How soon can you make it?

His reply was immediate.

I'm there.

Rena grinned and tapped her screen.

Text me when you are and we'll work something out.

She closed her laptop and was just leaving the room when another text arrived.

Make sure you're not followed!

She hurried to the bathroom to freshen up before any of the others could hog it.

CHAPTER 65

Hazel could hear Detective Bennett talking on the phone but knocked on his office door.

'Need a second!' he yelled.

Turning to the long row of chairs against the wall outside, she briefly scanned the stern faces assembled there and found an empty seat at the end. Hazel became aware of crying and leaned forward. At the other end was a scrawny, thirty-something woman. She wore a grubby yellow baseball cap screwed down over her long tangles of sorrel hair and was clutching some sheets of paper. She wiped away a tear with her thumb and nervously jigged her denim-clad leg. The laces of her dirty white plimsolls were untied.

'Here, keep the pack.' The Hispanic woman seated next to her offered her some tissues from her handbag.

'Thanks.' She took them.

'You on your own?' the woman asked her.

'No. Waiting to hear from my husband.' She turned over her phone with nicotine fingers.

'I'm sure they'll find your daughter.'

The crying woman rose and proffered one of the pieces of paper to the next person. 'This is my daughter, April. She went to Blue Grove Park today and hasn't come home.' Her voice quivered. 'Have you seen her?'

They shook their head.

'Please pass it along.'

It reached Hazel, and she examined the yellow photo of the freckled little girl. Her image was split by lines where the printer head had run out of darker ink.

'Anyone seen her?'

Everyone shook their heads.

But Hazel had recently stood in Blue Grove Park and remembered what it was like to be a child there.

'My husband's scoured every inch.' She made eye contact with Hazel. 'You haven't seen her?' she asked, desperately.

For the mother's sake, Hazel looked down at the picture again. 'Sorry. How old is she?'

'Seven. Said she was meeting some friends.'

'Afraid I haven't.' Hazel offered the photo back to her.

'I don't know what we'll do if… ' Her features froze, mucous dripping from one nostril.

'Mrs Weeks?' A young, plain-clothes officer had opened the door of the office to their right. 'This way.'

From his expression Hazel could tell that he was too young to know how to deal with her. 'I really hope you find her.'

Mrs Weeks nodded absently and followed the officer inside.

'Do you want this back?' Hazel still held the image.

The door closed, and Hazel looked for somewhere to leave it for her.

'OK, Miss Salter!'

She entered Bennett's office, and he remained seated behind his desk. He was apple-shaped, rounder than he'd appeared on TV, a patch of his thinning white hair in a static tuft above his forehead.

'You're late,' he stated.

Hazel was sure she wasn't but fought the temptation to glance at her watch. Folding and pocketing the picture of April, she closed the door but didn't sit in the leather chair in front of her. The office smelt of sweat and whatever half-eaten pasta was congealing in the open carton next to his phone.

'Heard you've been having a few problems up at Fun Central.'

'Nothing we can't handle. Any news about Henrik Fossen or Jacob Huber?'

'Not as yet. As you'll appreciate, I don't have many men to spare.'

Hazel hoped the situation wouldn't be the same for Mrs Weeks. 'So, why am I here? Second thoughts about an interview?'

'No. We've all had enough cameras, Miss Salter.'

'Officer Soles was happy to talk to us.'

'Was he?' Bennett's dark eyes gave nothing away.

'Yes. Any reason I shouldn't be comfortable with him as a contributor?'

'I know what you're doing, Miss Salter. But I won't be drawn. I'll speak with Officer Soles. His input is immaterial.'

'Why?'

'He's not qualified to comment.'

'He knew Meredith Hickman.'

'Everybody knows the Hickmans.'

'Seems Officer Soles was more than acquainted with Meredith. And Wade Hickman seems to think he was intimidating her.'

Bennett snorted. 'From what I hear, my officers had plenty of reasons to call at their turkey farm. Don't think that place has been used for its proper purpose since the nineties.'

'What goes on there?'

'You're buddies with the Hickmans now. Why don't *you* ask them? But there'll be no more interviews with my officers,' he said, categorically.

'Why not?'

'Only official releases, and you can get access to those online.'

'I really don't understand. My documentary could revitalise your investigation.'

'I've told you, it isn't my investigation any more. The FBI won't even return my calls.'

'Then tell me that. On camera. Vent. Your frustration is a part of this story.'

'Like Fossen's and Huber's disappearances?'

She didn't like the sardonic look on his face.

'You wouldn't have my officers running around on a wild goose chase just to give you some drama for your camera?'

'You might have heard – I was assaulted today.'

His expression didn't alter. 'And how come you didn't clue me in on the fact you grew up in Broomfield?'

Hazel hadn't been prepared to answer that.

'Been doing some of my own research.' Bennett picked up a document from his desk and put on his half glasses to read it. 'You lived here longer than I have. Anything else you've failed to tell me?'

'It's been twenty years.'

'Still a pretty major piece of background history you omitted to mention. Ashamed of where you're from?'

'No.'

'Look, I don't care if you have a personal beef with Broomfield or just want to do a hatchet job on small-town America but I called you down here to officially warn you – unless you want to be charged with filing a false police report, I need your reassurance you're not misusing my limited resources on whatever bullshit you're cooking up at Fun Central.'

'You really believe I'd do that? Besides, it was Eve Huber who reported her brother missing.'

'All I know is what some of your media colleagues were capable of last time around. They made my department look like a joke and me an asshole.'

'Then use me to set the record straight.'

'That's all I have to say, Miss Salter. We'll be keeping a close eye.'

'With your limited resources?'

'You can show yourself out.'

Despite her protestations, Bennett wouldn't discuss it further.

* * *

She left the station and drove back to Fun Central. What was he insinuating about the Hickman family turkey farm? Or was that to misdirect her from Soles's pursuit of Meredith? But as she glided through the dark streets of Broomfield she considered Bennett's accusation about her past and wondered if she really had concealed it for the sake of preserving an objective commentary for the documentary. Or did she not want to be called out for using her connection when she hadn't set foot in the town for two decades? She'd have trouble convincing anyone she still felt an association. But the fact was she did; more than she'd foreseen. And Hazel guessed one of the reasons she still held affection for and valued the days with Meredith in Blue Grove Park and Holtwood Forest was because they formed part of the short period when she still had a family of her own.

CHAPTER 66

Rena left the crew slouched around one of the tables in District Burger, eating leftovers and talking in low tones. They had nothing planned but an early night but she wanted to make herself scarce in case she was collared to do a last-minute booze run for Lucas in his Toyota.

She slipped through the main entrance and strode across the parking zone to the edge of the forest. Keeler had had over half an hour to make it from town while she'd showered and changed so he was probably already there. She halted at the top of the track and sent a text.

@ the pond?

Ready and waiting.

came the instantaneous reply.

Come meet me in the lot so we can find another spot.

Rena kicked at some jagged stones for half a minute before her phone vibrated.

Am just ready to go skinny-dipping. Really want to miss this?

It was freezing so this she had to see. She trotted into the trees feeling safer that Keeler was at the end of the short track. She used the torch on her iPhone to illuminate it but when she reached the jetty he wasn't there. She hastily typed.

Where R U?

An incoherent whisper came from the birches to her right.

Rena followed the sound to the side of the jetty, expecting a naked Keeler to suddenly expose himself to her.

'Rena.'

She took another pace forward but stopped. It didn't sound like Keeler. 'That you?'

No response.

Rena speedily tapped her screen.

Come out now or I leave.

She sent it and a phone buzzed just ahead of her as the message arrived. 'I heard that. I can see where you are.' She recalled the ringtone deep in the forest when Hazel had called Jacob's number.

Still no reaction.

'Look, we haven't got long. Get your hairy ass out here or I'm leaving.' But Rena took a few steps back.

The beam of a phone torch shone at her from the fringe of the trees and started to move quickly towards her. Rena shielded her eyes against the glare. She could see the silhouette of a figure behind the light but couldn't tell if it was Keeler.

Rena decided not to hang around to find out. Maybe it was creepy Henrik, Jacob Huber or a tweaker. She pelted back up the track and could hear footfalls pound hard to catch up with her.

She reached the top of the ridge and peered down but there was nobody behind her. Was Keeler messing with her? But she was sure it hadn't been him that had spoken down there. She hit one key and sent it.

?

A buzz then a rustle immediately to her left. Rena turned and saw the figure rushing at her from the cover of the trees. They'd skirted the track and were now beside her. A fist slugged her jaw and she was rolling back down, her phone slipping from her palm as she tried to break her fall. She landed heavily on her chest only a few feet from the jetty.

Rena's lungs closed against the impact, and she attempted to draw breath as a hand gripped her ankle firmly and heaved her anticlockwise. Then she was yanked backwards, her chin scraping along the sharp fragments of the track before it bounced on the end of the jetty and across the damp, rotting boards.

She was still dazed by the blow but twisted and flipped onto her back. Rena screamed when she saw who had hold of her leg. They jumped off the edge of the jetty and into the black pond.

Rena's spine lifted from the planks and then icy water closed over her face and rushed into her mouth.

Knuckles struck her left eye socket before she could jerk her head out.

CHAPTER 67

Cold currents trembled Rena's gut and sudden recollection jerked her back to night-time. She was still in the pond, stripped naked, on her knees and facing the edge of the jetty, which was only a couple of feet away. Her head and shoulders were above the surface, and her left eyelid was swollen and heavy.

Spluttering and spitting out putrid liquid through the coating on her lips, she attempted to push herself upright but her right hand was leaden. Rena awkwardly lifted it and saw, in the weak moonlight, she was holding a machete. The handle of it had been bound to her palm with a bandage that had been wrapped around it several times and knotted at her knuckles.

Her left hand was free, and she groggily tried to untie the bandage.

A dragging noise focussed her eyes ahead and, as they tilted up to the person on the jetty, her vocal muscles unlocked to emit a sob.

It was Keeler, lying on one side with his lifeless fingers extended towards her. Keeler's moment of death contorted his black features and the whites of his eyes were half-closed. They were being pushed shut by rope wound tight to his forehead. The person who had dragged Rena into the pond was standing behind his corpse.

She rose, backed away and felt a tug around her neck. Then she registered the rope that extended upwards from Keeler.

He was rolled into the water and sank out of sight.

As it snared her, Rena grabbed the noose around her throat but Keeler's bulk raised her from the pond, her feet churning up foam. Looking up at the quivering rope she could see it was slung over a thick branch about thirty feet above her. The other end was attached to Keeler.

Now his head and shoulders emerged. Rena's weight was hoisting him out but Keeler was much heavier and, even though she dropped a few inches, her toes could barely touch the surface.

Rena couldn't support herself on the rope. Her wrists were too weak, and the machete fixed to her strongest hand wouldn't allow her to get a grip. She chopped at the rope above her but couldn't get enough power behind her upward strikes. The only way to exert any force was to use both hands.

As she swung towards the jetty again, Rena yelled silently for help but the person there just watched impassively and blinked against the spray she was thrashing up.

Her pink toenails scraped the slimy boards and, momentarily, she dug them into the rotten wood and held herself in place – relieving the pressure. But her calves quaked and gave way and Rena juddered off it again; the soles of her bare feet skimming the icy water, and the sound of her strangulation amplifying inside her head.

Rena pedalled at the jetty, slamming the bridge of her foot painfully against the solid wooden edge and kicking Keeler's face.

She lashed out at her captor with the machete, but the blade whistled harmlessly out of reach. Her heartbeat pounded in her scalp.

Directly below her Keeler's corpse was still visible, his back against the jetty. Rena knew what she was expected to do and that there was no time for second thoughts.

As she wobbled above him, Rena seized the weapon rigidly in both palms and swiped the machete downwards at the double coils around his head. The metal impacted his skull with a hollow clunk but the rope remained intact.

Swinging it again, her cry of revulsion was unable to escape her constricted windpipe.

The steel lodged deep in Keeler's scalp, and Rena was suddenly motionless as the blade anchored her.

Rena couldn't gag but saw she'd severed the first rope and blood was oozing from the deep wound she'd inflicted. But both coils had to be cut. Wriggling and yanking on the machete, she attempted to release the wedged blade.

It unstuck and she was still directly over Keeler but couldn't steady herself on his head. As her feet slid off his dank skin, Rena's eardrums were at bursting point. She only had a few seconds left. Detonating a scream inside her chest, she spurred her arms into frantic action.

She attacked Keeler, cleaving fragments of bone; her frenzy bouncing Rena in the noose and squeezing her throat until her face turned blue.

But Rena remained suspended. Her squirming subsided and fingers relaxed their grip on the handle. Darkness crowded her brain, suffocating the panic as her limbs sagged and toes dipped to the pond.

She'd almost cut through the second coil and had left only a few tendrils of rope holding it to Keeler.

They snapped.

Rena didn't feel the frayed end whip at her face on its way up but regained consciousness as she landed in the freezing water and her body jolted against the bottom.

CHAPTER 68

Rena sucked pond water into her mouth. The noose had slackened but not enough to allow her to breathe properly. She got her fingers under the rope and scrabbled her nails at chafed skin as she struggled to unfasten it. If she didn't, Rena knew she would pass out and probably drown.

She sat up, loosened it, and retched as she wheezed in a few shallow breaths. The jetty emerged from the black fog in her eyes. Nobody there.

Keeler's body had listed and was drifting towards her, and she could see the damage his head had sustained. The left side of his cranium was gone and a flap of it had hinged away from the pulverised interior.

Rena recoiled and was upright but tottering backwards to maintain her balance. She landed amongst a flotilla of plastic bottles.

Getting unsteadily to her feet, she kept watching the empty jetty. Rena had to climb out the other side and warn everyone at Fun Central about who had attacked her. She glanced fitfully around but couldn't spot any movement at the edge of the pond.

Still disoriented, she turned and staggered towards the bank behind her. Ploughing her thighs through the trash that had set in the scum there, Rena dug her fingers into the cold, soft sludge and painstakingly dragged herself out.

Her limbs felt weak, and her whole body seemed to beat erratic time with her traumatised circulation. Digging the bloody blade of the machete into the grey muck, she used it to lever herself towards the reeds at the perimeter of the trees and was just stumbling for cover when she was violently hauled backwards by the noose still around her neck.

She slid rapidly down the slippery bank on her spine. Her head went under the freezing water and the impetus rolled the rest of Rena's body on top of her. She'd barely stood again when another heave lurched her further into the pond.

Her attacker was standing in the middle of it, reeling her in with the cut end of the rope.

Rena burrowed her fingertips under the noose to release it but it was wrenched again and she was on her knees, sliding along the bottom as they lugged her nearer.

As she slithered forward, her left knuckles grazed a rock. Rena grabbed it and the next tug pulled her hand and sucked it free from the silt. She lifted her right palm clear of the water and hefted the machete.

She was only five feet away from her attacker, and they froze when they saw the blade. In that moment, Rena lifted the rock and hurled it at them. In her weakened state it only skimmed the surface but, as the figure ducked, she quickly lifted the noose over her head.

Rena dashed for the bank again, her progress slow as the littered water restrained her. Behind her she heard feet slogging powerfully through it. Finally, a scream ruptured its way out of her larynx. It propelled her up the mud incline and Rena threw herself through the reeds and into the pitch-blackness beyond.

CHAPTER 69

Holding out the caked machete and her free hand against any obstacles, Rena sprinted into branches that lashed her face and naked skin.

For minutes her bare feet pounded leaves and mulch and splashed through muddy puddles. Then her palm told her she was about to slam headlong into a thick trunk. She jogged right but Rena's shoulder buffeted against it and her body twisted away.

She managed to steady herself and felt around the tree, using it as cover to look back. Her heart punched her aching throat and, momentarily, it was all she could hear. Then Rena discerned footfalls.

A torch glinted through the gaps in the birches some distance away. It zigzagged towards her. She wasn't brave enough to double back so decided she should keep going, even though she had no idea what lay the other side of the forest.

But now she was seeing two lights. Rena observed them jinking identically as her view of the woods tilted. Her oxygen-starved brain was playing catch-up. She pressed her fingernails into the crumbling bark. She couldn't lose consciousness, not now.

There was a patch of solid blackness below the tree to her right. Peering at it, Rena realised it was a hollow in the roots. She crept over, extended her free hand to the hole and waved it in the interior. It didn't connect with the sides so there was obviously a considerable recess. Big enough for her? Rena bent and thrust her arm inside until she made contact with the moist rear of the cavity.

The hiss of leaves was getting louder.

Pulling her shoulders in tight she crammed herself through the damp opening, the strong aroma of mildew immediately overpowering. Her knees sank and squelched into its soggy floor, and dense roots scraped her shins as she slipped awkwardly inside.

The chilled interior closed around Rena and she balled herself to fit, sliding in the machete and gripping the handle with both hands in front of her. As she waited and attempted to gulp air through her bruised windpipe, her short breaths bounced off the humid wall half an inch from her face.

The swishing boots were almost adjacent with the tree. Rena stopped breathing but was sure the confined space was amplifying the noise of her chattering teeth. Her stomach quaked, and she put her hand over her mouth to prevent any sound escaping. If she were found now, there would be no way of defending herself. Her weapon was useless if she was assaulted from behind.

She anticipated fingers against her exposed back or around her ankle. But the feet kept moving.

Their zigzagging meant it took some time for them to fade altogether but, when Rena was sure they'd gone, she emerged from her hiding place.

Rena saw the light vanish through the trees a hundred or so yards ahead and was once more in darkness. She returned the way she'd come, taking care not to tread too heavily and looking back every now and then to see if the torch had reappeared. There was no sign of it. She would try to find the pond. From there she could pick up the track to Fun Central and raise the alarm.

Her wrist still pulsed from striking Keeler's head.

Choke on it, loser.

Rena remembered what she'd contributed to the WhatsApp discussion. She used her left hand to feel for branches, the other she crossed over her breasts so the blade was at her side. Now her panic had partially subsided, she was suddenly aware of how freezing it was. Her hair was still soaking, and the low breeze scalded the icy droplets on her skin.

She halted and looked behind her again, wondering how long it would take her attacker to realise they'd missed her. There was a good stretch between them now though so she moved faster.

But Rena was suddenly out of ground. She'd wandered to the edge of a deep ditch and couldn't prevent herself from falling.

She had the presence of mind not to scream, however, and waited for her body to make contact with the earth again. It did, four gut-jolting times, before she came to a standstill.

Rena looked up at the stars but felt like she was still rolling. She'd struck her head against something and the pain buzzed in the already swollen left side of her face.

Do not black out was the last thought Rena had before she did.

CHAPTER 70

Hazel didn't sleep and knew no one else would have either. She'd made a list of what they could still feasibly shoot but when she examined their remaining options she wanted to re-interview three key people. Soles clearly concealed a deeper involvement with Meredith. After her dialogue with Bennett, however, she was positive getting the officer in front of the camera wouldn't be easy. First though, she was going to visit the Hickmans.

Had the detective been deliberately baiting her? Whatever his motives, Hazel wanted to take her crew to the turkey farm. Plus, even though the Hickmans had left Fun Central long after Jacob Huber, was there a chance they'd run into each other? After Wade and Jacob's confrontation, she imagined what would have happened if they had.

Ironically, it was Wade who had said the answer to Meredith's murder lay closer to home. But where did that leave the lone tourist theory? Meredith Hickman, Denise Needham, and Caleb Huber – all three deaths were connected to what they'd tweeted.

Who had she heard in the forest? The two voices were definitely male. Was one Jacob Huber? It was his phone they found. And was it really possible Henrik could be trying to dupe them by setting fire to the shrine as well as his own clothes? Or were the arson and her attack in the forest because she was getting closer to the motive behind Meredith's death?

Maybe Sweeting was right to be as uneasy as he was. But Hazel wasn't going to leave until she had answers to the questions that seemed to stack higher the longer they stayed in Fun Central. She'd call the Hickmans first thing.

Lucas still hadn't come to bed. Hazel decided she might as well shower and head back to the production office. Rising, she slipped on jeans and sweatshirts and grabbed her washbag. She stumbled along the corridor and yelled as she butted into someone.

They yelled louder.

'Lucas?'

'Weiss.'

Her hand scrabbled for the light switch and found his there. The strip bulbs flickered on.

Hazel picked up the washbag. 'Still up?'

Weiss was fully clothed but wasn't wearing his spectacles. 'We're nearly on the clock so I thought I'd hit the shower.'

Leaning down had reactivated her throbbing bruises. 'Have you seen Lucas?'

'Why?' He sounded defensive.

'He's not in his bed.'

Sweeting came through the door at the end of the corridor, wearing his parka. His skin looked raw. 'Who's yelling?'

Weiss turned. 'Where have you come from?'

'Roof.' His teeth chattered. 'I've been keeping watch but I fell asleep.'

Hazel could see a half-empty spirit bottle in his fist. 'You could have frozen to death.'

'Feel safer up there than in my room. Thought I heard a shout from the pond so I went up to listen.'

'When was this?' she asked.

'Hours ago. Just as I was turning in. Didn't hear anything after though.'

'We should take a look anyway. Where's Lucas?' She fixed Weiss again.

'Last time I saw him, he was in the burger place,' he offered reluctantly.

Their recreational drug use was no secret to her. Why was he being so cagey? 'Let's head to the pond. If none of us are sleeping, we might as well be shooting.' She hurried towards her room. 'Somebody get Rena up.'

Weiss called after her. 'OK if I pee first?'

CHAPTER 71

Hazel walked onto the concourse and headed for District Burger, but halted as Lucas emerged from the ball pit. Seemingly deep in thought, he stopped dead when he saw her.

'Did you hear any shouts from the pond?' It was the second question she wanted to ask but figured she'd give him the chance to explain what he'd been doing there.

He tightened his lips and shook his head.

'Have you just been with Weiss?'

Lucas seemed to consider denying it. 'Just hanging out.'

Didn't answer her question. What the hell was he hiding? 'Look, whatever the two of you were doing down here is none of my business… '

Lucas nodded and wiped invisible dirt from the palms of his hands. His gaze shifted to the door as Weiss and Sweeting came through it, and he seemed grateful for the distraction.

At that moment, Hazel didn't want to press him further. 'Anyway, we're going over to the pond to check it out. Thought we'd take the camera with us.'

'Sure.' He agreed a little too readily and trotted off to Neptune's where they'd stashed the equipment.

Hazel had anticipated refusal and knew Lucas's willingness was to excuse him from being probed further. 'Rena not with you?' she asked Weiss.

'Not in her room.'

Sweeting zipped up his parka. 'I saw her slipping out just after dinner.'

'Did she say where she was going?' But Hazel had a pretty good idea.

'No. I assumed she might be running an errand for you.'

Weiss was alarmed. 'I didn't know she'd left when I locked the entrance.'

'Keeler was staying an extra night. Maybe she's at a motel with him.' Hazel fumbled in her pocket for her phone.

'I'll call her.' Weiss took out his and speed-dialled. He listened for a moment. 'Straight to message.' He spoke into the mouthpiece. 'Rena, Weiss, look it's… ' he glanced at his watch, 'just after six a.m. Give us a call when you get this, OK?' He hung up.

'Don't panic. Rena had a key so she could let herself back in.' Hazel rang Keeler and listened to his answering service while she observed Lucas emerge from Neptune's with his Lumix. 'Keeler, Hazel. Just want to make sure Rena's OK. Let us know if she's with you.'

'We lost Rena as well?' Lucas said drily.

She acknowledged how quickly he'd composed himself. 'I think she's with Keeler. We'll wait for them to get back to us.'

Sweeting squinted through the main entrance at the forest. 'So you want us to go in there again, even though we might run into Jacob Huber?'

'You're the one who heard the noise. But stay put, if you want. Lucas?'

'I'd rather we all go. Strength in numbers.'

'Have we got anything heavy we can defend ourselves with?' Weiss looked about them.

'Shame I didn't bring the Emmy. Would have been good for something,' Hazel quipped but nobody laughed.

Sweeting was still peering outside. 'It's getting light now anyway.'

Hazel used her key to unlock the sliding doors. They rattled and squealed as she pushed them apart.

'Let's do this then,' Sweeting said grudgingly.

The four of them stepped into the parking zone, and Hazel pulled the doors back in place and secured them. There was a ground frost and the sunbeams spiking the grey clouds had just started gilding the white trunks of the birches. They couldn't help but briefly take them in.

'Perfect lighting.' Lucas shouldered the camera.

Hazel touched his elbow. 'Start running.'

CHAPTER 72

Dogs barking far away frightened April. Whether she was outside or safely tucked up in her bedroom, she always pictured how ferocious they looked and them bounding in her direction.

Early morning light fractured the grubby sky and, as April shivered and padded cautiously home, she wished it were only the far-off dog she could hear that was hunting her. A hundred barking dogs even, instead of the grown-up. There were so many trunks that could conceal them.

Had they given up chasing her? Their circling of the tree had stopped just before sunrise.

April wondered if she should have stayed up there until she'd been found. When the search party had given up in the park they'd obviously start looking for her in other places.

Even though it was day again, did it mean she was any safer? She just had to keep on walking until she reached her house. If she spotted the grown-up, she would flee and not stop running until she was at her front door. But she knew they could move faster than her, scoop April up and drag her back into the forest.

She slowed, glanced back and saw the figure there.

They were in the distance, briefly illuminated by the sunshine as they passed under a gap in the canopy.

April cast her eyes frantically around for somewhere to take cover, but she couldn't find a tree that had as many leaves as the previous one. She stepped up onto the roots of the nearest but there wasn't a knot to get her foot into, and the lowest bough was way out of reach.

She raced to the next. Grasping a jagged branch stump, April hoisted herself up between the 'v' of the trunk.

Had they seen her? They were getting near. April hastily climbed through the sparse foliage, going as high as she dared.

CHAPTER 73

Walking onto the bank of the pond, the crew's reflections in the black litter-strewn water shimmered as a keen breeze disturbed the surface. Nobody said a word as Lucas silently panned the Lumix around. They all assembled in front of the jetty and listened. The wind sizzled the leaves overhead and eddied the dead ones around their feet.

'You heard a shout?' Hazel whispered to Sweeting.

'Hours ago.' But he nervously scanned the trees.

'Well, there's nobody here now.' Lucas stopped recording and lowered the lens.

'Let's all do a circuit. See if we can find anything. Meet back here in five.' Hazel began skirting the right bank, but turned back to Lucas. 'Shoot anything that moves.'

Lucas nodded.

Hazel's eyes were drawn to the junk floating in the middle of the pond. The day before, it had all been gathered at the far end. Must have been a strong wind to shift it from where it had been lodged in the thick scum. Weaving her way through the trunks to her right, she examined the ground for any sign of footprints.

This looked like a waste of time but breakfast was imminent, which always improved everyone's mood. That was when she'd tell them about the new schedule. It would keep them busy while they waited to hear about Henrik and Jacob.

Her phone vibrated. It was a text from Keeler.

Rena with me.

A small nagging worry had been allayed. Hazel responded.

Ask her to grab bagels for the crew on her way back.

She couldn't lecture her again. Not having taken her down a peg the night before. In fact, Hazel couldn't afford to rub anyone up the wrong way today. If someone walked, it was likely to have a domino effect. Besides, it was still early. Rena was probably hoping to sneak back so nobody would notice she'd left.

Her phone buzzed again.

She's hung-over.

Hazel sighed.

Tell her she needs to rally.

Keeler's reply was swift.

Will use cattle prod.

Hazel smiled and quickly typed.

We need her at location as soon as possible, you dirty dog.

She was about to finish her lap when another message arrived.

I'm right on her ass.

CHAPTER 74

Rena's prostrate body was concealed beneath an overhang of mud so it was impossible for her to calculate how far she'd fallen. Her throat was nearly closed up and she could barely swallow let alone scream for help. And she figured she shouldn't even attempt that if her attacker was still looking for her.

The back of her head was against a rock, and she couldn't get any of her limbs to respond. Was she permanently paralysed? Over hours she'd cried tear channels through the dirt on her cheeks and begun to soberly resign herself to the fact that perhaps nobody would find her.

Rena wasn't sure if her right hand was still holding the machete or if it had been dislodged in the fall. Even if she still had it, she was unable to turn her face in its direction let alone grip with her fingers.

She couldn't feel the cold any more, only the occasional currents of air goosing her numb flesh and sending a fuzzy reminder of its presence up to her brain. And she was terrified to move. When she had she'd heard a creaking sound from her vertebrae and assumed she'd fractured it or something worse.

Was she going to die here? She'd been surprised to still be alive to see the daylight breaking.

When she didn't turn up at Fun Central, however, Hazel would try to contact her. But she'd dropped her phone at the pond. Rena considered the texts she'd exchanged. She'd been effortlessly lured there.

But she knew, sooner or later, she had to budge. Despite what might happen when she did, Rena had to warn the others about who killed Keeler.

She delicately tensed her neck muscles again but the crunch inside her head was deafening. Was it only the pressure of the rock behind Rena holding her skull together, and should she risk exerting herself any more if help might arrive?

CHAPTER 75

'Still no reply.' Hazel dumped her phone on the cracked plastic table in District Burger.

Weiss was chewing on the last cereal bar. 'Rena? I thought you said she's picking up breakfast.'

'I'm trying to get hold of the Hickmans.'

'You interviewing them first?' Lucas drained his coffee and grimaced. 'Jesus, this instant's rank.'

'Detective Bennett gave me some food for thought. Maybe they even know where Jacob is.'

Lucas ditched the cup. 'You think he and Wade might have come to blows?'

'They had unfinished business after their little face-off. Wade and Tamara drove back after he left. Maybe they bumped into him on the way home.'

'And you mean "bumped into him".' Weiss sucked granola out of his teeth.

'They live near. I think we should swing by.'

Sweeting had returned from the bathroom. 'We wasting more stock?' He straddled a chair backwards. 'Christ only knows what goes on at that turkey farm.'

Hazel put on her jacket. 'Sounds like a good reason to go. And if Rena's hung-over we'll probably be there and back before she rolls up with the bagels.'

Sweeting sagged. 'Wasn't the plan to finish the interviews so we can get out of here?'

She zipped up. 'Yep. And I want to start with them.'

Lucas stood. 'What the hell. If it's only down the road, I'll take any excuse to get out of this place for a while.'

Weiss nodded agreement.

Hazel picked up her phone. 'We'll take my car.'

Sweeting was the last to move. 'Does your insurance cover me getting savaged by guard dogs?'

CHAPTER 76

'It can't be this way,' Sweeting said for the second time.

Hazel was guiding her silver CX-5 along a tight, rugged road bordered by two overgrown hedges. Brambles dragged at the bodywork as she nudged the touchscreen of her TomTom. 'According to this it is.' But the display had frozen. She recalled her father driving her down the same country tracks but they'd never been this neglected.

The raised dirt in the middle of the trail scraped at the bottom of the car.

'We're being swallowed,' Weiss warned.

She looked in the rear-view mirror to where he was sitting with Sweeting. They were both peering out the back window at the branches closing behind them.

'I'd stop now. We might not be able to reverse if we go any further.' Lucas was in the front passenger seat, nursing the camera in his lap.

'I'm sure this is it.' Hazel kept her foot on the pedal; out of the corner of her eye she caught him shake his head.

Soon they couldn't see further than a few feet.

'This is a Mazda not a John Deere.' Weiss leaned between Hazel and Lucas.

The car slewed and graunched as it hit a trough. Leaves were already building up on the wipers. She switched them on.

Eventually the vegetation thinned out and they were in a dust bowl bordered by stacks of slate and roof tiles. Beyond them were three one-storey corrugated outbuildings.

Hazel turned off the engine. Was this really where Meredith had grown up?

'Looks derelict.' Weiss pulled the handle of his door.

'Stay in the car.' Sweeting folded his arms. 'We're trespassing.'

Hazel tapped the TomTom screen again but it was still motionless. 'This is definitely their zip code, and it was the only place on the map for miles.'

'Then try them again.' Lucas grabbed Hazel's phone from the dash and handed it to her.

She speed-dialled and put it on speaker. Engaged tone.

'Come on; as we're here, let's take a look.' Weiss got out.

The others followed, and Hazel slid her phone into her back pocket and led them through a gap in two stacks of the tiles to the plot the other side. 'May as well record this.'

Lucas lifted the Lumix and nodded he was running, hanging back to get them all in frame.

They came to the end of another narrow road that wasn't clogged by bushes.

'That must be the *right* way in,' Sweeting griped.

Hazel made for the first structure. It had two buckled aluminium doors that were chained and padlocked. She tried to get a glimpse through the gap in them, but the interior was pitch-black. A sour smell from within wrinkled her nose. She moved to the next outbuilding and halted as something bumped inside it.

She put her finger to her lips. Was it livestock?

They all listened.

No other sound came so Hazel continued until she was adjacent with the doors. They were secured in the same way.

'That doesn't sound like my fucking problem.' Wade emerged from the furthest outbuilding, talking on his phone.

The four of them waited to be discovered, but he started striding in the opposite direction.

'Mr Hickman!' Hazel called after him.

He rounded the corner and disappeared from sight.

'Jesus, they do live here.' Lucas lowered the camera.

Hazel gestured for him to keep shooting and hurried after Wade.

'We shouldn't be creeping up on him like this.' Sweeting caught up with her.

Hazel glanced into the dark recess of the third outbuilding. A large TV screen was showing a rerun of *The Middle*. Around the corner she found Wade getting into his blue Tacoma pickup.

He saw her and paused at the open door, his features flitting between hostility and recognition. 'I didn't give you permission to come out here.'

Hazel turned to Lucas, but he'd vanished. Then she spotted his shadow at the corner of the outbuilding. He was hiding with the Lumix. Weiss and Sweeting had registered this so were staring straight-ahead at Wade. 'I've been trying to contact you.'

'Phones are for shit out here.'

Hazel's gaze dropped to the one in his grip.

'What's so important anyway?' He seemed agitated.

'The police are looking for Jacob Huber,' Weiss piped up.

Wade kept his attention locked on Hazel. 'What's that got to do with me?'

Hazel held up her hands. 'We just wanted to make sure you hadn't seen Jacob since your last conversation with him.'

'Why would I have?' He swallowed and his leather necklace slid tightly up and down his throat.

'Perhaps you saw him on the road back into town?'

'No. And if the cops think I had something to do with it why am I not talking to them?' He darted his tongue into the hollow of his cheek.

'You might be soon.'

Wade rolled his eyes to Weiss. 'Thanks for the warning but I advise you all to go now. Tam's nearly back from walking the dogs.'

Hazel remembered Meredith mentioning her mother's secret target practice in the woods and imagined how she'd punish unwanted guests. 'We're really sorry to come busting in like this… ' but she could tell from Wade's expression that her apology wasn't cutting it. 'OK, let's move it, guys.' She followed Sweeting and Weiss back the way they came but couldn't see a sign of Lucas.

CHAPTER 77

Lucas had crossed the yard and was crouching the far side of the middle outbuilding with the Lumix still running when the rest of the crew walked by. Hazel turned briefly in his direction but didn't react. She looked quickly away, and Lucas figured Wade must still be behind them and she didn't want to signpost his hiding place. He padded to the rear and slipped around the corner, leaving only his lens protruding to record their exit. Wade didn't follow.

A few moments later, he heard the Mazda start up. The engine noise got louder. They were leaving via the second road, and the motor quickly receded and left the scene in silence.

They'd probably stop as soon as they were out of earshot. Lucas checked the battery supply – seventy-two per cent. He rested the camera on the ground and put his phone on silent.

A door slammed. Lucas waited. Another vehicle fired up, and he saw Wade glide by in his blue pickup, leaving the same way as the crew. He had hardly any reception so quickly texted Hazel.

W on his way.

She responded.

Have pulled off road. Shoot what you can.

Lucas grabbed the Lumix. He didn't feel safer with Wade gone. Sounded like Tamara would be here soon, and he guessed what sort of dogs she'd have with her.

* * *

When Wade's pickup had faded and he was satisfied she wasn't around, Lucas emerged and skirted the rusty wall of the outbuilding.

Something thudded inside, and he stopped and put his ear close to the corrugated iron. Were pigs kept in there and, if so, shouldn't they be making more noise?

The front entrance was padlocked so there was no way he could investigate. But Lucas could see a gap in the warped side panels and had an idea. He reached into his pocket and took out one of his miniature spy cams.

'Here he comes.' Sweeting leaned back in the front passenger seat, as if it would make him even more invisible.

Through the overhang of trees that concealed them at the side of the road, they watched Wade's pickup zip past them as it headed towards town.

'We'll give him twenty seconds then follow.' Hazel put her foot on the pedal in readiness.

'What about Lucas?' Weiss asked from the back.

'We'll let him shoot around the farm awhile then come back for him.'

Sweeting shook his head. 'I don't like this. He's trespassing and we've been given an explicit warning to stay away.' He folded his arms tightly. 'I really don't know what you're trying to achieve with this, Hazel. Are we tailing him out of boredom?'

'You can get out here, if you want. Walk back to base or find Lucas.' Hazel knew he was going to stay put.

'Well?' Weiss prompted him when he didn't answer. 'Are you in? We're losing him.'

'Of course I am. But I want you both to remember I think this is a fucking stupid idea.'

'Noted.' Hazel pulled out after the pickup.

CHAPTER 78

April had her eyes firmly shut and thumbs back between her teeth. If she couldn't see the grown-up, they didn't exist and she'd decided to stay like it until the search party found her, or she was an old woman.

There were insects on the branch she was lying along, crawling all over her hands. Without peeking, April couldn't work out how many of them there were. Two, three, five thousand? She imagined herself covered.

Their tiny legs pricked her skin, each tingle adding to the solid ball of a scream enlarging in her stomach. Soon it was going to be too big and burst out of her.

But although the bough was riddled, it concealed her completely. The grown-up wouldn't be able to spot her from the ground, even if they looked up directly. But perhaps they were playing a game now. Maybe they'd watched her climb the second tree and were just teasing April by making her think they'd left.

But then April could hear the familiar sound of their distant boots on leaves again and squeezed her eyelids so tight the blood boomed in her ears.

CHAPTER 79

Lucas squinted across the yard to the outbuilding Wade had emerged from. There were no windows and its aluminium door was now sealed. No sign of Tamara.

If he were discovered, Lucas would say he got split from the rest of the crew and was looking for them. He decided to run the camera from under his arm. That way it wouldn't appear as if he were recording. He checked the viewer to confirm the frame was elevated enough and stepped out of his hiding place.

Lucas awkwardly covered the yard to the closed door, trying not to tread too heavily or act as if he was being stealthy. Tamara could be watching him, and he anticipated dog barks or even gunfire. Around the doorway crack he could see there was a light on. Did they really live in this hovel?

He deliberated whether to check the interior or do a swift circuit of the dilapidated structure first.

Hazel took her foot off the pedal as soon as they rounded the corner and caught sight of the top of the blue pickup winding through the hedges ahead.

'Slow down.' Sweeting's shoulders were rigid.

But before the tall shrubs obscured it she saw Wade take a sharp right. 'He's not going to town.'

'I can't see him.' Weiss was craning through the front seats.

'He's just turned off. Keep an eye your side.' But Hazel spotted the tight track before he did and swerved the Mazda down it.

The wheels popped over gravel.

'How are we going to explain this if he realises it's us?' Sweeting gripped the buckle of his seat belt.

'There he is!' Weiss exclaimed.

'I can see him.' She applied the brakes and allowed the pickup to draw a good distance away before she accelerated again.

'Maybe he knows we're following and is leading us somewhere to butt fuck us at gunpoint.'

'Maybe that's exactly what you need.' Weiss leaned into Sweeting's ear from the back seat. 'Might make you less uptight.'

He angled his face away. 'Happy for you to take one for the team.'

'Where's he gone?' Hazel picked up speed.

'Careful, you'll be on top of him in a moment.' Sweeting braced himself.

'He must have been shifting to leave us this far behind.' She resisted the temptation to go up a gear as they glided around another corner and there was still no pickup.

The three of them were silent as they waited to catch a glimpse.

'There.' Weiss pointed.

They'd almost missed it; the Tacoma was parked to their right by an opening in a hedge that led into dingy woods.

CHAPTER 80

Hazel stamped on the brake, and they jerked still a few feet behind the pickup. 'He's not in there.' She attempted to peer through the trees beyond it. Were they about to witness the kind of criminal activities Bennett had alluded to, and had Meredith regularly been party to them?

Weiss leaned forward to study the slow-moving TomTom. 'Nothing nearby. Why stop here?'

Sweeting glanced through the back window, as if expecting attack. 'He must have seen us.'

Hazel rolled the Mazda twenty feet past before switching off the engine. 'Let's follow him.'

'Fuck that. I'm staying right here,' Sweeting said, crabbily.

'Suit yourself.' Hazel was already exiting the car, and Weiss followed. 'If we're not back in ten minutes—'

'Jesus. Wait.' Sweeting got aggressively out.

'Don't slam it,' Hazel hissed and made for the gap in the hedge.

Lucas had circled Wade and Tamara's rudimentary living quarters and ventured through a copse to the rear. He found empty wooden kennels and some smaller corrugated outbuildings. The camera was still recording as he tried the handle of the first. It was locked. Moving to the next he expected the same but the spring of the mechanism creaked loudly.

He turned back towards Wade and Tamara's place until he was sure nobody was about then pushed the handle the whole way.

The metal door relaxed from its frame and swung heavily out at him. Lucas caught it and put his eye to the viewer as he pointed the lens inside.

It was stacked to the ceiling with plain cardboard boxes covered in dirty green stains. He entered, and the interior smelt of mould. Putting down the Lumix, Lucas slid one of the heavy boxes from the top of a pile and set it on the floor. He didn't have a knife with him to slit the wrinkled brown tape across the top but managed to unpick an edge and tear it up from the bottom.

He hesitated after making the ripping sound then picked up the camera and opened the flaps with his other hand. 'OK, let's see what you're stashing in here—'

The door slammed hard, and Lucas was crouching in pitch-darkness. At first he thought it was the wind or that its weight had closed it, but then he heard a key turning in the lock.

CHAPTER 81

'What the fuck is he doing?' Weiss whispered behind Hazel.

She held up her hand for silence.

The three of them had tracked Wade via a barely discernible dirt path that slalomed through the trees until they'd spotted him standing on the edge of a stream below them.

Wade jumped the water and began climbing the bank the other side.

Hazel waited for him to get a good few paces up it before continuing.

Sweeting grabbed her arm. 'This doesn't feel right. Why would he come here?'

'Exactly why we're following him.' She lifted her elbow from his grip.

'He's right.' Weiss still had his eye on Wade. 'What if this is a trap?'

'We'll keep him in sight. That way, he can't surprise us. But if we don't move now, we'll lose him.' She started down the path again.

After a few moments she heard Weiss and Sweeting fall in behind her.

'Hello?' Lucas felt foolish but it was all he could think of to say. He listened at the door and tried the handle again.

The action prompted several low canine growls.

Whoever had locked him in was outside with the dogs, and he guessed who it was. Lucas hadn't heard any footsteps away from the door. But, then again, he hadn't heard her approach either.

'Is that you, Tamara? I'm with the film crew and got separated. I was just trying to find them. Please, let me out.'

There was no response.

'We came to see Wade. You probably remember me. I was the cameraman when Hazel Salter interviewed you.'

Snarling and a soft scrape against the panel. One of the dogs was getting his scent.

'Look, I've got a phone. I can call her, and she'll drive straight back and open this door.'

'Phone reception's lousy here.' It was definitely Tamara's voice.

'Listen, Tamara—'

'So if you knew she'd left, what were you doing snooping back here?'

Lucas didn't have an answer. 'I've already sent her a text from here to pick me up so I know my phone *will* work.' Taking it out he punched the button so the screen lit up. No reception. He found the torch and switched it on. The musty atmosphere was getting overpowering. 'Please, just let me out.'

One of the dogs barked harshly.

'I'll walk straight out of here so they can pick me up from the road.'

After a few seconds, the door was unlocked.

CHAPTER 82

'OK, so what now?' Weiss halted on the hill and rested his palms on his knees.

Hazel caught her breath and scanned the brow. Even though they'd quickly crossed the stream and had been striding rapidly up the incline, Wade had already disappeared over the top of it. 'I don't mind heading up there on my own.'

'Don't be stupid.' Weiss gulped air. 'We're not about to let you go alone.'

'You did say we had to keep him in sight. We don't know what he's got waiting for us.'

Sweeting was chicken but she knew he had a point. 'Why don't we split up? I'll take the middle ground and you two take left and right.'

Weiss nodded. 'OK but I'll go up behind Wade or we don't go at all.'

'Deal.'

Sweeting sighed and started climbing, cutting diagonally and generously to the left. Hazel arced right, and Weiss continued on through Wade's tracks.

As the bank got steeper, her kneecaps ached. If Wade hadn't known they were there before, Sweeting's laboured breathing would certainly alert him now. She tried to make eye contact with him, but he kept his focus dead ahead.

The ridge of the hill came into view, and the three of them slowed so they were in line with each other. Weiss attempted to peer over from his position.

Hazel gestured him to stay still and trudged up a few paces. No sign of Wade. She took a couple more cautious steps so she was looking at a furrowed field beyond. On the edge of it was a ramshackle wooden hut.

'I would offer you some coffee but I'm behind with my chores.' Tamara was striding swiftly in front of Lucas, yanking the chained heads of her three Brazilian mastiffs behind her as she escorted him back to the main yard.

It was odd behaviour because she knew he'd opened one of the boxes in the outbuilding. When she'd swung the door, she'd held the black-snouted monsters at bay and looked down to where he'd parted the lid. There had been nothing but rusting tins of food inside. She'd said he was welcome to help himself to the flood-damaged stock and that she'd been on at Wade to dump it since it had gone out-of-date in 2013.

But Tamara didn't strike him as the sort of woman who would skip an opportunity to berate someone for poking their nose in where they shouldn't, and he'd been surprised she hadn't let the leashes go.

'I'll just walk you to the road.' Her dark, blue neon-streaked hair flapped behind her.

Lucas couldn't help but look at her tight ass in her jeans. What the hell did she see in Wade? 'Thanks, Mrs Hickman, but I'm good.' They were passing the living quarters and Lucas glanced briefly at the closed door again.

'No problem.' She marched purposefully ahead. 'Bruce!' She wound the chain tighter around her knuckles and prevented the burly creature from turning back in his direction.

Lucas wondered if he'd been let off the hook because of the Hickmans' involvement in the movie. Perhaps if he'd been a thief her reaction would have been considerably different. 'Really, I know my way from here.' He lifted his camera so it was lodged rigidly under his arm. It was still running.

CHAPTER 83

'Is he in there?' Sweeting crouched where Hazel and Weiss were. They had the cover of some ferns on the boundary of the field.

'Maybe this is where he works.' Weiss pulled him lower.

'I don't think Wade has ever grasped that concept.' Hazel registered there were no windows in their side of the hut.

'Perhaps it's his little man cave,' Weiss suggested.

'Shame Lucas isn't with us. He could bust in there and shoot him jerking his gherkin.' Sweeting tied his lace. 'What now?'

They all ducked as Wade emerged.

Wade pulled the door shut. He had an orange bucket in one hand and made for a gate at the far edge of the field. He opened and closed it and traipsed off down a track. He disappeared behind the hedge beyond, and his footfalls faded.

'I'm going to take a look.' Hazel rose first.

As she trotted quickly towards the hut, Weiss and Sweeting followed. When she reached the door, Hazel put her palm against it but paused. Although it appeared she was waiting for the other two to catch up, she was suddenly reluctant to go inside.

'Open it then,' Sweeting said impatiently.

Hazel pushed on the panel, and a vile smell rolled out at them.

'You don't need to walk me the whole way.' But Lucas could see Tamara was determined to. Even if she had to fight her dogs the entire distance. They were now passing the locked middle outbuilding, and her pace had sped up. Lucas still held the lens on her. 'Expect you've got better things to do.'

Tamara kept going until a human sneeze came from within the structure. She didn't stop but her step faltered. The mastiffs' ears pricked up, and they all swivelled their heads back.

'Mrs Hickman?'

One of the dogs started barking at the outbuilding, and Tamara accelerated.

'Was that? … '

She halted to slap the offending hound on its flank. 'Spike!'

It fell silent but the animals kept their gaze trained.

'You OK the rest of the way now?' Her surly nod told him he'd have to be.

'Yeah. Thanks for the escort.'

Tamara waited impassively for him to leave.

Giving her and the dogs a wide berth, Lucas cleared them, kept walking and flinched in anticipation of the mastiffs on his back.

CHAPTER 84

'This is fucked up.' Sweeting had joined Hazel and Weiss inside the hut.

Hazel waved humming flies from her face. A small LED lantern yellowed the dismal space. It was empty except for a concrete post jutting from the middle of the floor. A metal hoop was attached to it and, to that, a pair of handcuffs. The smell of stale urine and human faeces was overwhelming. Hazel wondered if Meredith had known about this place.

'What *has* he been doing in here?' Weiss covered his mouth.

'Jesus wept.' Sweeting gagged and exited.

Hazel hurried out, and Weiss followed.

'We're calling the cops.' Weiss ushered her back to the ferns.

She kept her eyes on the hut and the gate Wade had left by. There was no sign of him. As they reached the brow of the hill, she pulled out her phone. 'I have to get Lucas out of there.'

Weiss nodded and kept watch over her shoulder.

Sweeting wasn't waiting for them and had started stumbling down the slope. 'You're not going to get any reception here.'

But Hazel was surprised to find a tiny amount and speed-dialled Lucas.

Lucas felt his phone buzz in his pocket and was glad of an excuse to stop and check where Tamara was. He turned and made a show of taking it out. She and the dogs were standing where he'd left them. The Lumix was still recording, and he knew he'd taken in the outbuilding before nicely framing her.

'Hazel?'

'I'm about to lose the signal.' Sounded like she was on the move. 'Are you still at the Hickman place?'

'Just on my way to you now,' he said with enough volume for Tamara to hear. 'You're just pulling up?'

'What's going on there? Are you with Tamara?' She was starting to break up.

'Yeah.'

'Leave as soon as you can. We followed Wade. He's got a shack where he chains people up.'

He heard that loud and clear. 'OK. I'm sure Tamara won't mind if you drive up the road to meet me. That OK with you, Mrs Hickman?'

She didn't reply and studied his performance stony-faced.

'We're coming, Lucas. But we're a few miles away.'

'Great, you'll probably see me in a few seconds.' Lucas pocketed the phone and stuck his thumb up to Tamara. 'They're here.' He put his back to her and strode faster.

A mastiff slammed into Lucas and then he was looking at Tamara's black leather boots as they circled him. Teeth pierced his left calf muscle and then something solid struck the crown of his head.

CHAPTER 85

'It's right turn for town!' Sweeting exclaimed from the front passenger seat as Hazel accelerated in the opposite direction.

'I'm picking up Lucas first. Then we go to the police. How's the reception on your phone, Weiss?'

He was holding it up in the back. 'Shit.'

Hazel snatched up hers from the dash and glimpsed the display. 'Mine's stacking again.' She passed it over her shoulder. 'Call the cops and tell them we'll meet them on the edge of town.'

'What are you talking about?' Sweeting tried to intercept her phone but Weiss plucked it away. 'Just tell them what we've seen and where they can find Wade.'

'Lucas can shoot the arrest, even if it's from a distance.' Hazel steadied the Mazda.

'So, we're picking up the camera first and Lucas second,' Sweeting said caustically.

'Lucas will want to be in on this as much as us.' Hazel's eyes darted to her rear-view mirror and the pickup that had suddenly appeared behind them. 'It's Wade.'

Weiss turned to see the blue vehicle surge towards them. 'Floor it!'

But Hazel already had and pulled away.

'Slow down!' Sweeting's attention was locked on the narrow road ahead.

They'd hit a sharp bend and, as she tugged the wheel, the rear of her car whipped around and the back tyres lost contact with the dirt. The front swung ninety degrees, ramming Hazel against the side window.

CHAPTER 86

When she came to, Rena blinked sluggishly and wondered how long she'd been unconscious. The daylight had dimmed, and a slight breeze grazed her eardrums.

She discerned a different noise to her right. Sounded like nail clippers. Was that what had woken her? Rena took a breath and identified the dark shape skittering at the periphery of her vision.

Burnished black eyes stared back at her – uncomprehending observation. The rabbit seemed only slightly wary of Rena as it stripped tiny leaves from a gorse bush with its teeth. It had brown fur and a yellow white belly that quickly rose and fell as it watched without any concept of her predicament.

Rena slowly raised her right hand, and the animal's chewing froze. She considered it might be the last living thing to see her alive. And that it would probably sniff around her corpse before the scavengers did.

The rabbit hopped away but, briefly, she hadn't been alone. Rena attempted to follow its progress but could still hear the crunch at the rear of her head. She examined her raised, bandaged fingers. The machete had been dislodged. Her arm trembled with the exertion but it was the most she'd moved since the fall. What did she have to lose now? Should Rena just lie here semi-conscious or try to escape, irrespective of the consequences?

Nobody had come looking for her. Even if they'd gone to the pond, there was no reason to think she'd ventured into the forest. So there was only one person likely to find her like this, and she'd rather die than have to endure whatever torture they wanted to inflict on her.

Rena hinged up the other arm to the same height and inspected the deep cut across the heel of her left thumb. But she knew lifting her skull was the real test. She allowed her palms to rest on her face, breathed against them and warmed her nose.

She counted and raised her head on five.

It was only elevated an inch from the rock, and she anticipated loss of sight as her spinal column disintegrated or her brains poured out of her skull. But as her tendons shook, there was no sign the action had wrought any further injury.

Rena took her grubby hands from her cheeks and focussed on them. She still had vision. Linking her fingers tight into a double fist, she gritted her teeth and gradually levered herself into a sitting position.

Pain distributed itself along her limbs and now she could see her legs and blue feet. Only her familiar pink toenail varnish made them seem part of her. But even though a new agony was needling her right shoulder, Rena gradually inhaled. Had she been in deep shock since her ordeal in the water?

Her blood buzzed from its sudden animation. Rena delicately touched the back of her neck, expecting to find exposed bone. The skin felt raw but her fingertips didn't encounter anything alarming. She massaged the tops of her legs and felt for breaks down their length.

Rena carefully swivelled her head and heard the same grating sound but was already casting her eyes about for a way up and out of the ditch.

CHAPTER 87

Somebody said Lucas's name and he opened his eyes. He blinked against the glare from the TV, which was the only light source in the room. The volume was down. Hazel was seated above him and, in the flickering blue glow; he saw a frown pinching the muscles over her nose. But she wasn't awake.

'Haze.' He was lying on his stomach on the floor with his hands tied behind his back but he didn't know what with. His ankles were secured as well. He guessed where he was. The rug smelt of stale dog dust.

'Lucas,' Weiss whispered.

Lucas couldn't turn his head to see where he was. 'How did you get here?'

'I've been waiting for you to come round.'

Christ knows what Tamara had slugged Lucas with. 'What happened?'

'Hazel was trying to get away from Wade and we ran off the road.'

Lucas heard leather squeak as Weiss struggled. He breathed in the rank carpet and craned up at Hazel again. Her eyelids were quivering. 'Haze,' he hissed louder.

'My hands and feet are tied as well.' Weiss continued to squirm. 'And Sweeting's not here.'

A door slammed, glass jingled – a refrigerator.

Lucas listened to a bottle cap being twisted off and heated conversation between Wade and Tamara in the kitchen. He couldn't make out the words though. He rolled onto his spine, and the movement prompted a tight pulse at the back of his head and a cold prickle in his calf. He sat up, used his hips to slide his body back to Hazel's armchair and nudged her leg hard with his elbow.

He watched her expression react irritably to it, and then she opened her eyes.

CHAPTER 88

Hazel struggled to sit up. 'Lucas?' She recognised the outline of his shaved head below her, silhouetted by the TV screen. 'Where are we?'

'The Hickman place.'

'Keep quiet; they're in the next room.' Weiss was hidden in the shadows to her left. 'Can you move?'

'Jesus, he must have dragged us out of the car.' Hazel realised she was sitting against her hands. The restraints were so tight she could barely flex her fingers, and the ones around her legs were cutting deep into her ankles.

'We don't know where Sweeting is.' Weiss creaked on his leather cushion as he writhed against his bonds.

Wade and Tamara's conversation ceased. They waited. There were footfalls outside before the door opened.

'My sincere apologies for this.' Wade's face was in darkness. He switched on the light.

Hazel squinted against it but quickly took in their positions around the grubby peach plastered TV room: Weiss on a leather armchair against the rear wall; Lucas sitting bound on the carpet, and no sign of Sweeting. Hazel was seated in the only other armchair, her feet coiled by a green, plastic-coated chain.

'Necessary though.' He tugged at his leather necklace.

'Where's Sweeting?' She knew it was useless shouting for help. Nobody was going to hear.

'Had a concussion. Wasn't wearing a belt. None of you were. Surprised you didn't all come off as bad.'

'Untie us.' Weiss had his hands behind his back as well; his ankles shackled by a similar chain.

'I just need to talk to you all first.'

Lucas rotated on his buttocks to face Wade. 'You haven't answered the question.'

'I took him to the hospital.'

'Bullshit.' Hazel's eyes followed Wade as he walked to the TV and bent to turn it off.

He stood away from it. 'You two were unconscious but your injuries weren't serious. Your friend was delirious and had a badly gashed head. I took him to the ER.'

'You're a liar.'

'Hazel,' Weiss cautioned her.

'Had to tell them I found the car mashed up by the side of the road and skipped out of there before they could ask me any more questions. He's getting the treatment he needs now, so I'm sure he'll be fine. Call the hospital if you don't believe me.' He sealed the door.

Nobody responded. Whatever agenda he had, they had no choice but to be part of it.

'I need to make a few things clear before you do though.'

'We're not going to say anything.' Lucas eyed the door.

Wade leaned against it. 'That's what I was hoping.'

'What you do in that hut is your business.' Weiss shuffled forward and attempted to stand up.

'But you saw to it that it isn't any more. Even after me and Tam agreed to take part in your movie. You had no right coming out here.'

'Stay in your seat.' Hazel glowered at Weiss.

He kept trying to rise. 'We're sorry. Really. Just take these off us and we'll walk out of here and pretend this never happened.'

Hazel could see the gash in his left eyebrow glistening. 'Sit down.'

'If he's more comfortable on his feet, that's fine with me.'

'Weiss, for fuck's sake,' Lucas said through his teeth.

But Weiss was upright. He wobbled slightly on his heels. 'I don't feel so good.'

'Sit back down then. All I want to do is talk to you.'

'I'm going to pass out. Can you loosen these?' Weiss swayed and fell backwards across the armchair, eyelids shut and his spectacles at an angle across his nose.

They watched him noisily slide down the leather and listened to his constricted breathing.

'Out cold.' Wade crossed the room to where he lay diagonally on the cushions and started repositioning him.

Lucas turned; Hazel locked eyes with him then nodded towards the door. He blinked acknowledgement, and she stood dizzily up from her chair and took tiny steps towards it. Lucas was on his feet a second later and rammed his shoulder into Wade.

'Tam!'

The door opened before Hazel could reach it, and Tamara was standing in the passage, a Brazilian mastiff snarling at the end of a chain. The beast lunged forward, snapping its jaws, and almost garrotting itself in its eagerness to attack Hazel.

She twisted back to Lucas. He was lying on top of Wade and Weiss but got elbowed in the gut, rolled off the arm of the chair and dropped hard onto the floor.

Hazel's attention returned to the animal and Tamara grimacing as she tried to restrain it. The mastiff barked, and its slavering black jowls whipped around its teeth.

Wade's hands firmly restrained Hazel's shoulders.

CHAPTER 89

Tamara allowed the dog to stretch the chain another few links then slammed the door in Hazel's face.

'Let's sit you down.' Wade's lips were at her ear.

He manoeuvred her over the armchair and she dropped back onto the leather seat. Lucas struggled into a sitting position again.

The mastiff's claws scratched repeatedly at the panel as it attempted to dig its way into the room.

'And let's all take a breath.' Wade returned to his post at the door. 'Need to explain what you think you saw.'

Hazel focussed on the soiled fawn carpet. What did it matter? Sweeting had to be dead, and Wade couldn't let them walk.

'I think it's really important you guys finish this movie.'

Hazel glanced sharply up at him.

Wade nodded. 'And we still want to be part of it. Tam and me.'

Hazel tried to hide her incredulity. Lucas met her gaze but neither of them spoke.

'We didn't want this situation. And it's got nothing to do with what happened to Meredith.'

Hazel swallowed. Was there really a chance he was going to let them go? But whatever he was trying to convince them of, she knew they had to go along with it.

'That little den you found. I know how it looks. But it's there to help people.'

Hazel was sure Wade was deranged. Did he really think any story would justify what they'd seen in there? With Wade and Tamara as parents there was little wonder Meredith had been corrupted, and she suspected whatever they'd embroiled her in at the farm had to have led to her murder at Fun Central.

The beast's scraping at the flimsy door still hadn't subsided.

'It's why people still call this place the turkey farm. Ain't been livestock on this land since my father owned it in the nineties but people come here for a different kind.'

Hazel's attention returned to where Wade was leaning.

'Tam was an addict. I went through the whole withdrawal hell with her. Now we help others do the same.'

Lucas was the first to respond. 'So… who's locked up out there?'

'Some city slicker. Not the first time he's been here neither.' Wade thumped the door with his heel. 'Spike!'

The hound barked a couple of times then retreated.

'After Tam got clean, a few of her friends came up here for the same, then a few of their friends. Soon people are approaching her from all walks. Don't misunderstand me. She doesn't do this out of the goodness of her heart. This is her specialist accommodation service. Tam gives them isolation. Monitors them while they work the junk out their system. We're cheaper than a high profile detox clinic and they can remain anonymous. Unless a film crew rolls up. The last thing that guy out there needs is to be on the big screen.'

Hazel recalled the concrete post in the floor. 'You imprison them inside that filthy shack?'

'It's never pretty. But they only need shelter – and no way of escape. I don't think anyone will ever be writing us up on TripAdvisor though. Plus Tam's hygiene standards probably don't meet industry regulations. When you said the cops were going to be sniffing around here, I went out there to get it ready for Tam's guest. Haven't used it in around six months but I knew I could relocate him there quickly.'

From his bemused reaction Hazel could tell Lucas also thought Wade's explanation seemed too bizarre to be a lie. 'So, why did you run us off the road?'

'I didn't. Tried to catch up with you but you pulled away too fast and came off at the bend.'

Hazel had no recollection of what happened after the pickup appeared behind her. 'So, Sweeting really is in the hospital?'

'Told him to keep his mouth shut or you'd all come to harm.' Wade produced Hazel's phone from his pocket. 'Afraid I might have ladled it on. He seemed pretty shook up when they took him in. Call him. I just need your word you'll delete anything you've recorded here with your camera. Tam got spooked when she saw it. It's why she got so heavy-handed.'

'Before you tied us up and scared the living shit out of us.' Lucas readjusted his leg and grunted. 'And where *is* my camera?'

'Short, sharp shock treatment is how we roll here. I had to have your undivided attention.'

'Just keep that dog away from us.' He turned to check on Weiss. 'Besides, I could have smashed it up.'

Lucas flinched. 'But you care too much about the movie, right?'

'For Meredith's sake.' Wade respectfully nodded. 'It's safe.'

'Look, I promise I'll delete everything I shot here. Right, Haze?'

But her fear had swiftly been supplanted by anger. 'So as well as helping people out of addiction, are you still helping them into it?' She remembered what Wade had told her about Meredith dealing.

Wade shook his head at her, as if it were a naïve question. 'Like everyone else, we're just trying to make ends meet.'

'Like everyone else—'

'Want me to untie you or not?'

CHAPTER 90

After Wade released them and they revived Weiss, Hazel immediately called a petrified Sweeting and assured him they were all safe. He'd discharged himself from the hospital, had made his way to Broomfield Police Station, and was just standing outside it, deliberating whether or not to go in.

'That fucking psycho told me if I breathed a word, he'd cut your faces off and swap them around.'

'Don't bother the cops. Just get yourself back to base. We'll meet you there.'

'Positive you're all OK?'

'Yes, shaken and still a little sceptical.'

'As of now then I'm out. I didn't sign up for this shit.'

'Sweeting—'

He hung up.

She tried to call him back, but got his answering service. 'Sweeting's not coming back.'

'And there's a trace of surprise in your voice because? ... ' Lucas lightly touched his bruised scalp.

Wade was hovering. 'Better let me put your minds at ease.'

While Tamara kept the mastiffs in the kitchen, Wade led them out of their temporary prison to the outbuilding across the yard. He produced a key and released the padlock securing the corrugated doors.

A sinewy, tanned man in his thirties with dark dreadlocks, wearing only a pair of Speedos, was lying motionless on a mattress at the back of the empty poultry shed. His clothes were strewn about the floor, and a black bucket lay on its side to the left of him.

'Jesus.' Weiss was still unsteady on his feet and supported himself in the doorway.

Wade went inside and righted the bucket. 'Hey.'

The figure eventually stirred.

'You're doing good. But these people need to know you're OK and here of your own free will.'

He slowly sat up and used his hand to shield his lean face from the daylight.

'Quiz him if you want.'

Hazel bent to her knees. 'Do you want to come with us?'

'No,' he said weakly.

'Are you being harmed?' Lucas asked.

He shook his head then looked up at Wade. 'What is this?' Aggression ballooned. 'This isn't a fucking freak show. Get them out of here!'

'They might wanna talk to you some time soon.'

He started curling into himself. 'Get them the fuck out of here.' His voice had wilted again.

Wade patted his bare shoulder and walked back to Hazel, Lucas and Weiss. 'I don't know these people. Tam looks after them. She'll have a cell number. You can contact him when he's done if you need to. He's not going to remember any of this.'

CHAPTER 91

Rena didn't know if she was limping back to Fun Central or heading deeper into the forest. She thought daylight would be an ally but realised she might go around in circles until it fell dark again or her body succumbed to exhaustion. Not having the first clue about navigating by the sun, she was suddenly regretting being so inattentive on the myriad camping trips her parents had forced her to go on.

Her neck was getting stiffer, and she could only rotate her right arm from the elbow down. Either her humerus or shoulder was broken. Rena's right leg was also delicate to walk on. She'd unwrapped the bandage from her hand and wound that tight around her tender ankle but her hip smarted as well.

She was dehydrated and low on blood sugar and had expended most of her energy crawling out of the ditch and looking for the machete. Rena hadn't found it and had had to rest behind a fallen tree for some time before continuing. That had been a mistake. She'd almost lost consciousness again.

Rena had forgotten her state of undress and was fixated on recognising something from the night before, like the hollow she'd hidden inside. If she spotted that, the pond would be near.

But every direction she turned seemed to offer the same vista of trunks and mulch pools. And, any moment, she anticipated running into the person who was still probably hunting her. If they caught her now, Rena didn't have an ounce of strength to fight back.

She pushed herself off the dirty white bark of a tree and listened again for any sounds that could lead her back to civilisation, but knew there was slim chance of hearing any traffic on the road up to Fun Central. The crew were alone there, and she wondered if they were in more danger than her. She strained her ears for crows squawking about the jetty, but there was little noise except for her wheezing breath.

Rena's right foot sank deep into marsh, and the action of tugging it clear was excruciating. But she covered her mouth to stifle a scream and began hobbling along the boggy channel between the birches.

Resting again would be fatal because Rena knew that, if she did, her injuries wouldn't allow her to get back up again.

CHAPTER 92

Wade dropped Hazel, Lucas and Weiss at Fun Central in the pickup and said he'd drive to the Mazda crash site and assess the damage. If it were roadworthy, he'd tow it back that evening and leave it outside. Hazel's car keys were still in it.

They observed him accelerate across the parking zone and bounce down the ramp.

'What are we going to do about the turkey farm?' Weiss spoke first.

Hazel rubbed the red chain indentations around her wrists. 'There's nothing *to* do. What they get up to on their property is none of our business. We were trespassing. Nothing's changed.'

'Apart from emotional trauma and me needing a rabies shot.' Lucas put down the camera and examined the wound to his calf that Tamara had grudgingly dressed.

'I'll get Rena to drive you to the hospital.' Hazel was focussing on logistics but was as shaken as the other two after their ordeal. She attempted to slide the entrance doors apart, but they were shut tight.

Weiss sighed. 'Rena's still not back?'

Hazel felt anger burn through her empty stomach. Extracting the key from her pocket, she unlocked and rolled one open. 'I thought Keeler was getting her in gear.'

Lucas picked up the Lumix and followed Hazel and Weiss inside.

'Appears our associate producer might have eloped with him.' Weiss lightly touched the congealed cut on his left eyebrow.

A thud came from overhead, and all three of them looked up and waited. It was followed by a slam and footsteps.

'Is that her?' Lucas turned to the others.

'Sounds like they were in the production office.' Hazel's eyes settled on the entrance to the stairs.

Feet stomped down them and the door opened. Griff Needham emerged.

'Jesus!' His startled expression confirmed he wasn't anticipating company.

'What the hell are you doing up there?' He was the last person Hazel expected.

'You scared me half to death.' Griff put his palm against his chest and made a performance of breathing a few times. He contemplated Lucas's bandage and then Weiss's injury. 'What happened to you guys?'

Hazel suspected he was playing for time. 'Answer the question.'

He tugged off his beanie and ran a hand through his flattened mousy hair. 'I was looking for you.'

'How did you get in here?' Weiss paced towards him.

Hazel touched Lucas on the elbow. 'Record this. We might have to show it to the police.'

Lucas put the viewer to his eye.

'Wait, the police, why?' Griff took a step forward.

'The doors were locked.' Weiss shifted sideways to block his route to the entrance. 'This is breaking and entering.'

'Got in through the back of the burger joint,' he casually explained.

Hazel wondered if he'd make a run for it that way. 'Why? What are you doing here?'

'You wanted me here.'

'I didn't send for you.'

'You did. I got a text this morning.'

'No, you didn't.' Hazel watched the side of his mouth twitch.

'Well, your assistant sent me a text and told me to be here this afternoon. I asked her what time, but she didn't get back to me.'

'Rena sent you the text?' Weiss glanced dubiously at Hazel.

Griff nodded. 'Yeah, that's who I was looking for. When nobody let me in, I thought you might all be busy shooting in a different part of the building.'

'Show me.' Hazel extended her hand.

'What?'

'The text.'

'I left my phone back at the motel.'

'Very convenient,' Lucas snorted from behind the camera.

'You took it off me the last time I was here so I thought I'd leave it charging.'

'You're full of shit,' Weiss snapped.

'Frisk me if you want.' Griff hoisted his arms.

'OK. Turn around against the door.' Weiss gestured.

Griff hesitated before complying.

Weiss patted the pockets of his oatmeal hoody. His fingers paused. 'So, what's this then?' When Griff didn't reply he pulled it out and held it up for the lens. 'One phone.'

Griff faced them again. 'I meant to leave that behind. Give it back.' He snatched it from Weiss.

'Show us the text then, Griff.' Hazel joined Weiss, and Lucas hovered.

He pocketed it. 'No point. I deleted it.'

Lucas came in closer. 'Jesus, Griff, have you ever seen *World's Dumbest Criminals*? That's the only place this footage is going.'

Hazel folded her arms. 'After it's been to the cops. Why are you lying to us?'

'OK. I didn't get a text. I just wanted to come up here and snap a bunch of photos for my Facebook page.'

'Why d'you think I asked you to sign a non-disclosure agreement?'

'I know, and I'm sorry. But when I got here and there was no one around, I figured it wouldn't do any harm.'

Hazel indicated the Lumix. 'Is this how you want to be portrayed? I've got your permission to use any of this.'

Griff looked mortified. 'Don't do that.'

'I'm going to have to ask you to give me your phone until we're finished.'

He reacted as if she'd just asked him to hack off a limb.

'That's the deal. Otherwise we're done with you.'

Griff reluctantly fished it back out and surrendered it to Weiss. He slipped it into his jacket pocket.

Wind juddered the roof of the concourse.

Hazel listened for other sounds of movement. 'And you haven't seen anyone else since you got here?'

He shook his head.

Hazel found Lucas training the camera on her. 'OK, I suppose, as he's here, we might as well make good use of him.'

CHAPTER 93

'In our first interview, you told me you feel no animosity towards Henrik Fossen.'

Griff Needham fidgeted in his pink plastic oyster chair as green and blue fish shapes gyrated on the walls. Despite Weiss protesting, Hazel had chosen the location to disorient him.

'Maybe now you can tell me how you personally felt after your stepsister's death.'

He slightly relaxed. 'Sure.'

Hazel guessed Griff was relieved she wasn't going to interrogate him about his trespass but it was that behaviour which was going to drive her interview. 'Were you close to Denise?'

'I'd say so.'

'But you obviously didn't grow up with her.'

'Lived with her for about a year after my dad remarried. She moved out soon as she got her nanny post.'

'So, you weren't really that close.'

'I shared a house with her for a year.' He regarded her blankly, as if his response was sufficient.

Hazel held his eye. 'What was your reaction when you were told she'd been gunned down?'

'I wasn't. I found out online.'

'Your parents didn't tell you?'

'Dad had walked out.'

'What about your stepmother?'

Griff thought about it. 'I left her to deal with it in her own way.'

'You didn't grieve with her?'

A laugh scraped his nose, as if it was a ludicrous concept. 'She locked herself in the bedroom for three straight days.'

'And you didn't talk about it to anyone else?'

'First thing I did was put an announcement on Denise's Facebook page.'

'That was the appropriate thing to do?'

'I think so.'

'And did that act as a positive introduction to Denise's network of friends?'

He hesitated, knew where she was leading him. 'So, you're going to tell me how much I've benefited from her death as well. Like Henrik Fossen did when you were interviewing those cops.'

'You had your own conversation with him?'

'We shot the breeze.'

'What did he say?'

'I must have made a real impression because he said he'd rather talk to Denise's killer.' He smirked.

'And why's that so funny?'

Griff considered his reply. 'Because I'd been so looking forward to meeting him.'

'Even though your stepsister may be dead because of him?'

'I've told you; I don't believe that.'

'Why are you so sure?'

'Suggestion doesn't make you pull the trigger of a gun.'

'What does then?'

'Hatred,' he said simply.

Hazel pushed him. 'Anybody hate your stepsister?'

'Nobody… apparently.'

'Apparently?'

'Have you ever seen anyone murdered and their friends and family on TV saying they were cheap and vain?' He shot the lens a waggish look.

'You think there were people who hated her then?'

'I didn't really know her.'

'But you said you were close.'

He scowled.

'Denise was an attractive girl. Did you have feelings for your stepsister? Maybe ones you shouldn't?' She anticipated Griff's immediate denial.

He was silent; his features momentarily withdrawn.

She had no grounds for the suggestion but Hazel realised she'd hit a nerve. 'Were you in love with her?'

His face shifted, as if he'd made his mind up about something. 'I wanted to fuck her if that's what you mean.' He seemed suddenly cavalier. 'But I categorically didn't love her.'

'Why not?' A different person was sitting opposite her. Had he been more guileful than she'd given him credit for?

'Because one man from our side of the family was enough for her.' His expectant expression waited for her to fill in the blank.

'Your father?' Hazel hadn't envisaged the interview taking such a left turn.

'It's not rocket science: marrying a cougar with a hottie for a daughter. It's why he had to leave and Denise had to rapidly find her nanny post. I ended up sharing my parents' house with a pill popper.'

'Are you still in touch with your father?'

'Occasionally but it's awkward talking to your dad when he's soiled your sexual fantasies. It was golden with stepmother though. I kept busy for her, curating Denise's online memorial.'

Hazel believed she'd had the measure of Griff Needham. Now she wasn't so sure. 'And what was your motive for doing that?'

'I certainly didn't do it for Denise. When I started to get bombarded with all the sympathy online, I was making her give back. I used her, and I lied to all the people who got in touch to say what a terrible waste it was that such a beautiful person had been taken away. That's when I tweeted @BeMyKiller. Said "wishing you a lethal injection" for the benefit of anyone who thought I was sad to see the bitch gone.'

Hazel watched his resentment brimming over and knew he didn't need further prompting.

'She was a lie. I remember her coming out the shower singing and how I would always go straight in after. It smelt so fresh in there. My father had probably done her in the tub and in the bed he used to share with my mother. So I was happy to keep the memorial going. I was using her as currency.'

'And you're still doing it now. Posting furtive images of an involvement with us that wouldn't exist without Denise.'

'Without both of us,' he said flatly.

'So you think the two of you are inextricably connected now?'

'Denise only tolerated me so I think she'd hate that.'

'But that pleases you?'

He nodded, tight-lipped. 'Yeah. It feels like I'm violating her.'

Hazel was chilled by his matter-of-factness. 'And was that your specific sexual fantasy?'

Griff's contemplation of her didn't change.

'Did she deserve to die, Griff?'

He chewed it over. 'Funny thing is, before she did, *I* nearly tweeted as her to @BeMyKiller. I knew all her passwords. Logged into her Twitter account and was ready to drop her in there.'

'But you didn't?'

'No.'

'Why not?'

'It was a moment of weakness.'

'Understandable though; you had severe issues with her. Why was it weak?'

'Because it wasn't like me actually pulling the trigger.'

Hazel leaned back in her swivel chair, unsure if she was still simply talking to an online opportunist. 'You were in a different state when Denise was murdered.'

'I was. But there was always going to be a bullet with her name on it. Maybe she just speeded up its arrival.'

Hazel swallowed. 'Anything else you want to tell me?'

He put his hands in his lap. 'No. But we've been talking a good while. I need a break.'

CHAPTER 94

'Jesus, I need a power shower after that,' Lucas whispered to Hazel as she watched Griff exit Neptune's Party Zone.

'He's been playing the part of the bereaved stepbrother since her death.'

'So why fess up today?'

'Before that interview, I would have said it was because he's an attention-seeker.'

'And now?'

'I'm changing my whole perception of him.' Hazel rose from her swivel chair.

'And what about this private meeting with Henrik?'

'Makes me wonder if it was just that one occasion.'

'You mean Griff might have visited Henrik at the pond? He's just a kid.'

'A kid who's constructing a whole career out of his stepsister's death. And, after that performance, he knows I'll have no choice but to use the interview.'

'Think he's lying about his parents?'

'I don't think so. I'll have to contact them. But neither have spoken publicly since Denise was killed.'

'If it's all true, they won't want their private lives dissected on-screen.'

'Griff hasn't left them any choice. But I can at least give his parents the opportunity to dispute what he's told us.'

'He must really hate them.'

Hazel couldn't deny Griff's casual animosity towards his family had more than unsettled her. 'Enough to have Denise killed?'

Lucas knitted his brows. 'Stretching things a bit?'

'Griff has an airtight alibi. He was with his stepmother at home the day Denise was shot. Doesn't mean he wasn't party to it though.'

'The guy doesn't have a job. Where would he get the money to hire a hitman?'

Hazel's gaze returned to Griff's empty pink oyster chair. 'If it *was* a hitman.'

Weiss took off his headphones. He'd been listening to their conversation. 'And where does that leave your lone tourist theory? Wasn't proving that the reason we're all here?'

'I want to get him back in front of the camera as soon as he's ready.'

Her phone buzzed. A text from Keeler. She'd left messages for him and Rena since returning from the turkey farm. Hazel read it aloud: '"Rena laid low. Hope you survived without bagels".' She was furious. They both knew better. 'We can manage without Sweeting *and* Rena.'

'No associate producer. How will we ever survive?'

She ignored Lucas's sarcasm. 'We can operate with a skeleton crew.'

'We were a skeleton crew. Now we're down to a wishbone.'

Keeler texted again:

Don't worry. I'll take care of her.

CHAPTER 95

Griff Needham felt exhilarated, drew deeply from his e-cigarette and considered what his responses would be when the interview resumed. He'd enjoyed watching Hazel's reaction as he'd told her about Denise and his father's infidelity.

There was no going back. But his online existence was about to morph into something much more exciting. So many of the friends he'd been duping would recoil from him, but people exactly like Griff would quickly replace them – other pretenders, other catfish.

But now he had nothing more to fabricate. Griff would be out in the open – a person orchestrating his own starring role who had finally gotten away from the reek of Denise's corpse.

A movement to his right caught his eye. Beyond the empty parking spaces at the edge of the forest, somebody was stealing past the gaps in the birch trunks. They halted, as if they'd become aware of his observation, and beckoned him.

Griff turned back to the open entrance but the others were still in Neptune's Party Zone. He took another toke on the cigarette and strolled over to the trees.

CHAPTER 96

April counted backwards from twenty and opened her eyes. In the dim light she could see ants scuttling across the backs of her hands. The rotten bough was alive with them. But she couldn't scream. The boots had moved away, and if she did she knew they'd come back.

She silently flicked off the ants and clambered swiftly back down the tree, hitting her elbow and hissing out the pain as she descended.

April paused at the lower branch and listened, her eardrums thumping as she strained for any signs of movement on the forest floor. No footsteps. Should she go now? Looking down to the mulchy leaves she told herself she could always climb back up.

But once her feet touched the ground she was going to run all the way home. She felt tears building and starting to hurt her nose. April just wanted her parents now. A solid bubble of fear ached painfully in her chest.

She held her breath and swung down from the lower branch, put the soles of her feet against the trunk and slid awkwardly down it. Now she was standing on them and quickly glanced around in all directions. Was anybody coming?

Leaves hissed. The wind? April didn't stay to find out. She pumped her legs and shot off down the path, watching her footing then looking up sharply to check the way ahead.

A thud from behind her.

April didn't look back. She'd won races at the school sports day. They would never catch her if she kept on sprinting and didn't stop.

More thuds. Somebody was definitely after her.

A squeak of panic escaped her lips but she ran faster. April didn't care if she made herself sick.

'Stop!' It was a man's voice.

April grunted and prayed she wouldn't slip.

'Come back!'

She didn't know the voice. It had to be the grown-up.

'I'm not going to hurt you!'

April jumped a root sticking out of the mud.

'Stop, or you'll be in a heap of trouble!'

Something tugged at her – the instinct to obey adults like she did at home and at school. It was difficult not to halt and respond, but April didn't break her step.

The footfalls got louder.

'Wait!' The voice was at her shoulder.

April shrieked and tried to dodge to the left and away from the command, but then her view ahead was blocked. He'd put a sack over her face. She couldn't see but kept running.

Fingers tightened around her waist.

She yelled again, and it was deafening inside the cloth.

His weight was on top of her, and she was lying on her front. April could smell her own breath as she kicked her arms and legs and cried for help.

'Lie still. Just lie still.' His voice was being nice again now. 'I'm not going to hurt you.'

But April knew he was telling lies and that the stinking sack covering her was probably the one she'd seen inside the black sports bag.

CHAPTER 97

Hazel scanned the empty parking zone.

Lucas was lamely walking towards the ramp while Weiss was trotting along the border of the forest.

'Griff!' she called. Why would he have wandered off in the short time they'd taken a break? He'd only been outside a matter of minutes.

'Griff!' Weiss shouted randomly into the trees.

Had she been too hard on him in the interview, and was this exactly why Henrik Fossen had fled? Or maybe this was more attention-seeking. Perhaps Griff was hiding in the undergrowth, watching them panic. Was he even in cahoots with Henrik? He'd told her the two of them had 'shot the breeze'. But Hazel could feel alarm rapidly escalating. He was the third person to vanish, and they couldn't even call him. Weiss had the phone she'd confiscated from him.

'No sign!' Lucas was at the top of the ramp squinting down and beyond it to the road into town. He headed over to Weiss.

'Griff!' Weiss barked before his ragged voice echoed back at them from the pond.

Hazel cupped her hand around her mouth. 'I'm going to search for him behind the burger place!' She jerked her thumb in its direction.

Lucas nodded, and Hazel observed them both duck through gaps in the birches. She made her way to the rear of the complex where the heaps of old kitchen equipment were dumped.

CHAPTER 98

Rena's progress had gradually lost momentum until she was resting for minutes at each trunk before lurching a few paces to the next. She was sure she'd been staggering in a straight line and had expected to find the edge of the forest by now.

But she knew the energy expended trying to blank out the pain of her injuries meant she might not have focussed on heading along the path she'd thought. She was becoming delirious as well; had been hearing voices she was learning to ignore.

Rena couldn't swivel her neck, and her right ankle wouldn't take weight for more than a second. She pushed herself off the tree she was leaning against and limped unsteadily to the one on her left, collapsing against it and quickly drawing breath to stem the pumping in her foot.

She had to keep moving and tensed her muscles in readiness to stumble to another resting post. But dizziness suddenly canted the ground under her bare feet.

Rena gripped the bark as she wrestled with unconsciousness and dug her nails hard into it so the pain kept her awake. Clinging tightly on, she had the sensation of being horizontal; the tree, the ground and gravity pinning her there so she could let go with her hands. She did and slid to her knees.

Pulling herself upright was going to require strength she no longer had. She touched her swollen ankle and realised the bandage had unravelled and been left behind. Rena's head got heavier until her chin was on her chest and her eyelids closed like a landslide.

Conversation – but distinct and familiar this time. She turned to see which direction the sound was coming from.

It was Lucas and Weiss. They were walking together, about fifty yards away. Behind them, through the branches, she could just catch a glimpse of Fun Central.

Rena said both their names, but her lips scarcely moved.

CHAPTER 99

'Griff!' But Lucas suspected they were wasting their time.

'Maybe we're next.' Weiss paused at the jetty and contemplated the polluted water. 'We should leave this to the police and split.'

Lucas joined him there. 'What a fuck up.'

'This or us?'

Lucas didn't immediately reply but lit a cigarette with his Zippo and exhaled.

'I'm happy to bide my time while you work through your conflicted emotions, Lucas. But remember, yours aren't the only ones at stake here.'

Lucas took his second and third puffs and nodded. 'I'm still turning it over in my head.'

'Just be honest. But start with yourself. I know you're scared. I was as well.'

'But you were nineteen.' He stamped his cigarette.

'Think that was easier?'

From his anxious expression Lucas realised Weiss needed the secrecy to end sooner than he'd implied. He squeezed his shoulder.

Weiss touched Lucas's hand but didn't look up from the plastic bottles on the surface. 'Sorry, I should be more patient.' But it didn't sound like an apology.

Hazel retreated from the trees, hoping her painstaking footsteps wouldn't give her presence away. She'd found nothing behind the burger joint and had followed Lucas and Weiss into the forest to help with the search.

She emerged back into the parking zone, heard Weiss call Griff's name again and released the breath she'd been holding.

Hazel had to focus on finding Griff. Concentrate on just that.

She gazed around but wasn't seeing anything. Lucas and Weiss. There was nothing about their tactility that left her in any doubt.

Just keep looking. Griff was the priority.

Lucas and Weiss. Hazel rifled her memory for tell-tale signs.

'Griff!' She shouted in the direction of the main entrance. More for Lucas and Weiss. They couldn't know she'd overheard them. 'Griff!' Hazel yelled it harder.

She fumbled out her phone. Griff had disappeared in a matter of minutes. She had to call the police.

CHAPTER 100

'Listen to me carefully,' April's captor said through the oily-smelling canvas. His voice was almost a whisper, and he was breathing fast. He'd been carrying her in the sack over his shoulder, so her body gently struck his spine with each step, but now he'd stopped. 'I'm going to put you down but I want you to stay very still. Do you understand?'

April nodded and wiped sweat from her face. She felt the ground against her behind again as he set her carefully on the leaves. They were still in the forest.

'What's your name?'

She took her thumb from between her teeth. 'April,' she croaked.

'Pretty name. April what?'

'April Weeks.'

'And where do you live?'

She wasn't going to tell him that.

'Answer me.'

'The Hollows.'

'What number is your house?'

'Number seven,' she lied.

'Did you make that up?'

April shook her head hard. The grown-up outside the sack didn't say anything for a while and, momentarily, she thought he might have gone.

'You took something that didn't belong to you, April.'

'I didn't mean to.'

'You didn't mean to steal?'

'I can tell you where I hid the pictures.'

He snorted. 'Those belong to my friend. He likes to remember people. Would you like to be in one of those pictures too, April? Now, tell me the real number of your house. This is your last chance.'

'Two forty-four.'

'Two forty-four. And you live there with your parents?'

'Yes.'

'Do you want me to hurt them?'

April closed her eyes.

'Answer.'

'No.' Her tummy hurt because she needed to pee.

'Don't lie to me again then.'

April heard the man grunt, felt herself being lifted and then bumping against his hot back.

He started walking faster.

CHAPTER 101

Hazel was waiting apprehensively by Meredith's blackened shrine when Lucas and Weiss got back from the forest. Griff wasn't with them but, having eavesdropped their conversation in the forest, she was still trying to evaluate how she felt. She waited for them to speak first.

'Still no sign of him. You OK?' Lucas frowned.

She unfolded her arms and nodded.

'Need the bathroom.' Weiss headed for it. 'Then I think we should scram.'

Hazel waited for the sound of the door squealing open and shut.

Lucas breathed warmth into his cupped hands and uneasily glanced back to the main entrance. 'He's right. There's some fucked-up games being played here. We're probably better off getting the hell out.'

'Look, if you and Weiss need to take off … '

'As soon as you're ready.'

'Together I mean; I'll understand.' Hazel looked fixedly at him.

Lucas stiffened. He realised the conversation they were having.

'I've just got off the phone to Soles. I couldn't get anyone else. Least of all Bennett. Soles and Drake are on their way. With Henrik, Jacob, and now Griff missing I hope they'll bring in that backup they were talking about. But this is my responsibility. Head into town and stay at Rifkin Lodge tonight. The police might want to talk to you.'

Lucas shifted on the balls of his feet. 'You don't have to be a martyr, Haze.'

'The two of you get your gear together. I've still got to wait for my car to be dropped off.'

'We'll wait with you.'

'You and Weiss?'

He swallowed and nodded.

Hazel closed the laptop on the table.

Lucas hovered. 'I don't want you stranded here on your own.'

'I'll be fine.'

'We'll wait.'

'The cops will be here by the time you leave. Please, Lucas, I need someone to check on Eve Huber. She still hasn't returned my calls so I'm getting worried about her now as well.'

'Isn't she out looking for Jacob?'

'She can still pick up. I got hold of Sheenagh. She's going to stay put. Can you do that for me?'

'What about Criteria?'

'Maybe I'll stop returning their calls.'

'Haze—'

'Just… do this for me. I'll join you there soon.'

'Sorry this didn't work out,' he said eventually.

'The project?'

He massaged the shaved skin at the side of his head then made for the door to the stairs.

'Lucas?'

He paused with his fingers on the handle.

'Have you told Carrie about Weiss?' She attempted to meet his eyes as he lingered there.

His were on the floor between them. 'Not yet.'

'She deserves to know.'

CHAPTER 102

April could tell the grown-up was carrying her down a hill. She wasn't bouncing against his back as much, just lying against it while he walked in small steps. She was so hot. 'I can't breathe.'

'Don't speak.'

She juddered as he trotted down the bottom of the slope, and then she was being placed carefully on the ground again. No leaves crunching. Were they out of the forest? Wherever he'd taken her, April knew she was far from home.

He panted and she felt his bulk drop down beside her.

'I need you to be honest now, April. Can you do that for me?'

She nodded.

'I want you to describe me.'

April frowned.

'Do you know what that means?'

'Yes.'

'That's all I want you to do. Then I'll let you go.'

'I can't.' The figure in the forest had been too far away when she'd climbed the tree.

'You're lying again, April.'

'I'm not.'

'All I want you to do is describe me. I promise you can go once you've done that.'

'I can't.' She gritted her teeth against the pain in her tummy. She couldn't pee now.

'Then you'll have to stay in the sack and I'll have to hurt your parents. Do you really want that?'

'I can't,' she sobbed.

'Are you telling me you didn't see me?'

April didn't respond.

'So you did. Describe me.'

April was suddenly blinded. Light was getting in through the opening at the top of the sack.

'I'll drag you all the way home if you want. And do you know what I'm going to do to your parents when they open the door?'

April sprang from the sack and looked frantically around her. She was at the bottom of a grass bank and beyond her was a yard. The grown-up was already getting to his feet. She headed up the incline.

'Get back here!'

Her feet slipped on the wet grass but she grabbed a few thick clumps and heaved herself higher. She heard the grown-up attempting to climb after her, and April's scream shot her forward.

'April! No!'

She didn't look back, just kept yelling and running. She could see the trees at the top. April knew she had to flee back into the forest. A hand locked around her ankle.

'Come here!'

April screeched as she landed hard on her front and was dragged back down the wet bank. She turned and tried to kick him.

'April, enough!'

She saw his face. Now she could describe every detail of it.

CHAPTER 103

As she waited tensely for the police, Hazel's reflection glowed over her bleak, late afternoon view of Holtwood Forest through the production office windowpane. After she'd brushed off their objections, Lucas and Weiss had very reluctantly left to look for Eve. But there was still no evidence of a patrol car. Hazel surveyed the trees under the slate clouds. No sign of Griff either.

Her instincts had told her she shouldn't rekindle things with Lucas. But she still had to process what had been going on between him and Weiss right under her nose. And the notion of that compounded her frustration about failing to disentangle the multiple events that orbited Meredith Hickman.

She'd become too focussed on Wade and Tamara, but even after their explanation about the turkey farm, she still suspected they were concealing the reality of Meredith's life there. And she had to get Soles to be transparent about his relationship with her.

But Hazel's interview with Griff Needham had opened up deep-seated resentments she hadn't anticipated, and now he'd vanished as mysteriously as Henrik Fossen and Jacob Huber.

Where did any of that leave the lone tourist theory?

Hazel slid her hand into her back pocket and pulled out the piece of paper. She unfolded the photo of April that Mrs Weeks had given her and looked into the eyes of the seven-year-old. She wondered if she'd been found yet or if she was the fourth to vanish since they'd arrived at Fun Central. Hazel considered the little girl in Blue Grove Park she'd left behind two decades previously and adult Meredith's sadistic murder: a wretched event amongst a glut of others she hadn't even started to resolve.

Her phone rang and she checked the display. She thought it might be Lucas with news about Eve, but it was Rick Bloom from Criteria. She let him leave a message. Hazel had no choice but to put the project on hold. Soon she would be leaving Broomfield again, with more questions than she'd arrived with.

She attempted to contact Rena and Keeler, but neither of them were picking up. Hazel examined the texts from Keeler. When had she last actually spoken to him? She only had his word about Rena's absence.

Hazel had brought everyone to Fun Central. As her panic deepened, she tried Rena again and left instructions to call her back immediately.

CHAPTER 104

Rena collapsed backwards from her sitting position on the forest floor. Blinking at the birches above her, she waited for circumstances to play catch-up and sat painfully erect when they did. She flinched as she tried to angle her head towards the spot she'd seen Lucas and Weiss, but they'd gone.

It didn't matter. She was only two hundred or so yards from Fun Central and was already scrambling to her feet. Her right ankle was double its normal size but Rena bit down on the agony as she put her weight on it with each stride she took towards the parking zone.

She had to climb the dirt incline to reach it and clawed at the wet dirt and leaves as she drove herself forward.

Emerging from the branches, she paused to take a couple of breaths and looked down at her bare toes on the concrete. Rena lifted her head to the complex. There were no vehicles parked outside. She limped across the spaces, dreading finding the place deserted. Were they out searching for her?

A noise behind her made her turn to the trees. She waited and took three steps back. Was it just the bushes settling into place? Rena peered through the trunks for signs of movement.

She couldn't glimpse anyone there but ran as fast as her body would allow. Rena could feel the ball of her joint crunching in its socket as she put more pressure on her leg. She was only twenty feet from safety and hoped yelling against the dry grinding of her hip would attract the attention of someone inside.

Crows cackled and fluttered on the branches but Rena kept going until the doors slid open.

'Help.' She barely sobbed the word. The concourse was deserted. Where was everybody?

She teetered sideways to the Meredith shrine. The table was still positioned beside it, but there was no production laptop there. Had everybody split? 'Help!' Her throat was still swollen, and her lungs struggled to wring the jagged plea from her chest. She sagged against the sooty pillar and waited for a response.

As soon as the word finished echoing around the concourse, she turned back to the main entrance. If somebody were in the forest, she'd just telegraphed exactly where she was. And if they wanted to attack her now, she couldn't defend herself.

Feet clumped above her. They hit the stairs and stopped halfway down.

Rena launched herself from the shrine and grunted towards the door. Her bottom half had begun to feel warm. She thought it was because she was thawing out but, as the pain of her hip and ankle deepened, she wondered if it was the final warning her body was about to shut down.

'Who is it?' she demanded, as her palm gripped the cold metal handle.

The footsteps descended the rest of the way.

Rena yanked it, but her leg gave and she swung with the door; her skin squeaking down the panel before her face struck the tiles.

CHAPTER 105

Rena tried to locate the door handle above her but found she was lying, still naked, on one of the yellow coral tables in Neptune's Party Zone. The walls coruscated with green and blue fish silhouettes.

Rapid footsteps echoed outside the doorway. Sorely, Rena sat up and prepared to drop from the table top. She figured she could crawl under it to hide before whoever it was entered.

'Stay still.' Hazel's anxious expression emerged from behind a blanket and bundle of clothes she was carrying.

Rena felt the blanket being wrapped tightly around her and suddenly tears were running off her nose.

'What happened to you?' Hazel dumped a first aid kit beside her.

'The cab driver.' They were the words Rena thought she'd never utter. Her bruised throat barely allowed her to.

'Cab driver?' Hazel brushed Rena's matted pink locks from her face.

Her sobs remained paralysed. 'The guy who's been dropping people up here in the red Chrysler; he attacked me.'

'Jesus.' Hazel used a wipe to catch the string dripping from Rena's nostrils.

It burnt her raw skin and she jerked her face away.

'He picked you up from Keeler's hotel?'

The cucumber moisturiser smelt overpowering. 'Keeler's dead.'

Hazel's hand froze.

'The driver killed him. And tried to kill me... last night. He hung us both from a tree.' She recalled the machete blade in her palm and the solid jolts in her wrists as she struck Keeler's corpse. 'And he has our phones.'

'Where have you been since?'

'Lost in the forest.' Her jaw trembled.

'All this time?' Hazel was horrified.

'Where's everybody else?'

'Sweeting left. Lucas and Weiss have just taken off as well.'

Panic suspended pain and her eyes darted around the room. 'We're alone? We have to go now. Where's your car?'

'Long story. The cops are on their way though. Put these on.'

Rena grabbed the handful of garments, and her fingers shook as she attempted to unfold her blue cotton vest.

'Here.' Hazel pulled it over her head and shoulders.

Rena couldn't lift her right arm to push it through.

Hazel tore the seam down the side and gently tugged her elbow clear. 'I'm so sorry, Rena. I got texts from Keeler's number. I thought you were with him.'

Rena bent her left hand through the other armhole while Hazel knelt in front of her, carefully slipped her white panties around her muddy heels and tugged them up her shins.

'This looks broken.' Hazel was examining her swollen ankle.

'Don't worry about it.' Rena stood, tuned out the agony and pulled the panties up the rest of the way.

Hazel headed to the doorway. 'I'm calling an ambulance as well.'

CHAPTER 106

Hazel returned breathless to Neptune's, half expecting Rena to have passed out again. 'Somebody's just been in the office.'

Rena stiffened, sweatpants halted at her hips.

'My phone's been taken. And the laptop.'

'He's here,' Rena whispered.

'Where's Henrik's phone?'

'The cops took it. Along with Huber's.'

'Then we have to leave.' Hazel cursed Weiss for walking out with Griff's.

Rena quickly hitched the sweatpants up the rest of the way.

'Can you walk?'

She nodded vigorously.

Hazel crossed the room to the counter at the rear. There was a long-handled brush and scoop there. She brought the brush to Rena and inverted it. 'Use this as a crutch.'

Rena lodged the bristles under her armpit but the handle was too long.

Hazel took it back from her and tried to break a section from the end across her knee but the plastic was solid. She leaned it at an angle against the coral table and stamped hard on it. It broke in half. 'Fuck.'

'Screw it.' Rena took a few exploratory steps forward. 'Let's just go.'

'Slip these on.' Hazel snatched up a pair of Rena's blue leather loafers from the table top and dropped them in front of her. 'Put your arm around me.'

Rena delicately slipped her feet into them while they both watched the doorway.

CHAPTER 107

Hazel paused them outside Neptune's, both listening as they intently watched for movement behind the pillars. The wind briefly clattered the ceiling overhead. She waited until the sound subsided before shuffling them forward. Rena was clearly exhausted. Even supported, it didn't look like she could get very far on her ankle.

'Where are we going?' Rena flinched with every slow step they took.

'As far away from here as we can get,' Hazel whispered back.

'I'm not going back into the forest.'

'We'll stick to the road and hopefully meet the cops.' Where the hell had Soles got to?

They passed the grabbers and both fell silent as they came to the bathroom door. Rena clamped her jaw tight and they continued. As they drew in line with the entrance and the panels parted, Rena started to limp faster.

Outside, the dismal evening seemed in stark contrast to the charged atmosphere they were about to walk out of, and the only activity was a few leaves skipping lazily across the spaces.

Hazel glanced back at the deserted concourse and readjusted her grip under Rena's shoulder. 'Straight for the ramp?'

Rena inhaled slowly through her nose. 'You might have to roll me down it.'

Hazel guided her over the threshold. They made swifter progress than they had inside. She set the pace as Rena leaned hard on her and mostly hopped across the forecourt. 'We're doing good.' Hazel noticed Rena had her eyes firmly closed against the pain. 'Tell me if you need to stop.'

Rena shook her head. 'No stopping.'

Hazel focussed on the top of the ramp and calculated they were a quarter of the way there. 'Put all your weight on me.'

A car engine started behind them, and they were lit up.

'Turn, we have to turn.' But Hazel couldn't because her arm was locked behind Rena. She craned her neck but not enough to see.

Rena bounced and swung her body in time with Hazel's until they'd arced ninety degrees.

A Chrysler was parked against the right-hand side of the entrance, the headlights facing them.

Rena tensed around Hazel.

They hadn't clocked it there, and whoever was seated inside had been watching their progress. Hazel recognised the deep cherry bodywork. Wasn't that the cab that had brought Eve Huber out when she'd been looking for Jacob?

The vehicle accelerated diagonally across the parking zone, circled around and came to rest between them and the ramp. The door opened and the driver got out.

His expression was genial. 'Looks like you could use a ride.' The lenses of his spectacles magnified his blink.

Hazel hadn't absorbed his appearance during the shoot, but as she looked over her shoulder and took in his unkempt sandy hair and avocado shirt, she wondered if Rena could have been mistaken.

He got back inside his Chrysler, and Rena attempted to drag them back towards the entrance. They were stranded between the complex and the car, and they couldn't move fast enough out of his path.

'We have to go back.' Rena was still trying to retreat.

'Wait.'

She slipped free of Hazel. 'Run!'

The driver revved his engine, and the Chrysler surged towards them.

CHAPTER 108

As the vehicle accelerated, Hazel shoved Rena harshly sideways. But as she tried to throw herself clear, one of the wings grazed her right hip. Hazel spun and dropped to the ground hard.

The driver braked.

Adrenaline overrode pain and Hazel scrambled upright. 'Stay behind it!'

Rena rose from where she'd landed and hobbled over to her.

The Chrysler remained motionless about twenty feet away.

'Get ready to go left, if he reverses.' Hazel's whole frame pulsated from the blow. 'He can't turn as fast as we can.'

Rena nodded and didn't take her eyes off the rear of the car.

The engine revved and it shot back.

They dodged at the last moment, and it glided past them.

'Head for the entrance!' Hazel yelled. But she knew Rena was going to take triple the time it took her to get there.

The vehicle screeched to a stop.

'Right here!' Hazel waved both hands at him.

But he took off after Rena.

'Rena!'

She glanced back but there was no time for her to react.

Hazel heard a hollow thud and watched Rena shunted off her feet and travel into the air before she fell heavily onto the concrete.

The Chrysler halted abruptly a few inches from where she'd landed.

'Rena!' Hazel waited for her to move.

The car was reversing again, diagonally at Hazel. She bounced from foot to foot then cut left and sprinted towards Rena but the driver skidded to a standstill and catapulted forward.

Hazel could see Rena's eyes were closed and quickly darted right.

The vehicle would have to follow suit, which meant it would bypass Rena. She weaved her way to the complex and could hear the tyres scuff as they turned in whichever direction she did.

The entrance doors parted. Hazel was nearly inside but realised the concourse didn't offer any safety. He could easily drive over the threshold and run her down.

CHAPTER 109

As the gunning engine vibrated in her chest, Hazel pumped her arms and jogged left.

The car struck the edges of the open doors, shattering both panes of glass from their frames. The wing mirror smashed against her right elbow, and the Chrysler shot past and slammed into Meredith's shrine.

Hazel found herself sprawled on the tiles, her injuries only a vague buzz as she focussed on the motionless vehicle. The front of it was concertinaed against the pillar but the windshield was intact. The engine had cut out. Hazel shakily stood before there were several clicks and two heavy thumps from the driver's door.

It swung open violently. He'd kicked it with both feet. The soles of his tan desert boots touched the floor as he gripped the warped frame to heave himself out. It creaked under his weight, and he turned in Hazel's direction.

The driver adjusted his spectacles and fixed her with his enlarged blue gaze. But his attention shifted to the passenger door. He tugged it open and extracted an oily brown baseball cap with a dark leather peak. Jamming it tight on his head, he leaned in and pulled out a long, telescopic metal pole.

Hazel backed towards the main entrance. What the hell was that? She saw a white spark flare at the prongs and guessed. Turning to flee, the right side of her pelvis was suddenly numb, the leg below it buckling and almost bringing Hazel to her knees. She looked over her shoulder and saw the driver closing the gap between them, the cattle prod extended in readiness to incapacitate her.

She had to lead him away from Rena so made straight for District Burger. There was a way out at the rear where Griff Needham had got in. Hazel could escape via the junkyard.

The restaurant was only thirty feet away but her limb was suddenly a dead weight. Hazel could hear his steady footsteps echoing over her erratic ones. She anticipated a bone breaking.

Hazel reached District Burger, skidded inside and yanked down the shutter. She didn't know where the key was to lock it to the floor and was just darting her eyes around when his shadow fell across her. He angled the prod through one of the shutter holes, and it grazed her knuckle.

She recoiled in time but almost lost her balance as he withdrew it and bent to roll the shutter back up.

He got his fingers underneath.

Hazel was back on her feet and staggering to the counter. She heard a harsh rattle as he hurled up the shutter.

Lifting the red hatch, Hazel let it drop down behind her and barrelled through the swing door. She stumbled through the tiny prep kitchen and pushed on the next one. It only opened a couple of inches before it thudded into something solid.

She shoved against it, but the panel was immovable. Peering through the gap she could see that one of the old rusted chest freezers from the junkyard had been jammed there. Hazel threw her whole body against the door, but there was no way she could budge it.

CHAPTER 110

Hazel's head spun to the swing door behind her. The driver still hadn't appeared. He was probably biding his time because he'd positioned the freezer to block her escape. She returned to the aluminium workstation in the middle of the room. There weren't any tools she could use as a weapon, only stacks of dusty plastic tubs.

The driver entered, unblinkingly assessing her situation before extending the prod towards her.

'Don't fucking touch me!'

His eyes slanted as he stretched his arm so the telescopic pole bridged the length of the prep counter between them.

Hazel leaned away from it. He couldn't get nearer without moving down the longer side of the table. She could see that register in his eyes and, as he glimpsed briefly down at his footing, lunged forward and grabbed the prod an inch below the end.

She jerked it, but he maintained a firm grasp. They held the position for a few seconds and then he started circling the counter. She shifted in the opposite direction, towards the swing door that led back to the restaurant. The driver halted when they faced each other halfway along the surface.

The end sparked a few inches from her neck, and he started thrusting the prod towards her. Her hand shook as she tried to resist but he was forcing her spine against the tiled wall. Soon Hazel wouldn't be able to stop the prongs going into her throat.

As he put his whole body weight behind it, Hazel suddenly released her grip and dodged to the right. The driver fell forward into the stacks of tubs, and Hazel seized the weapon again.

He still wouldn't relinquish it so Hazel tipped the edge of the table towards him. His bulk slid down it, and she grunted and used both hands to hinge it on top of him. Hazel battered back out of the swing door, through the hatch and onto the concourse.

Dragging herself to the main entrance, Hazel paused at the bathroom and dared to look behind her but there was no sign of pursuit.

She inched towards the broken doors, all the time watching District Burger and anticipating him emerging. There wasn't another exit – unless he had the strength to bulldoze the freezer from the rear. Was he coming around the front of the complex to intercept her? She waited and listened. Where the fuck was Soles? Hazel's attention settled on the Chrysler against the pillar.

Hazel crossed the tyre tracks, tiptoed through the shards and peered in the open driver door. The key was still in the ignition; still no trace of the driver at the restaurant or main entrance.

If she made a run for it outside there was no telling how long it would be before her leg gave out. But if she took his car and picked Rena up, he couldn't catch them. That's if Hazel was able to get it started. And if she didn't, the sound of the engine would alert him to exactly where she was.

She dropped into the seat, softly closed the buckled door and turned the key.

The motor chugged a few times then cut out. Hazel checked the entrance and District Burger. No movement. She tried again and it strained longer. If he was inside Fun Central, there was no doubt he'd heard her.

She had to go. One more attempt.

Hazel yanked the key hard, and this time the engine started. She put her boot on the pedal and glanced in the mirror – still no evidence of the driver at the entrance. Putting the car into reverse, she scraped the compressed metal away from the shrine. But as soon as it broke contact, the vehicle died again.

She kept wrenching the key but it was silent. Now Hazel was rolling backwards towards the doors, the tyres crackling over glass and dead leaves.

Hazel applied the brakes and knew she'd left it too late to abandon the Chrysler. But, as she got out, the driver still hadn't come to investigate. If he hadn't emerged from the restaurant it was likely he was waiting for her in the parking zone. She had to find another route to Rena.

She hauled her leg over to the door that led to the stairs and opened it.

Footfalls behind her. Hazel swivelled to the main entrance and saw a shadow fall there. She was just about to enter the stairwell when she sidestepped it and ducked into the ball pit.

CHAPTER 111

Through the smoked glass of the ball pit entrance, Hazel could see the stiff hinges still hadn't allowed the stairwell door to close properly. She hoped the driver would spot it and head straight up there. As soon as she heard him ascend, Hazel would steal outside. By the time he'd searched the rooms, she could have Rena safely hidden in the forest – if she was still alive.

Hazel crossed the faded orange carpet tiles, lifted herself to the edge of the ball pit, slid in and kneeled down. The balls settled around her face. The smell of latex was potent, and her hot breath bounced off them. Her right elbow throbbed angrily, and it was the first time she'd registered the pain of being struck by the wing mirror.

Boot soles ground broken glass. She stopped breathing. They left the shards and got louder. They were approaching the door to the stairs.

'Hazel?' The male voice echoed along the concourse.

Hazel recognised it. Sweeting.

'Anyone?'

He'd come back. Had Sweeting had second thoughts or was he collecting his gear? If he'd been dropped off in a cab she'd been too busy trying to start the Chrysler to hear it. She had to warn him he was in danger. Hazel stood and quickly swung herself back over the side of the pool. She padded to the entrance and peeked out.

'Sweeting.' But it wasn't Hazel who called him.

She observed Sweeting, a bandage around his head, halt twenty feet from the stairwell door and turn to the main entrance. The driver was standing there.

'Where the hell have you been? We've been waiting for you so we can get started.' The driver marched towards him.

Hazel hung back. Did Sweeting know him?

'Thought you'd chickened out on us.'

'Where's Hazel? And who the fuck are you?'

The driver was still a couple of feet away but extended the prod from where he'd concealed it at his side.

'And whose car is that?'

Hazel opened her mouth but Sweeting convulsed, collapsed and rolled onto his side. She clamped her palm over her lips as she watched the driver zap him under his armpit three more times. Sweeting locked into a foetal position and the driver circled him, as if considering doing it again.

He looked up and down the fun zones, and Hazel took a step back from the door. She kept one eye trained on him as he crouched and plucked the turn-up of his chinos from his tan desert boot. There was a black sheath strapped to his leg. He undid the clip and withdrew a hunting knife with four holes along the brass handle. Slipping his fingers into them, he effortlessly jabbed the silver blade into Sweeting's neck.

Hazel bit her hand as he twisted it once and wiped it on Sweeting's shoulder.

CHAPTER 112

Hazel was lying flat on her back along the bottom of the pit. The balls were hollow and weightless but she could feel their contours pressing against her body and eyelids. If she needed to run, they'd slow her down. But the driver would have to climb into the pool to reach her in the middle, and there were four different sides to use as exits.

Maybe he'd intercepted Soles in the parking zone. But she hadn't heard his car arrive either. Whatever accounted for the officer's absence, she was on her own. Her stomach grumbled for the third time. Hazel heard the driver make his way to the Chrysler and assumed he was removing the key. If he'd been waiting outside for her as she'd tried to start it, he knew she was still in the complex.

The bathroom door creaked open and shut. No more footsteps. He must be hunting for her inside. She hastily took some lungfuls of stale air, and the balls rustled as her chest rose and fell.

Should she flee while he was in there? It would take her seconds to cross the concourse to the entrance but maybe that's what he expected her to do. Perhaps he'd simply opened and closed the bathroom door and was standing outside, watching for signs of movement. She wouldn't know for sure until she'd given herself away.

The bathroom door complained again. His footfalls recommenced but changed pitch. He was crossing to her side, and his soles became muffled as he walked onto the carpets of Neptune's Party Zone. It wouldn't take him long to confirm she wasn't in there.

She visualised him stalking the coral tables and, moments later, his feet echoed briefly back onto the concourse before entering the ball pit.

Hazel went rigid as she felt the soft impacts along the floor. He stopped as he surveyed the room. She was positive one breath in or out would make the balls shift and betray her hiding place. She couldn't even disturb them by blinking. Closing her eyes tightly she could hear the squeal in his throat. All his exertions were obviously taking their toll.

The driver remained motionless. He was listening. Hazel's circulation began to pummel her ears. There was no way she would inhale while he was still out there. She'd black out first.

Metal scratched across plastic sheeting. He'd put the cattle prod into the pool and was dragging it through the balls. Hazel fought her body's impulse to struggle against her lack of oxygen. She couldn't work out which direction the prongs were travelling. If he was moving in line with the side, she should still be out of reach.

Her stomach gurgled.

The activity stopped. Hazel's eyes opened.

All the balls around her quaked; he was getting into the pit.

His mass displaced and compacted them around her. He had to be within a few feet. As they continued to churn she curled into herself.

Over the clamour in her head she discerned the prod being forcefully jabbed into the pool at random but now a shadow was blotting out the dreary light. Hazel didn't know if it was the driver or impending unconsciousness.

As he waded forward, she anticipated an electric charge from the prod or the pressure of his boot on her limbs. The tide of plastic surged, and Hazel decided she had to spring up at him before he discovered her.

A loud thud.

He'd stepped over her and clambered out of the pit. But he was still loitering there, and Hazel had to restrain her shoulders from pumping. The light began to dim and move away from her, as if the bottom was dropping and the pool was getting rapidly deeper.

Still no sound of his exit from the room but, as her oxygen-starved brain began to close down, his presence no longer seemed to matter.

CHAPTER 113

Hazel clawed her way to the surface of the ball pit and tried not to vocalise the agony of her first breath. The air was cool on her perspiring face but she stayed on her knees as her heart stumbled around in her chest. Had the driver even left the room? She waited for the inky blobs in her eyes to be burnt away by the weak light and was relieved to see he'd gone.

She didn't know how long she'd blacked out but it could have been only seconds, which meant he was probably still nearby. The percussion in her ears slowed but she heard a different thud overhead. He was upstairs. She ploughed her way to the edge of the pit, heaved herself out and dropped quietly onto the carpet.

Hazel limped to the door. Sweeting's motionless body was in the middle of a large pool of blood.

The driver's footfalls above told Hazel he was working his way through all the rooms. He'd be back down as soon as he realised she wasn't there, and that was all the time she had to retrieve Sweeting's phone. She'd call Lucas.

Hurrying to where Sweeting lay on his side, Hazel hesitated at the circumference of the dark puddle. It had spread out from him by three feet, and she'd have to tread in it to reach his pocket.

Hazel's petrified expression was reflected in it as she carefully tested her good left foot on the liquid and allowed it to take her weight. She gradually leaned forward and extended her hand to Sweeting's parka. Feeling the pocket, she found nothing. Was it in the other? If so, he was lying on it.

The driver moved along the passage to the next room.

Sweeting's coat was open at the front. Focussing on the back of his spattered baldness, Hazel slid her fingers into the lukewarm blood on the floor and grappled under him for the other edge. It wouldn't budge. She needed more purchase, and her right boot slithered as she painfully repositioned herself in the slick.

Grunting, she tugged it clear with both hands. His bulk rolled further forward as she squeezed the soaked pocket. There was something solid in there. His head jerked as she waggled her fist inside and wrestled the phone out. Hazel stood but her boots skated. Yelping, she windmilled her arms to stay vertical.

Steadying herself, she listened for sounds of the driver returning. No feet on the stairs.

Hazel punched the button and the screen lit up red. Wiping her bloody fingerprints from it, she could see he was down to six per cent power. Hazel didn't need his passcode; there was an emergency call option which bypassed it. She made for the main entrance.

A firm hand seized Hazel before she could take her second step.

CHAPTER 114

Sweeting was still alive. Hazel looked down at him silently mouthing something at her, one half of his face deathly white, the other crimson from lying in his own blood. His grip tightened on the pocket of her jeans and an incoherent word hissed out of him.

'Sweeting,' she whispered.

He emitted a guttural sob.

Hazel bent to him. 'You have to keep quiet.'

Sweeting struggled to get upright and blood gushed out of the slit in his neck.

'Keep still.'

But he writhed around in the pool as he tried to escape it, and his weight was suddenly pulling Hazel forward.

Her left foot skidded sideways. 'Sweeting… '

Now the driver's boots were pounding down the stairs.

'He's coming. I have to hide.' His expression was only inches from hers, and she could see the terror in his eyes. 'You have to let go.' But he wouldn't release her.

The driver hit the bottom.

'Please.' She prised his fingers away, and he blinked once before they slipped from her.

Staggering straight she checked the door. It hadn't opened yet but, as the handle was depressed, she didn't have time to return to the ball pit. Hazel dashed to the wall on the other side and pressed her back against it as the panel swung out.

The driver emerged and halted a few paces from Sweeting.

Hazel saw the bloody footprints leading from the puddle to her.

Sweeting did as well then held the driver's gaze. He gurgled a 'fuck you' at him and started crawling towards the main entrance.

Hazel realised he was attempting to draw him away from her but the driver remained where he was, observing his progress. He had the prod in his left hand, and the hunting knife in his right.

The door gradually closed. Hazel slid across it.

Sweeting shouted another incomprehensible obscenity and heaved his body further, a red trail smeared in his wake.

Keeping her attention on the motionless figure between her and Sweeting, Hazel clasped the handle.

The driver's cap dipped to her boot prints, and he slowly followed them to where she was standing; large blue eyes censuring her from under the curved brim of his leather peak.

She turned, opened the door and hurtled to the stairs. As she scaled them, Hazel could hear the driver's shoulders scraping the walls behind her. On the eleventh step, she felt a sudden jolt to her left calf. Her muscles contracted and she was briefly suspended before she slid backwards. Sweeting's sticky phone slid from her palm.

Her right ankle was tugged the rest of the way, chin bashing the edges of each stair. Hazel was unconscious before she reached the floor.

CHAPTER 115

She awoke shivering.

April remembered the grown-up forcing her back inside the sack and carrying her across the yard. Then she'd heard a metal door opening and closing behind them.

He'd put April on a hard floor and told her not to move. He hadn't asked her to describe him again though. He'd paced around and sworn a lot when he tried to get someone on the phone. That was when she'd wet herself. She'd lain there like that for a while and then April recalled something hitting her head. How long ago had that been?

Now she was in pitch-darkness, and the sack was gone. April was lying on her tummy and tried to sit up. Her scalp struck something hard above her.

Feeling around she found freezing metal surfaces on all sides. She was inside a small box. 'Help.' April's mouth was dry but her voice sounded so big. What if he was still outside, listening? She waited but there was no reply or any sounds to tell her where she was. Where had he put her? 'Help!'

April beat her fists on the walls. No good.

Resting on her back she kicked up at the barrier above until her ankles hurt.

Was this a punishment or had he left her there forever? She could describe him now. Why didn't he want her to do that any more? She was so cold and thought about being at home. Maybe he'd gone there to hurt her parents. April started to cry.

CHAPTER 116

Lucas and Weiss had tried to find Eve Huber at Rifkin Lodge, but she wasn't in her room. Driving the Toyota down the illuminated main street of Broomfield there was no sign of her there either.

Weiss glanced at him from the passenger seat for the third time. 'You OK?'

He nodded.

'Really?'

'I've just said I am.'

'Look, I feel as bad as you do about Hazel.'

'What more could we do? I'm the last person she wants to be around right now.'

Weiss squinted at the dingy entrance to the tiny cinema. 'Hazel's got a lot on her plate, and our presence is probably the last thing she needs.'

'That was shitty timing though.'

'She confronted you.'

'I know.'

'It had to happen – sooner rather than later.'

'Now though? What the fuck—' Lucas had spotted a large crowd of people assembled outside the park. A patrol car was pulled over on the sidewalk with its lights flashing. The throng was being coordinated by two police officers. 'That's Soles and Drake.'

Weiss squinted through his specs. 'Oh yeah.'

'Hazel said it was Soles that was on his way to Fun Central.'

'And?'

'We didn't pass his car when we came into Broomfield. If he's been waylaid with this, Hazel's still there on her own.'

CHAPTER 117

Even though she was in virtual darkness, Hazel knew immediately where she'd been taken. Woozily lifting her head, she recognised the glow of the white reflective lines bisecting the go-kart circuit.

She attempted to touch her throbbing chin, but couldn't move her hands from their position behind her. It was the second time she'd been bound that day. Hazel peered down at her thighs. She was sitting on her swivel chair, wrists secured around its trunk.

Hazel could feel the same cold metal sensation about her ankles and the cool, rough track against the soles of her bare feet. Her boots had been removed to snap the second set of cuffs there.

Was the driver standing nearby, watching? As Hazel scanned the gloomy arena, her blood pumped harder against the restraints. She listened for his presence. If he were in here with her, he would soon make himself known.

Hazel shunted her buttocks. The chair rolled a couple of inches on its plastic wheels but slewed left. Using her toes and stomach muscles to guide it to the middle of the speedway, she wondered which direction to go. There was no opening in the tyre barrier until the finish. She had to follow the luminous lines. Was that what the driver wanted? Hazel considered reversing but figured moving forwards was the quickest route to the exit. She boosted her body ahead again and was just approaching a bend when she heard the sound of different wheels.

One of them squeaked under a steady trundling, and Hazel halted and waited for the source of the noise to appear. It was coming from the concourse.

The rumble got louder, dampening and crunching when the wheels hit dead leaves. Hazel pushed faster but veered right and bumped against the tyres. She thrust vigorously in the chair as she tried to free herself.

The squealing became distinct as it reached the entrance to Speed Zone.

Hazel strained to look back.

The wheels stopped and strip lights flickered on. Squinting, she struggled to arc around before she registered the now illuminated finishing line and the person seated in a chair behind it.

CHAPTER 118

Hazel couldn't recognise the charred corpse but guessed who it was.

Burn me in hell. #BeMyKiller

They were the words Henrik Fossen had tweeted to @BeMyKiller, and she recalled the incinerated tree they'd found in the forest and the scraps of his tee shirt nearby.

Henrik's features were consumed. No hair remained on his shiny obsidian skull, and his burnt-out eye sockets were empty. Some form of plastic had melted and fused to the bottom half of his shrunken charcoal face, partly coating the exposed teeth there.

The fire had eaten away his shoulders and exposed bone jutted from black flesh. The flames had scorched him to his midriff, and the skin around his navel was tightened and raw. But everything below his waist looked untouched. Only sooty streaks on his jeans intimated the trauma to his torso, and his new Reeboks still looked spotless.

Before Hazel's senses could recoil from what was sitting twenty feet in front of her, the wheels started turning again. She harshly jerked herself free of the tyres and rotated the chair.

Beyond the barrier, she could see the top of the driver's baseball cap as he leaned forward to push Rena's trolley in her direction. Sweeting was sitting on it, bloodied and naked, his back propped up against the handle.

He was bloated and deformed, his belly distended. One of the bright red plastic balls from the pit was stuffed between his lips like an apple in a hog's mouth, and the incision from his throat to his groin barely held in the ones that had been crammed into his stomach.

Hazel's repulsion twisted her wrists in the cuffs.

It looked like he'd been gutted; his innards removed to jam as many of the balls inside him.

She attempted to reverse, but shot across the track and struck the tyres on the other side.

You don't have any balls.

had been Sweeting's input to the WhatsApp discussion. The driver must have got hold of a crew phone.

He passed by, negotiating the trolley towards the rear of the arena before hitting a small rubber ramp covering some cables. It rattled the wheels, and several balls spilled and bounced away from the cavity of Sweeting's chest.

Hazel swivelled reluctantly to follow the driver's progress and saw where he was going. A naked cadaver was seated on a chair in front of the shuttered coffee stand.

Come get some, fuckface!

Hazel's struggling ceased as she saw what Keeler's message had wrought. His slashed face hung in ribbons, and large chunks of his cranium and brain tissue were missing; the top half of his head almost hacked clean away.

The driver positioned Sweeting a few feet from Keeler at an angle he seemed satisfied with.

As Hazel's hands and feet were so firmly secured there was no way she could resist whatever he had planned for her. She juddered away from the barrier and made for the finishing line, keeping her attention locked on him as he stood back to appraise his display.

Hazel was only about ten feet from the chequered floor, where there was a gap in the tyres. But what would she do, even if she reached it? Roll all the way out and back to Broomfield? The driver knew he could take his time. But the sight of Fossen's cremated carcass kept her feet shuffling in tiny steps.

As she edged closer, the driver ambled back to the entrance but changed course and vaulted the tyre barrier. His desert boots thudded onto the track and he advanced down the circuit towards her, holding the cattle prod in his hand.

CHAPTER 119

'Why are you doing this?'

The driver didn't break his leisurely stride.

Hazel's chair came to rest on the dirty white finishing line. She raised her head and shouted into the high ceiling. 'Help!'

He slowed a few feet in front of her and circled his free palm, encouraging her to do it again. 'Don't let me stop you.' The comment was softly spoken and amiable.

Hazel furiously waggled her wrists and ankles and felt the metal cut deep.

The driver blinked at her through his thick lenses then bent to one knee.

Spineless bitch.

They were the words she'd dropped into the WhatsApp discussion, and Hazel was sure they were about to tailor her death.

The driver used his left hand to hitch the leg of his chinos and unclipped the hunting knife from the sheath. He stood, showed it to her then forcibly stabbed the blade into the top tyre of the barrier behind him so the handle jutted upwards.

It appeared he wanted to take his time with the prod first and thrust it in her direction. She glided from him and hit hard rubber again. He paced towards her and Hazel leaned away, as she had in the kitchen, but now her scalp was pressed against the opposite barrier.

The driver held the prod under her nose and made it spark. Hazel could smell the charge. Then he touched her cheek with the prongs and moved them downwards, grazing her neck and tracing the edge of her shoulder. He drove them hard between her breasts then skimmed gently to her right nipple. He pricked her there and pressed them firmly through her bra.

Hazel waited for him to glance up. 'Fuck you.'

He shifted the prongs further down, circling her stomach and scratching the denim at her crotch.

Hazel squirmed and bucked in the seat, rotating herself away from the prod before he caught hold of the chair and swung her back to face him. His expression was irked, and he stuck the prongs hard into the top of her leg.

She stiffened against the jolt of electricity, her tendons rigid and shoulders shrinking in on her body. As the muscles of her throat stifled a yell of agony, Hazel knew she was unable to delay the fate she'd chosen for herself.

He went to retrieve the knife.

Groaning as she tried to galvanise her body, Hazel couldn't even scream against what was about to happen.

The driver reached the barrier and set the prod next to the knife. Then he paused, as if remembering something, and turned back to her. He rummaged in his pocket and pulled out a tube of glue. He frowned as he unscrewed the tiny lid.

Hazel recalled the footage of Meredith's death and how her eyelids had been stuck open so she had no choice but to watch.

The driver turned to put the cap on the barrier.

Hazel closed her eyes tight and waited; her stiff limbs anticipating his touch.

She heard a female scream. Was it hers?

A male choke of pain opened her eyes.

The driver slowly spun from the barrier. The knife was planted in his chest. As he slid down the rubber wall, Hazel recognised his attacker. She was the other side of the tyres.

Rena took a few faltering steps back, expression repelled and hands balled against her.

The blade was deep in his sternum, and he made no attempt to remove it. He blinked at Hazel from his seated position.

'Is he dead?' Rena's voice trembled.

Hazel couldn't reply. She watched the blood patch rapidly expanding under the driver's avocado shirt, and him puff some air out of his cheeks.

He stopped blinking soon after.

CHAPTER 120

It was minutes before Rena would take one step back to the driver's body.

As the effects of the prod wore off and Hazel's muscles began to relax, she assured Rena he was dead and told her to search his pockets for the keys to the cuffs.

Rena limped cautiously onto the circuit through the gap in the tyres by the finishing line. She sobbed when she saw Henrik's corpse.

'Don't look at him. And don't look back there. Focus on finding these keys.'

Rena nodded her tangled pink hair, warily approached the driver and gazed in horror at his darkened bloody chest.

'He must have them. Look in his top pocket. For car keys as well.' Hazel registered the black grit embedded in the side of Rena's raw cheek.

Rena extended her fingers but hesitated a few inches from him.

'He's dead.' But Hazel still anticipated his magnified blue eyes blinking.

Rena's hand remained where it was.

'Quickly.'

She tentatively grazed his top pocket. A button secured it, and Rena shakily fumbled it open.

Hazel heard the jingle of keys.

Rena wheeled the chair away from the barrier by the arms so she could get behind Hazel.

Hazel didn't shift her attention from the driver while the metal scraped about in the lock of the cuffs around her feet.

'It's awkward,' Rena said from her kneeling position.

One of the loops loosened from Hazel's left ankle, and the other quickly followed. She stretched her legs out to get the blood back into them. The cuffs clattered to the track, and Rena unlocked her wrists from behind the chair.

Hazel stood unsteadily and silently hugged Rena. They trembled against each other but Hazel knew they'd have to deal with the trauma of their ordeal later. She released her. 'OK, you get in the chair now and I'll push you out of here.'

CHAPTER 121

Hazel rolled Rena away from the Chrysler. Even though they hadn't found it on the driver's body, the key wasn't in the ignition. 'I'll wheel you right back to town if I have to. We're not waiting for Soles. Keep your feet on the legs.'

Rena eventually complied. 'I played dead, and he dragged me inside. Had to lie there while he cut up Sweeting.' Her words were sluggish.

Were they really alone? Hazel didn't want to stay there a second longer than was necessary. Especially with Jacob Huber and Griff Needham unaccounted for. But perhaps their bodies had been displayed elsewhere. She painfully pushed Rena to the main entrance and avoided glass shards with her bare feet as she tried to prevent the chair from listing.

They reached the smashed doors, and a hard rain blew in at them from the darkness. Hazel quickly shoved Rena over the threshold and blinked against the spray. As she drove her towards the ramp, they both shot a nervous sideways glance to the spot where the driver had waited for them before.

There was nobody there so Hazel returned her focus to the rows of empty parking spaces ahead. She froze when she heard an engine. A car was accelerating up the ramp.

Hazel recognised the battered orange Toyota and relief trickled through her. 'It's Lucas.' He was in the driving seat with Weiss beside him.

A patrol car was behind it.

She gently squeezed Rena's shoulder. 'They've brought the cops.'

Rena's body sagged as if she couldn't hold her exhaustion at bay a second longer.

The Toyota halted in front of them, and Lucas got out. 'What happened?'

Weiss quickly followed.

'Jesus… ' Lucas reacted to both their injuries.

Officers Soles and Drake joined them.

Hazel could barely summon any anger. 'Where the hell were you, Soles?'

'I'm sorry. I was organising a search party for a missing girl.'

'The cab driver killed Sweeting, Keeler and Henrik. And tried to kill us… '

'There's dead people in there?' Soles was incredulous.

'In the kart arena. There could be more.' Hazel felt suddenly faint. 'Rena needs a medic.'

'I'm calling for backup and an ambulance.' Drake relayed the situation via his radio.

'You mean the guy ferrying everyone from the motel?' Lucas eyed the busted Chrysler.

'Rena stabbed him. He's dead.'

'Any sign of Jacob or Griff?' Weiss crouched and studied Rena's pupils.

'Didn't see them but we got out as quickly as we could.' Hazel leaned heavily against Rena's chair.

'Rena? Are you OK?' Weiss touched her hand. 'I think she's gone into shock.'

'Ambulance on its way.' Drake stepped back into the group.

Lucas wiped rain droplets from his shaved head. 'We should take a look in there.'

Soles walked backwards over the threshold. 'This is a crime scene again.' He gestured for Drake to accompany him. 'Don't any of you move from there.'

Soles and Drake headed for Speed Zone.

'Rena?' Weiss passed his fingers in front of her face. 'When did she come back?'

'Let's get her out of the rain.' Hazel tried to move the chair but flinched.

'Here.' Lucas pushed Rena inside.

Weiss helped Hazel get under cover.

Another engine was gunned.

Everyone turned. A blue Tacoma pickup towing Hazel's battered silver Mazda appeared and parked thirty feet from the entrance.

Hazel squinted against the headlights.

Leaving the engine running, Wade Hickman got out and strode in their direction.

CHAPTER 122

'I don't like this.' Lucas sidled closer to Hazel.

Wade took in Hazel and Rena's injuries and hesitated as he saw Soles and Drake hurrying to intercept him. 'So, what have I missed?'

'What's your business here?' Soles reached the entrance.

Wade started walking again. 'Delivering this lady's car, like I promised.'

'Is this correct?' Drake had joined Soles.

Hazel nodded.

'Just hold it right there.' Soles held up his palm.

Wade didn't obey.

'I said hold it right there.' Soles drew his handgun. 'This is a crime scene. People are lying dead in there. I'll give you two seconds to tell me why you happened to roll up now.'

Wade slowed but kept coming. 'No need to pull that on me, officer.'

Drake brandished his. 'Not another step.'

Wade halted and raised his hands theatrically. 'You two arresting me?'

'Not just yet,' Soles sniffed, as if he didn't like Wade's scent.

'Mind if I come out the rain while you make your minds up?' His eyes darted between Soles and Drake before he covered the few feet separating them so he was under shelter.

'Stay where you are!' Drake extended his arm so the gun was only a few inches from Wade's face.

Wade circled towards the Chrysler. 'Shouldn't point that thing unless you're gonna use it.'

'If he doesn't, I will.' Soles followed him with his.

He stopped with his back to the Chrysler. 'Look, I'm just returning the car.'

Soles nodded to Drake. 'Cuff him.'

Wade raised an eyebrow at Drake. 'You heard him. Cuff me. For no good reason.'

'Put your hands behind your head!' Soles barked.

Hazel could see his finger start to squeeze the trigger. 'Officer Soles, what are you doing?'

'Somebody tell me what's going on here.'

Everyone turned to the figure that had just appeared at the entrance. It was Tamara Hickman, illuminated by the headlights and holding a double-barrelled shotgun.

CHAPTER 123

'I told you to wait in the pickup.' Wade dropped his hands.

Tamara's eyes flitted from Soles to Drake.

'I advise you to get back in your truck. This is a murder scene.' Drake didn't move his gun from Wade.

'Who's dead?' she demanded.

'You're pointing a weapon at police officers,' Soles cautioned. 'We've already had one psycho die tonight after going nuts. Let's not make it two.'

Tamara tightened her lips. 'We both know you don't have the balls to pull that trigger,' she goaded him.

Soles kept his pistol on Wade. 'Put the gun down, Tam. You don't want to be part of this.'

'It's a misunderstanding.' Hazel watched Soles's finger. 'Everybody just take a breath.'

'Lower your weapon,' Drake snapped at Tamara.

But Wade's gaze was now locked on his wife. 'What did Soles just call you?'

Tamara shot an ireful glance at the officer.

'Answer my question.' Wade took a pace towards her.

'Another step and this is going in the back of your skull, Wade.' Soles was losing control of the situation.

'You always told me you hated Soles. Now you two are on first-name terms?' Wade narrowed his eyes at Tamara.

'Ancient history,' Soles eventually said with some satisfaction. 'Now step back from her.'

Wade swallowed audibly but didn't move.

'How does *that* sit with you, Wade?' Soles bared his teeth. 'It was me Tam wanted, but I was already married to a better woman so she had to make do with your sorry ass,' the officer scoffed.

'You son of a bitch,' Tamara spat at Soles.

Soles continued: 'pleaded with me to leave Laurel, even though my wife was sick. I realised what a piece of work she was then. At least Laurel died not knowing how stupid I'd been.'

Wade rolled his tongue slowly around his cheek.

'Oh she did know.' Tamara glowered at Soles. 'I told her, Gene. In 2014. Paid her a little visit after you'd been getting too close to Meredith. Told her you had a daughter she didn't know about. Knew you two could never have kids. Laurel drank that weedkiller a few weeks later.'

Soles went rigid.

Tamara fixed her husband. 'That's why he was always hauling Meredith in, Wade. He wasn't victimising her, just trying to keep her out of trouble.'

'Growing up with you two freaks, she didn't have a chance.' Soles swung the barrel of his revolver to Tamara.

Wade looked down at Tamara's feet. 'Tell me this is bullshit, Tam.'

Tamara sighed. 'I did the math. Meredith is Gene Soles's child,' she admitted coldly and briefly rolled her eyes to Hazel and Lucas. 'This juicy enough for you? Don't want the cameras recording this? Told you taking part was a bad idea, Wade. But you couldn't pass up your chance of fame.'

Drake was eager to reassert his authority. 'Let's deal with one thing at a time. Everybody take a step outside.'

But Soles clenched his pistol tighter and kept it trained on Tamara. 'I still want to know how come you two breezed in now.'

'Better ask her.' Wade jabbed his finger at Tamara. 'I tried Miss Salter's mobile, but she didn't pick up. Wanted to leave it till morning, but Tamara insisted we head over now.'

She shrugged her shoulders dismissively. 'She needed the car, and I didn't want it cluttering up my yard.'

'You were desperate for me to drive it over and come with me,' Wade said contemptuously.

Tamara saw nobody else was buying her explanation. 'I wanted it off my property, and Wade's better at driving the pickup.'

'That's a lot of crap.' Wade scowled. 'You drive it more than me. And why the hell did you pack my shotgun?'

'I found it in the truck.'

'It was locked in my cabinet. You must have thrown that in back.'

She didn't respond.

Wade studied her intently. 'You knew something was going down, didn't you?'

'You're talking crazy, Wade. You know I hate guns.'

'That's not what Meredith told me,' Hazel declared.

Everyone turned to her.

She couldn't conceal their connection any longer. 'I used to live in Broomfield. Knew Meredith when I was a child. Twenty years ago.'

Lucas's reaction was the most conspicuous.

'She told me about your secret target practice in Holtwood Forest.'

Tamara was momentarily stunned.

'"Target practice"? What else you been hiding from me? I repeat: why the fuck did you have me drive over here?' Wade barked at his wife.

Tamara gritted her teeth and briefly closed her eyes, as if coming to an inward decision. 'I told Wade not to get involved in this documentary, but he wouldn't listen.'

Hazel forgot the weapons that were poised and ready to fire. 'Tell us what's going on, Tamara.'

She dipped the barrels of her shotgun and inhaled. 'I knew you people weren't safe here.'

'Yeah?' Weiss said scornfully. 'How?'

'Spit it out, Tam. These people are waiting,' Wade pressed her.

'Or we could do this down at the station,' Soles threatened.

Tamara blinked rapidly as she arranged her thoughts. 'Last year, a guy came to the turkey farm. Really fucked-up. While he was going through withdrawal he did a lot of talking. He'd killed a bunch of people in the line of duty. Ex Black Ops, dishonourably discharged. Then he started ranting about civilian casualties. It sounded like the people I'd heard about on the TV news. Said they'd gone online and asked for death. He couldn't believe they were making jokes about what had put him in therapy. Said if they really wanted to be executed he'd be more than happy to oblige. When he was rational, I didn't let on. But he knew he'd said too much. I saw the way he looked at Meredith. Tried to keep her away from him after that.'

There was silence as everyone absorbed the implications.

Wade grimaced. 'What happened?'

'He called me the night she died. Said he'd forced her to send a tweet from her account before he took her to Fun Central. Said if I breathed a word about him, Wade would be next.'

'You expect me to believe that?' Wade sneered. 'That you were protecting me? And you only ever tolerated Meredith. Wasn't she just a reminder of a life with Soles you never had? Hanging around you like a bad smell?'

'Fuck you.'

Hazel wondered if Meredith's killer had been chained up in the shack. 'Who was he?'

'Ryan Kirby. I had a cell number for him. Called it and told him I was worried about the movie you were making because Wade agreed to take part. Said I'd tried to talk Wade out of it. Kirby told me he was going to come back to Broomfield when the movie was being shot. I begged him to stay away.'

'Jesus.' Soles's gun hand was trembling.

'He's dead back there.' Hazel clenched her hands, and they were still sticky with Sweeting's blood. 'And there's three other bodies lying with him around that track.'

'Sir?' Drake looked uncertainly to Soles for an order.

'You fucking liar.' Wade sprang forward and grabbed Tamara by the throat.

CHAPTER 124

Officer Soles watched Wade strangling Tamara but did nothing.

Hazel took a step forward to help her.

'Stay back!' Soles halted her with his weapon.

'Give it to me, Tam!' Wade grabbed hold of Tamara's shotgun muzzle.

'I'll pull the trigger.' Tamara waited for him to meet the intent in her eyes.

He didn't and started prising her hands away.

'Wade,' she warned.

He twisted and jerked it from her. 'Now… ', he turned, the gun aimed at Soles, 'still smug about screwing my wife?'

The first barrel blew a hole out of Soles. He staggered backwards several paces, the force almost toppling him. His chest was black and bloody; shirt and flesh hanging in tatters. He looked at Wade with incomprehension then sank to his knees.

Drake fired, and Wade's shoulder was obliterated. He spun away but didn't relinquish the firearm. He discharged the other barrel at Drake.

The blast caught him in the neck and he crumpled.

'And this is for you.' Wade started butting Tamara in the face with the stock of the gun.

She screamed and collapsed to the floor and, despite his injury, Wade bent to her and kept pummelling.

Hazel threw herself onto Wade, crooking her arm around his neck and trying to tip him back with the weight of her body. Wade kept striking Tamara and busted her nose.

Lucas tried to wrench the shotgun from Wade's fingers.

Hazel crushed his throat and felt his Adam's apple solid against her bicep.

'Get the fuck off me.' Wade bent forward, flipped Hazel over his head and against Lucas.

They both went down, and Hazel bit her tongue as her scalp slammed into the tiled floor. Wade remained upright and raised the weapon to strike Tamara again. He froze there, and the report seemed to come after.

Hazel could see Drake had weakly lifted his gun arm and shot Wade from behind.

Wade keeled hard onto his face, and Tamara scuttled out of the way. He didn't get up again.

The sound of grunting returned their attention to Soles. He was still on his knees, his hands hanging uselessly at his sides. He hinged backwards, the impact splaying out one of his arms while the other came to rest on his stomach.

'Jesus Christ…' Weiss was standing motionless, uncertain if all the bullets had whizzed by him.

Hazel got to her feet but could barely hear. Her eardrums were deadened by gunfire.

'Wade?' Tamara crawled over to where he lay, blood and mucous pouring from her nose.

Hazel helped Lucas up.

'Wade.' Tamara rolled her husband over but his features were expressionless.

'Weiss, make sure Rena's OK.' Hazel rushed to Drake and put her fingers to his bloody neck. 'Weiss!'

He snapped out of it and checked her over. Rena was still seated in the same position, her head bowed.

Drake didn't have a pulse. Hazel glanced over to Soles. He was staring up at the ceiling with vacant eyes. She stood. 'Call more police.'

'On it.' Lucas already had a phone to his ear. 'I don't think Rena even knows what just happened.'

'There's a first aid kit in Neptune's. I'll get it.' Hazel limped sorely back along the concourse; before she passed through the doorway into the party room she saw the corpses shimmering under the green and blue lights.

CHAPTER 125

There were four.

'Hazel, you shouldn't be – fuck—' Lucas was behind her.

On the yellow coral table, where she'd clothed Rena earlier, the hulking form of Jacob Huber had been deposited in a sitting position; his buttocks on the edge, feet on the floor and his head bowed. He'd been disembowelled, and his glistening intestines were heaped between his boots.

Hazel choked and took a step back, recalling Eve Huber telling her which message Jacob had tweeted to the killer the night they'd all been fooling around online.

Ain't got the guts? #BeMyKiller

Then she recognised Griff Needham. He was lying on the carpet in front of Jacob, a length of Huber's intestines wrapped around his bicep like an addict's belt. Three syringes were stabbed into his blackened forearm.

Wishing you a lethal injection. #BeMyKiller

There was little left of Eve Huber but Hazel knew the dismembered trunk of gnawed flesh was hers because the exposed bones and sinew remnants had been arranged over her mobility scooter.

Bite me. #BeMyKiller

'Cox—'

Her location manager was propped up on a pink shell chair. He'd never made it to his next gig. She swallowed against nausea. His mouth was just a jagged hole; his lips torn away, and his expression blackened by fumes. She remembered what he'd suggested to the crew WhatsApp group.

Blow me.

Rapid footsteps followed them in. It was Weiss.

'Hazel—' Whatever panic had driven him into the room briefly drained from his face as he took in the mutilated bodies.

'What is it?' She watched his features contort. 'Weiss?'

'It's Tamara. I tried to stop her.' His eyes remained fastened to Eve's remains.

'What has she done? Weiss?' Lucas snapped.

'She went into the arena.'

Hazel hobbled quickly back to the concourse.

When they reached the go-kart track, Tamara had found Ryan Kirby.

'You fucking son of a bitch!'

She'd taken the knife out of him and was repeatedly stabbing his dead body with it. Ryan's head hung down and bounced with each impact. Tamara's hand glistened red as she carved fragments from the middle of his chest.

CHAPTER 126

Hazel limped her way along the curtained bays in emergency and found a doctor redressing Lucas's dog-bite wound that Tamara had bandaged. 'Hey. You good?'

'Never mind me. You OK?'

'They don't think I've broken anything.' She lightly touched the plaster under her chin.

'What about Rena?'

'They've taken her up to X-ray.'

'Poor kid.'

'Doctor says she's still in shock. Where's Weiss?'

'Getting some air. He's pretty shaken up. Any word about Tamara?'

Hazel dropped into a plastic chair opposite him. 'The officer with me had a message on his radio. She's just called Broomfield PD and wants to make a statement.'

'Then why the hell did she take off in the pickup?'

'Good question.' She supported her bandaged and aching right elbow with her other hand.

'You trust her story?'

'No.'

'Me neither.' He flinched as the nurse tightened the new bandage.

'Don't understand why she suddenly chose tonight to feel protective about us. And where has she been since she split? The farm? Maybe we should check it out while she's with the police.'

'I have to go back there anyway.'

'Why?'

He raised an eyebrow at Hazel.

'Lucas, what did you do?'

'Need to pick up a piece of gear I left there.'

CHAPTER 127

The grown-up had gone, and April knew it didn't matter how many times she called out for help. Nobody was going to hear.

She thought about her bedroom at home and how the sun hit the orange curtains and turned the walls the same shade. She thought about breakfast with her father and how he watched the TV over the top of his spectacles while he ate his crispy eggs. And she thought about her mother crying, like the time she'd caught her doing it in the bathroom when she didn't think anyone was listening.

She'd be crying now. Wondering where April was. And crying even more when she didn't come home.

'Help,' she sobbed weakly.

The water went inside her mouth, and it tasted like earth. April kept pedalling her legs, treading it like her teacher had shown her. She was so tired now. And she couldn't tell the difference between the water and the darkness around her.

Had to keep her legs moving, even though her teeth chattered with the cold. Her head dipped under the surface, and she quickly lifted her face out again. She was falling asleep. Starting to dream. Or maybe this was a nightmare and she was about to wake from it.

April breathed the liquid into her nose again.

'April!'

She lifted her ears clear of the water. Had the grown-up come back? The voice sounded nearby.

'April!'

Should she answer? Did he care?

'April!' A lady's voice now.

Who was up there? They were having a conversation. 'Down here!'

Torchlight hit her, and she screwed her eyes against it.

'Jesus, she's still alive,' a man said.

It didn't sound like the grown-up who had put her there.

'Hold on, April!' the lady yelled. 'We're coming down to get you.'

'Help,' April responded feebly, because she couldn't think of anything else.

She waited, sluggishly kicking her legs even though she could barely feel them any more. There were more lights above her. It was the search party. The one she'd been waiting for since she'd climbed the tree.

A few minutes later, a big man was beside her.

'Just hold on, sweetheart.'

Then she was being carried out. When she was shivering against the cold night air she was disappointed not to see her parents. And the search party wasn't that big either. There was a TV camera though. It belonged to the big bald man. And with him was a lady with blonde hair, a bandage around her hand and a plaster on her chin.

CHAPTER 128

Hazel's feet were aching in her heels but she was way too jumpy to sit amongst the audience for the screening so just hung around at the back. Despite efforts to adjust it, the air con was on full blast and everyone was still wearing coats.

There was about ten minutes left of the movie. Like the rest of the cut, it was a combination of real footage and actor reconstruction. Criteria had insisted upon it. Against her wishes, another director had been brought in to hastily shoot the additional scenes in Vancouver, and Hazel hadn't even been introduced to him.

Hazel's earnest expression filled the cinema screen as she addressed the lens. Her talking head had been recorded in a sound studio. Fun Central was still a no-go area.

'After Tamara Hickman's frenzied attack on Ryan Kirby's body, she fled. I wasn't convinced by her story. Why try to warn us that particular night? A spy cam that my cameraman left positioned at the turkey farm recorded the revealing low-grade footage that follows. He'd jammed it between two of the corrugated panels of the poultry shed he'd concealed himself behind prior to us being taken prisoner by Wade and Tamara. It seems Wade Hickman had no idea what was going on right under his nose. The man inside the shed Wade had shown us wasn't a recovering addict. Only Tamara knew who he really was and had been conducting a secret relationship with him. This was the reason she was so eager to protect him from the intrusion of my crew. This first sequence is real and was recorded in low light, which has been enhanced.'

Her features were replaced by a bleached fisheye POV of the poultry shed interior. Its lean prisoner was now clothed in jeans and an olive field jacket, his dark dreadlocks tied in a ponytail. He was standing below a single bulb, hurriedly loading a rifle but displaying no signs of the withdrawal he'd exhibited when Wade had taken Hazel, Lucas and Weiss in there. The sound of raindrops striking the corrugated roof was discernible, and when his phone rang he hit speaker and continued hastily feeding in the bullets.

'Where the hell are you?' Tamara's tremulous voice fought with the engine of the pickup.

'I got held up. Been trying to call and text you.'

'I was with Wade. I couldn't answer my phone.'

'I caught the little girl who's been poking around at Fun Central and stole from Kirby's bag of tricks.'

'Where is she now?'

'Just locked her in one of the old feed bins. Wanted to find out if she'd seen my face.'

'Jesus. Did she?'

'She has now.'

'Shit.'

'You driving?'

'It's all gone wrong. Maybe I should go to the cops and make a statement.'

'What happened?' he demanded; temper barely restrained. 'Jesus, Tamara, all you had to do was send Wade in there so Kirby would kill him before I took care of Kirby.'

'Kirby didn't finish the crew. They were still alive when I got there with Wade. And the cops had arrived. You didn't show!'

'I've been dealing with the kid.'

'And I had to find out what the fuck was going on. Wade started a shoot-out. He's dead. So are the two cops.'

He nodded and absorbed this. 'What about Kirby?'

'Dead as well. One of the crew stabbed him.'

'But this is good.'

'No. I had to think on my feet. Told the crew about Kirby staying at the farm.'

'What the fuck for?'

'Had to justify why I got Wade to drive out to Fun Central. But I said Kirby killed Meredith. Don't think they bought all of it though. Maybe we should run.'

He shouldered the rifle and was silent for a few seconds. 'No. Make your statement about Kirby but get it dead straight in your head first.'

'What are you going to do with the kid?'

'We'll let Kirby take the blame.'

'Don't kill her. Better we make it look like an accident. Head to Third Base. There's a natural well. Push her in there. Nobody goes out that way any more.'

'OK. I'll call you when I'm done. Just hold your nerve.'

The footage froze, and Hazel's voice-over continued.

'But Tamara didn't know about my attack in the forest. It was obvious to me that two men were involved. Working in tandem, Ryan Kirby and his accomplice had easily achieved the murders of the online victims as well as those at Fun Central.'

A montage of snapshots depicting Ryan Kirby in combat uniform followed.

'Ryan Kirby was ex-military and had been discharged on grounds of substance abuse and mental instability after killing civilians in Syria. He'd found an ally through a PTSD chat room, and they'd both been drawn to Fossen's @BeMyKiller Twitter timeline, choosing the victims whose comments inspired them before stalking them for sport.'

A car arrived at the mocked-up Vancouver turkey farm. The actor portraying Tamara appeared from the Hickmans' living quarters, and the actor with dreadlocks playing the unidentified killer emerged from the driver's side. He opened the rear passenger door, and they pulled out a Ryan Kirby lookalike. He was delirious as they helped him to the poultry shed.

Hazel picked up her narration. 'The unidentified man we know only as Killer 2 brought Ryan Kirby to detox at the turkey farm just after Kirby had shot Denise Needham and he had mutilated Caleb Huber. Neither of them stabbed Kristian O'Connell. Police have now arrested a dealer for his murder.'

The scene cut to a two-shot of the actors playing Tamara and Killer 2 naked in bed having an intimate conversation.

'Killer 2 had got clean at the farm the previous year and had begun a secret relationship with Tamara. It was during Kirby's recovery that Tamara saw a way of disposing of Meredith.'

The scene wiped to the Tamara actor talking in the woods with a Meredith lookalike and haggard twenty-something man.

'Tamara was also a small-time dealer but she hadn't let Wade know it was more than just a sideline. She used Meredith and others to sell crank at Fun Central. But Meredith began blackmailing Tamara after she witnessed the way she dealt with a pusher who had been stealing from her.'

The Tamara actor pulled out a handgun and shot the man point-blank in the chest. The image froze.

'To avoid implicating herself, Tamara plotted with Killer 2 to murder Meredith and make it appear it was part of the @BeMyKiller executions. Tamara sent the tweet from Meredith's account shortly before she was taken to Fun Central by her lover.'

The scene dissolved to a replica Meredith shrine being doused with petrol by the actor playing Killer 2. He touched a match to it and the pillar went up.

'Both killers took it in turns to methodically target the documentary being shot at Fun Central. Kirby posed as a taxi driver to get close to the participants. After they'd dispatched their targets, Ryan Kirby believed they would end their lives in a suicide pact, preferably on film. But Killer 2 and Tamara planned for all the executions to be laid squarely at Kirby's feet. Tamara would dispose of Wade, her husband, by getting him to arrive at Fun Central during Kirby's killing spree, and then Killer 2 would shoot Kirby and make it look like suicide.'

A low definition still of the real Killer 2 taken at the poultry shed in Broomfield slid into the frame.

'Tamara didn't make her statement. But she was picked up by police a few days later and confessed. Given what we'd captured with our spy cam, she had no choice. She's now awaiting trial. Killer 2 vanished. Little is known about his identity or whereabouts. If any viewers think they recognise this man, please contact the number at the end of the credits or our production website. At the time of this movie release, a police manhunt is still ongoing and, until he's captured, the hashtag #BeMyKiller remains subject to a social media ban.'

CHAPTER 129

As the rescue of April Weeks was re-enacted, Hazel slipped out of a packed Studio One and into the lobby.

Rena was schmoozing Criteria's representative. 'All done?'

'Going to quickly grab some air.'

'You know Vance?'

Hazel regarded the tan, twenty-something exec but didn't. None of the seniors were going to make tracks to a tiny independent cinema in Broomfield. The movie was going to premiere at the Toronto International Film Festival and was set for an October theatrical release but she couldn't think of a more appropriate place to have an advance screening than her home town.

Like the rest of the crew, Rena had been reluctant to return but had insisted on coordinating the reception.

'How was the audience?' Vance asked glibly, clearly more interested in getting back to his cosy conversation with Rena.

'I think most of them were too busy trying to keep warm. The air con only seems to have a wind tunnel setting.'

'Hazel?'

She halted by the main door and turned back to Rena.

'You will be attending the party.' It wasn't a question. The gathering was being held in an aseptic cocktail bar a few blocks away.

'Of course. Somewhere else I need to be first though.' She pulled the handle and escaped into the chill air.

CHAPTER 130

Having found The Hollows housing project on her TomTom, Hazel pulled into the driveway of 244, switched off the engine and got out of her Mazda. As she walked up the short paved path to the front door, the curtain at the window ahead of her was pulled aside and a blonde head appeared over the ledge. She smiled but it dropped out of sight.

Hazel rang the bell and heard feet squeaking up the hallway.

Vanessa Weeks opened the door. 'Hey,' she whispered.

'Hi.'

Vanessa gestured for her to come inside. Hazel could smell baking.

It was only the third time Hazel had met April's mother. The first had been at Bennett's office when Vanessa had reported her daughter missing; the second when she'd been driven out to Hazel after she and Lucas had pulled the little girl out of the well at Third Base. Minutes later and they probably would have been too late. April had been close to exhaustion when they'd found her.

After Tamara Hickman had told Broomfield PD she would make a statement, Hazel and Lucas had driven to the turkey farm and found it deserted. Lucas had retrieved the spy camera and they'd viewed the footage of the conversation between Tamara and the unidentified killer. Third Base was where Tamara told him to dispose of April. It was only Hazel's childhood recollection of her trips there with Meredith to spy on the older kids that had allowed them to locate the missing girl so quickly.

Third Base was a place name that only existed on the lips of Broomfield residents. Perhaps even the most unexceptional past held something worth retrieving.

'Hi there.' Ben Weeks was whispering too. He was a thickset man with bushy sideburns and he loitered awkwardly at the doorway to the lounge.

'She's been looking for you through the window all evening. Now she's hiding.' Vanessa pointed into the kitchen.

'How is she?' Hazel peered through the doorway but couldn't spot April at the dining table.

Vanessa and Ben swapped a look.

'She still won't leave the house.' Vanessa's expression sagged and wiped away the lines of her smile.

'But she went out into the yard yesterday,' Ben added quickly, eager to emphasise progress.

'Can I say hello?'

Vanessa pursed her lips. 'She'd like that.'

Hazel went into the small country-style kitchen. The oven was purring, and the baking aroma was stronger. But there was no sign of April.

Hazel got onto her hands and knees by the table and lifted the cloth. April was cross-legged underneath. She was wearing dungarees and had her hair in plaits. 'Hi there.'

April didn't reply.

'Remember me?'

April nodded.

'I've got something for you.' Hazel unclenched her hand and showed her what it held. 'Do you know what this is?'

She nodded again.

'So you know this is a friendship bracelet.' Hazel had bought the kit from a craft store in town that afternoon and had braided and knotted the rainbow string as adeptly as she had when she was ten. She gave it to April. 'That means we'll always be friends.'

It's what she'd said to Meredith, when Hazel hadn't been able to conceive how the years in Broomfield would change her.

April started tying it around her wrist.

'You know you're safe now, don't you?'

April secured it but her face was unconvinced.

'Here with your parents. They're keeping extra watch.'

But the man who had taken April was still loose, and she knew Vanessa and Ben wouldn't sleep until he was caught.

Hazel had already started building a file on Killer 2. She had a small lead and was steadily tracing him via the PTSD site he'd signed up to under a false name.

'And I'll be watching too. Making sure you're safe. I promise you that.'

A LETTER FROM RICHARD

It's always my intention to attempt to do something different with each of my thrillers so I really do appreciate you giving it a chance. Thanks for the time you've spent with this book and, if you did enjoy it, I really would be grateful for any words you can leave as a review. Its success depends on them but with so many other great books out there to be read, I certainly don't take the time this requires for granted.

Follow You is, of course, a dark and mischievous work of fiction and, I believe, there are more instances of good on the Internet than there are of evil. It's a tool we should employ with the same respect and courtesy we would in our face-to-face lives but one that I hope to explore again in my next story for Bookouture.

I'm always happy to hear from readers via my website, Twitter, Instagram and Facebook so please do get in touch. If you'd like to go on my mailing list to receive updates about my books just visit: www.bookouture.com/richard-parker

Thanks
Richard

 www.facebook.com/groups/RichardJayParkerFans/

 @Bookwalter

www.richardjayparker.com

ACKNOWLEDGMENTS

Incalculable gratitude to my wife, Anne-Marie, for love and steadfastly indulging my need to live in a world of my own and to Mum and Dad for teaching me how to make the real one such a warm place. Huge thanks have to go to my editor, Natalie Butlin, for allowing this one into her head and for some very smart notes and suggestions. It's so much better but I'm happy to say, no less twisted. Thanks also to Janette Currie for invaluable input. A special mention for Kim Nash and the positive team at Bookouture – I am so glad to be allowed on the bus with so many other exciting authors. Last, but by no means least, thanks to Phil Light for being my hardware consultant. Cheers all!